Sex in the Kitchen
A Wicked Words short-story collection

D1638763

Look out for other themed Wicked Words Collections

Already Published: *Sex in the Office, Sex on Holiday, Sex in Uniform*

Published in May 06: *Sex on the Move*

Published in August 06: *Sex and Music*

Published in November 06: *Sex and Shopping*

Sex in the Kitchen

A Wicked Words short-story collection

Edited by Kerri Sharp and
Adam L. G. Nevill

BLACKLACE

Wicked Words stories contain sexual fantasies.
In real life, always practise safe sex.

This edition published in 2005 by
Black Lace
Thames Wharf Studios
Rainville Road
London W6 9HA

Cooking Lessons	© Teresa Noelle Roberts
The Food Critic	© Tammy Valentine
Midnight Feast	© Primula Bond
Dinner Service	© Monica Belle
Chocolate Delight	© A Colorado Woman
Ginger Tart	© Fiona Locke
Trencherman	© Nuala Deuel
Over a Barrel	© Maya Hess
Sweet Chilli Dipping Sauce	© Candy Wong
Butter Fingers	© Maddie Mackeown
All About the Ratings	© Sophie Mouette
Ice Creamed	© Heather Towne
Off the Menu	© Toni Sands
Stone Touch	© Natasha Rostova
Vanilla with Extra Sauce	© Jessica Donnelly
Salsa	© Estelle Blake

Typeset by SetSystems Limited, Saffron Walden, Essex
Printed and bound by Mackays of Chatham PLC

ISBN 0 352 34018 5
ISBN 9 780352 340184

Contents

Introduction and Newsletter

Food and sex have been strange bedfellows for a very long time. Perhaps because they are two of the most accessible and hungrily sought after sensual pleasures we have at our disposal. From the feasts and orgies of the classical age to the modern romantic dinner for two, good food and drink are timeless preliminaries to sex, not to mention accessories during sex. They are as much a part of the anticipation of sex, and the intention to seduce and please, as dressing to impress a lover. Sharing good food, preparing it together or cooking for someone special are all effective forms of bonding and intimacy. Also, with so many foods allegedly bestowed with sexual charms or acting as boosts to virility, it won't come as any surprise that Black Lace found the temptation to cook up a themed Wicked Words collection too strong to resist.

And as *Tom Jones* and *Nine and a Half Weeks* have proven, not only is food, and the act of eating it, compatible with story-telling, food stuffs can be a useful, messy and multi-sensual prop to erotic fun, as our authors gleefully illustrate in this imaginative and carefully prepared menu of short fiction.

And we're offering a varied selection to suit all tastes. Palates that prefer the spicy and exotic dish might find themselves reaching for a glass of water or milk after getting stuck into Candy Wong's Thai tale, Estelle Blake's South American sojourn or Natasha Rostova's Indian adventure. Those unafraid of getting their hands sticky or chins greasy should delight in Monica Belle's *Dinner Service* and Heather Towne's *Ice Creamed*. Fans of the handsome male chef will be licking their fingers after reading *Cooking*

Lessons, *Midnight Feast* and *All About the Ratings*. All-you-can-eat enthusiasts should find *Trencherman* a treat, and we defy those with a sweet tooth not to be sated after reading *Chocolate Delight* and *Vanilla with Extra Sauce*. And if you believe there can be a thrill in a reprimand for inappropriate behaviour at the table, bad service or having to find another way to pay your bill, then waste no time and tuck straight into *Ginger Tart*, *The Food Critic* and *Over a Barrel*.

So forget the fast and the diet, and disregard sensible nutrition; satisfaction is our aim. At last, excess, gluttony, over-indulging and wickedness can be fully and freely enjoyed without a hint of guilt or weight gain. The greatest feasts will always be in the imagination. Enjoy.

Kerri Sharp and Adam L. G. Nevill, Editors, Spring 2005

Want to write for Wicked Words?

We are publishing more themed collections in 2006 – made in response to our readers' most popular fantasies. *Sex on the Move* and *Sex and Music* are the next two collections for 2006. The deadline for the *Move* (Transport) collection has now passed, but if you want to submit a sizzling, beautifully written story for *Sex and Music* (deadline for submissions January 06), or *Sex and Shopping* (deadline for submissions April 06) please read the following. And keep checking our website for information on future editions

- Your short story should be 4,000–6,000 words long and not published anywhere in the world – websites excepted.
- Thematically, it should be written with the Black Lace guidelines in mind.

- Ideally there should be a 'sting in the tale' and an element of dramatic tension, with oodles of erotic build-up.
- The story should be about more than 'some people having sex' – we want great characterisation too.
- Keep the explicit anatomical stuff to an absolute minimum.

We are obliged to select stories that are technically faultless and vibrant and original – as well as fitting in with the tone of the series: upbeat, dynamic, accent on pleasure etc. Our anthologies are a flagship for the series. We pride ourselves on selecting only the best-written erotica from the UK and USA. The key words are: diversity, surprises and faultless writing.

Competition rules will apply to short stories: you will hear back from us about your story only if it has been successful. We cannot give individual feedback on short stories as we receive far too many for this to be possible.

For future collections check the Black Lace website.

If you want to find out more about Black Lace, check our website, where you will find our author guidelines and more information about short stories. It's at www.blacklace-books.co.uk

Alternatively, send a large SAE with a first-class British stamp to:

Black Lace Guidelines
Virgin Books Ltd
Thames Wharf Studios
Rainville Road
London W6 9HA

Cooking Lessons
Teresa Noelle Roberts

I studied the ingredients that Zak had assembled on the counter. Tomatoes in a bowl, already peeled and chopped. Peanuts. Two kinds of chillies, one in a can, the other soaking in water. Allspice berries. Small, hard reddish seeds labelled ANNATTO BERRIES. Cloves. Cinnamon sticks. Olive oil flavoured with garlic.

And a bar of bittersweet chocolate.

I started singing, 'One of these things is not like the other . . .'

Zak laughed. 'I thought we'd make Mexican chicken with red mole. The chocolate is the secret ingredient. Trust me.'

'We' was being generous. This was my third time having dinner at Zak's. The first two times, he made the kinds of meals you'd pay big money for in a restaurant and I helped by chopping vegetables and doing other things that didn't require much in the way of real cooking skills. 'Of course I trust you. You are the master chef and my guide in all things culinary.'

'Stop. You're making me blush.' He was smiling, and while he did turn a bit pink, it was more what I'd call a flush, the slight change in colour that shows a fair-skinned redhead is feeling good about life.

From that brief description, you probably picture freckles and light eyes and a full name along the lines of Zachary O'Connell. Actually his name is Itzak Meyer. Amend your mental picture to include brown eyes, ivory skin with a warm undertone and thick curly hair a deep, rich red that you'd never call auburn or carrot. Add a Caravaggio saint's sensual mouth, which seems out of place with a tall, big-boned Eastern European build and a face created to study the Kabbalah by flickering candle-light. I'd fallen for him while watching him eat a particularly decadent chocolate-marzipan torte at a mutual friend's party. The luscious mouth and blissful expression sparked my interest; watching the passion and precision with which he cooked stoked it. He liked things hot and spicy and complex. This I took as a good sign.

There was one problem. Zak's culinary boldness didn't extend into other areas. Some guys move too fast. He was the other sort, the guy who's clearly interested, but so determined not to be pushy that a girl ends up having to take matters into her own hands. That was my plan for the evening. But I didn't want to rush things either. For one thing, a sauce that combined chocolate and spices was just too intriguing to miss. I wasn't the cook that Zak was, but I liked good food.

'So, molé,' I said, hoping it sounded casual. 'Where do we start?' I put my hand on his arm, looked up at him and leaned in more than was necessary. He echoed my move-ment so we were definitely in each other's personal space. A little closer and we'd be wrapped around each other.

So far so good.

'Well, first we taste-test the chocolate.' Zak popped a square into his mouth, then broke me off a piece. I could almost see him thinking through how to give it to me. I was delighted when he held it up so I could eat it from his hand.

Naturally, I took the bait. I made eye contact the whole time, nibbled the tips of his fingers as I took the chocolate, and then licked them to make sure I got any melted bits. It was fine bittersweet chocolate, not that I would have expected anything less from Zak, but it didn't taste nearly as good as he did. By the time his fingers were clean, I felt as melted as the chocolate had been.

He made an exaggerated 'cool me down' fanning

motion. 'Oh yeah, that's good. And the chocolate wasn't bad either. Where were we?'

'We'd just gotten started.'

I hoped he'd pick up on the suggestion, but he was either clueless or hungry and determined to make this meal. I opted to believe the latter. 'We need to roast the peanuts and the spices, and then grind them. If you'll chop the chillies that are soaking, I'll start that.' I don't think I imagined that he sounded a little flustered, or that he was a little more flushed.

The peanuts went into the oven, a pile of spices into a dry skillet. Meanwhile, I went to work on the chillies, removing the seeds and stems and chopping what was left into fine pieces. They were ancho chillies, not super-hot, but with a rich, smoky, raisiny aroma that the chopping released. From the stove, the fragrance of spices and nuts filled the air, tempting my taste buds and tickling my nose. I could recognise clove and peppercorns, but roasting peanuts smelled surprisingly wonderful, and other aromas – annatto and allspice, I guessed – added complexity. Delicious.

Zak came over behind me. 'You can do big chunks,' he said, leaning over my shoulder. 'We'll be putting them into the food processor.'

I set the knife down and leaned back as if stretching, knowing this would bring me into contact with his body. He didn't pull away, so I wrapped my arms around him and cupped his butt, despite the awkward angle. 'Thanks for inviting me over.'

He slipped his arms around me. 'My pleasure.' The contact was lovely, but not enough. Feeling him against me, I immediately flashed to how wonderful it would be if I were leaning on the counter and he was pushing into me from behind, hitting all the right spots, gripping my hips decisively as he moved. I wriggled a little at the delicious image and he pulled me closer in a way that suggested his thoughts were heading in a similar direction.

Unfortunately at that point we both noticed the aroma of spice was getting more intense. I'd already learned from an earlier adventure in Indian cuisine with Zak that spices burn easily, so I wasn't offended when he wheeled around to pull the skillet from the heat. Disappointed, but not offended. 'That was close. The peanuts should be ready now too.' He pulled them from the oven and set the tray on the counter. 'We should let it all cool before we grind it.'

'Good,' I said. 'That'll give us a few minutes.' And then I kissed him.

When you catch someone off-guard with a kiss, you expect a second or so of confusion – more than that and you should probably stop kissing and start apologising. I figured Zak, being shy, might need a little extra time before he relaxed.

He didn't. He took me in his arms and returned the kiss as if he'd been waiting his whole life to do so. The sheer force of his pent-up desire came through on his lips, his hands on my back and ass, the heat of him against me. And I don't mean that in a he-hadn't-had-a-date-lately sort of way. This felt personal, and it burned straight into me, hot as chillies and sweet as chocolate. I buried my fingers in his hair, tried to pull him even closer. I didn't realise that I'd instinctively started grinding my pelvis against his until I felt him getting hard against me.

I was wet already, and that caused flooding. There were about a thousand things I wanted to say to him, but that would have meant using my mouth for something besides kissing. And there were about a thousand things I wanted to do and with him, all crowding into my head at once (frankly, some of them had already been camped out there for a while), but they could all wait a while so we could enjoy the moment.

He didn't rush, either. He kissed with the patience of a man who made bread and the passion of one who'd drive a hundred miles to get the perfect ingredient, and I realised that what seemed like caution might have been a matter of waiting for the right moment. He wasn't doing anything but holding me and kissing me, not attempting to rip off my clothes or anything, but the word *kissing* covers a lot of territory. Nibbles and licks and sucking my tongue and lower lip. Gentle mouth-caresses and fierce kisses that threatened to devour me whole. And I was giving back as good as I got. By the time we had to pause for air, he was rock-hard against me and I was trembling.

He let me unbutton his shirt, showing off a broad, furred chest, but when I reached for his fly, he took my hand and gently but firmly moved it away. 'Oh no,' he said with a wonderfully evil smile, 'we need to finish making the molé. But first . . .' He didn't let go of my wrist. Instead, he put it behind my back.

Such a small gesture, but it had such a weight of possibilities behind it, possibilities I hadn't even really considered where quiet, seemingly shy Zak was concerned. Vanilla is a lovely flavour, but it's not my favourite one. I drew a sharp breath, both delighted and excited, and felt my knees go a little weak.

Catching my reaction, he grinned approvingly. 'Just as I thought,' he said. Then he used his free hand to unbutton my blouse with a deftness that up until a few minutes ago would have surprised me.

He definitely wasn't shy or overly cautious. Zak had been stalking his prey, and I'd walked right up to him thinking he was harmless. I was wrong.

Lucky me.

My breasts are of the smallish, perky variety, so my red lace bra was more decorative than structural. Even one-handed, Zak was able to move it out of the way easily, baring my nipples. He traced the ring in the left one with one finger and was rewarded with a sharp, pleasured intake of breath. 'Now that's a nice surprise.'

'Glad you like.' I don't think I was talking above a whisper.

'Oh, yes.' He bent down, took the ringed nipple in his mouth.

Damn, that man had a clever tongue. And he didn't make the mistake of assuming that because I was pierced I must like rough handling from the word go. He was exquisitely delicate, even while the firm grip on my wrist promised that this would not always be the case. It made me writhe, took me to that place where even a light touch on my clit would have pushed me over the edge.

He didn't do it. Instead, he reduced me to the point of gibbering, weak-kneed idiocy, and then drew the bra back up over my nipples. 'More later,' he said, again with that evil grin.

'Do we have to finish the sauce now?' I was whining, I admit.

'It won't take much longer. Then we'll have a few hours while the chicken marinates – and another hour while it cooks.'

That put us eating dinner at about ten o'clock. I'd do something like that by mistake, from boldly setting forth to cook something without reading through the recipe all the way or something equally foolish, but Zak wouldn't. 'You planned this.'

'Hell, yes, I did. I've had my eye on you since the night we met. But you screwed up my timetable – I was going to start things once the chicken was marinating. And I'm still going to, because otherwise we'll have to order out.' It was clear from his tone that ordering out would be a defeat for him. But he didn't let go of me as he said it.

'So let's get cooking!'

Reluctantly, we peeled apart from each other. Not too far, though. It's hard to cook with one person holding the other's wrist, so he did let go eventually, but we kept in contact as much as we could.

We whirred the peanuts in the food processor, then puréed the anchos I'd chopped and the canned chipotles, throwing the tomatoes in with them. The roasted spices and a cinnamon stick went into a spice grinder, filling the kitchen with an even headier aroma as they were reduced to powder. We kissed over the grinder, inhaling the fragrance and setting ourselves on fire again.

Zak poured olive oil into a skillet and turned up the heat. When the oil was steaming, he poured in the purée and spices, then stirred in the peanuts.

Everything had smelled good to begin with. As it heated together, the perfume became even more extraordinary, and the garlic in the olive oil added its own notes to the olfactory symphony. 'Get the chocolate,' he said. His voice had such a husky quality to it that he might have been saying, 'Get the condoms' or even 'Get the whip.'

I did.

He let me stir in the melting chocolate, the almost-black streaks spreading out, then turning the brilliant red sauce to burgundy. 'Taste,' Zak said, practically making it an order.

Explosions on my tongue. Smoky and complex and spicy, yet not overly hot. The chocolate had melded with the many other components, adding depth and a hint of subtle sweetness. If I hadn't helped make the sauce, I wouldn't have guessed chocolate was the source of that dark, rich undertone. 'Oh my God. This is so good. How come I've never had this before?'

'Stick with me, baby,' he said, doing a remarkably bad Bogart imitation, 'and you'll get to taste a lot of new things.' He accompanied that with a lovely little hip-grind against me.

I don't know how we got the chicken into the marinade without spilling something major, because we certainly weren't being careful.

As soon as it was safely in the fridge, clothing began to fly. My bra ended up in the sink with the dirty dishes, but I failed to care, being more interested in getting a good look at Zak. I'd expect a hedonistic gourmet cook to have a little belly rather than six-pack abs, and I was right, but he looked fine to me: muscled arms and good, broad shoulders, nice legs, not a runner's but not a couch potato's either. And any woman who complains about a paunch when there's all that, an attractive face, a creative and sensual mind and an erection you could use as a flagpole doesn't know when she has it good.

He lifted me up and set me on a corner of the kitchen counter. I took the hint and opened my legs, resting one foot on the counter to give him better access, and wriggled down a bit to put my crotch on a better level. I don't fantasise about men kneeling at my feet in a high-heeled-vixen-with-a-whip sense – my kinks are more on the other side of the fence – but there are certain lovely things one can do from that position. When he knelt down I shuddered with anticipation, already knowing that Zak had a talented tongue, patience and a bit of an oral fixation.

He started by kissing and nibbling my mound, not touching the slick lips or straining, swollen clit below. Just enough to inflame me, just enough to send hot, sweet bolts of desire surging through me. I gripped the edge of the counter and squirmed against him. Now he let one finger trace each of my lips, feeling their plumpness, as he kissed my inner thighs, followed the crease of the joint with his tongue. 'Tease,' I panted. He laughed deep in his throat but didn't say anything. He had better things to do with his mouth.

Just when I thought I couldn't take any more teasing, he let his tongue go where his fingers had been, licking along my slippery outer lips, making me shiver and croon. Little, delicate, entirely controlled licks, reaching ever closer to my most sensitive areas, but not actually touching them. Delicious, but not enough, so far from being enough. My hand closed in his hair. I meant to pull him closer and end the glorious frustration, but there was an almost impercep-tible hesitation on his part. I got the point – that he was doing things on his own timetable, not mine – and con-tented myself with playing with his flame hair.

At last he relented and turned his attention to my clit. Focused, precise and intense as he had been in his teasing, he began to lick.

After the long build-up, I exploded almost instantly. I felt it all over my body, radiating out from my clit until every bit of me, including, I swear, my hair, was tingling and shimmering. I bucked against his face, gripping the edge of the counter with one hand and his shoulder with the other and moaning.

When Zak stood up again, he had to catch me – I was so limp I was ready to slide off the counter. I nestled against his chest, playing idly with the curly pelt there, catching my breath. I even wrapped my legs around him to hold him closer.

That was what made us realise that the counter would be useful again, this time as something to brace against.

Before I had time to wonder how I'd get to my now-distant purse without letting go of Zak, he pulled a condom out of a nearby drawer with a flourish, like a magician pulling a rabbit out of a hat. I was almost too eager, clumsy as I rolled it onto his straining penis. His cock was thick, hot under my hands. It jumped with anticipation at my first touch, and my cunt jumped in response.

There would be time to play with this pretty thing later, to lick and suck and swallow. Right now, though, I just guided him to my pussy lips and said, 'Now. Please.'

I expected him to tease me, to take his time as he had before, but he drove it straight home, lifting me up with the force of the thrust. His eyes darkened to an unlikely espresso as his pupils widened. I wrapped my arms and my legs around him and lost my mind.

More bone-melting kisses. I couldn't move all that much in that position, but he made up for it, driving fiercely into me, moving me against him with his strong hands. I did what I could, moving my pelvis in a small circle (I knew those jazz dance classes would come in handy for something!) and tightening myself to grip at him. Pretty soon my pussy set up a rhythm of its own, and it was a good thing I didn't need to concentrate on it because I no longer could.

My last semi-coherent thought was, I hope he doesn't mind being scratched, as I clawed convulsively at his back. Then everything was dark red, red as molé sauce, behind my eyelids and I startled the remote part of myself that could still care with the insane-wildcat noises I made as I came. Zak grunted and began moving even faster, keeping me locked in ecstasy as he drove towards his own climax.

He cried out, wordless and triumphant, lifting me away from the counter so he supported all my weight as he came. Our mouths locked again, and we sank to the floor together, too spent to crawl somewhere more comfortable.

Zak's first words were, 'And that's only the appetiser. I think we'll need to rest a little before the entrée, though, and maybe make it to the bedroom.' He was grinning like a fool – not that I blamed him, because I was too – but I had a feeling that he was serious about this being just the beginning of a long and very interesting night.

I made a happy-animal noise and snuggled against him, breathing deeply. The kitchen smelled like spices, chocolate and passion.

The Food Critic
Tammy Valentine

Donna spotted him as soon as he sat down at his table. She hadn't seen many in her time but he carried several of the trademarks she recognised: neatly turned out, he wore a smart tweed jacket and co-ordinating tie; he was meticulous about the place setting, adjusting cutlery to suit his position; and – the biggest giveaway of all – he studied the menu minutely, peering over his thin-rimmed glasses, reading every item with care. A suit would have been nice, she pondered, given that he might hold her future in his hands, but she couldn't really complain.

As a rule, Donna hated food critics. Like the notorious Butcher of Broadway in the world of theatre, their influence far outweighed their value. In this cut-throat business at the best of times, the most important of them had the power to make or break reputations, to close down the unfortunate victims of their savagery or guarantee a long line of prosperous customers with a generous review. Donna wondered which avenue awaited her.

Watching through the porthole in the kitchen door, she felt the hackles rise on the back of her neck beneath her crisp white blouse. This was the moment she had been dreading since she first opened the doors of La Prima Donna a few short weeks earlier. She knew it had to come, and she had done everything within her abilities to prepare for it. She had, she was sure, one of the top chefs in town and she had worked hard at building a team with him to present the ultimate face of fine cuisine to her discerning clientele. The opulence was beyond doubt – she'd spent enough on fittings and furnishings, after all – and she reminded herself that Guillermo's food was sublime. Relax, she thought, as she watched Lorenzo shake out the man's napkin and lay it across his lap. Things are going to be fine.

The first sign that things were not going to be fine came with Harriet's unfortunate slip of the spoon. Reaching in front of him to retrieve the lobster thermidor dish, she snagged the sleeve of her blouse on the spoon, which flicked a splash of liquid in a perfect, slow-motion arc onto his immaculate tie. Harriet was distraught – Donna had already warned the staff to pay particular attention to table eleven – but only made things worse with her clumsy attempts to wipe away the smear. Donna crossed the room in three steps and manoeuvred her smartly out of the way.

'I'm so dreadfully sorry,' she gushed, a little too fawningly, as the man eased his chair away from the table and began dabbing the mark with a corner of his napkin. The scowl was unmistakable. 'Let me get you a cloth, Mr Porter,' she added, grateful for having taken the time to research his name in the bookings diary.

'There's no need. It's only an old tie.' There was a definite tone of irritation, but Mr Porter's voice was warm and resonating. He shook out the napkin again and replaced it on his lap, covering up the impeccably pressed cream trousers. Then he pulled himself back to the table and reached for his wine glass.

Donna's brainwave hit with such an obviousness that she was furious she hadn't thought of it before. 'Mr Porter, may I show you to our private dining room? I'm sure you'd be more comfortable there.'

He hesitated momentarily. 'I'm not sure ...' he began, but Donna was already in motion.

Seamlessly, and with an assured confidence that left him little choice, she took up his napkin and wine glass and led him across the busy restaurant to a panelled door near the kitchen. Slipping a key from the ring on her waistband, she unlocked the room and swung the door open.

'After you,' she said, giving Mr Porter her best smile and standing aside to let him in.

As she followed him into the private dining room, constructed and reserved specifically for her most important customers, he slipped off his jacket and draped it over one arm. Donna couldn't help noticing the tightness of the buttocks now on view in front of her. The cream trousers hugged his firm outline deliciously until, below the crevice, they dropped away like a cliff face. Donna had always had a thing for taut buns and this pair gave her a distinct tingle as she appraised them approvingly.

She let him cross the room to the single, well-dressed table against the far wall, her eyes taking in the rest of his elegant frame. She put him in his late thirties and he certainly knew how to make the best of himself. His hair, greying discreetly at the temples, was sleek and beautifully groomed. His skin was smooth and obviously well cared for, while the limbs moved effortlessly under the smart clothes, hinting at a fit, toned body beneath. She had barely begun to contemplate that particular prospect when he turned back towards her to take his seat on the bench that ran along the wall beyond the table. At that moment she was staring at his long legs, and she was sure he caught her with her gaze roaming.

Flushing slightly, she smiled again. 'Please, make yourself comfortable,' she offered. 'It's the least we can do after ...' She waved vaguely at Mr Porter's tie and her words trailed off into feeble silence. He looked at her over his glasses in the same way he had when he first studied the menu.

'Yes, well, I have had less clumsy waitresses, I must admit,' he said, his words clipped and formal.

Donna could detect no discernible accent and put it down to a public-school education. That tallied with the overall look, she reasoned, and maybe contributed to the tightness of the buttocks: if what she'd heard about public schools was true, then it was little wonder he walked about with his bottom ready to repel boarders.

He sat gently and lifted his arms away from the table, looking expectantly at Donna. Stupidly, she realised she still held his napkin and glass in her hand, and she hurried across the red velvet carpet to return them. She laid the glass in its place with one hand, then reached across him to spread the napkin for him.

She hadn't intended it to happen, but it gave her a shock of excitement when it did: as she shook the napkin out over his lap and let it fall into position, her right hand brushed the bulging crease in the front of those beautifully pressed trousers. She let out a tiny gasp.

Her embarrassment coupled with a jolting thrill, she was unsure whether he had even noticed the contact, or heard her emission. As a wave of panic swept through her, her mind raced from fulsome apology to feigned ignorance and back again, all in the space of half a second. In the end she did nothing.

Mr Porter reached up, took his glasses from his nose and laid them precisely to one side, near the wine glass. Donna was rooted to the spot, hovering ridiculously at his left elbow, mouth gaping awkwardly.

'Do you do that to all your guests?' he asked simply.

Donna was speechless. He'd certainly answered the question of whether or not he'd noticed, but his directness appalled her. She'd been skewered as effectively as a butterfly on a collector's board and she had no escape.

Mr Porter clearly had no intention of letting her escape either. He shifted his position so that he was facing her a little more, and looked up straight into her face. The eyes – dark and piercing, she saw at this range – pinned her as impressively as the comment had and, when he spoke again, it was with a clarity and sternness that made her catch her breath.

'I only ask as it seems a particularly intimate way of getting to know your customers.'

Donna managed to regain her senses enough to take a half-step backwards. She stood upright again from the stoop where she'd frozen and clasped her hands in front of her nervously. This was disastrous. Harriet – the stupid, clumsy girl – had set in motion a chain of events that now threatened Donna's very livelihood. This man before her, whose crotch she had managed to fondle just moments ago, had the potential to destroy her and the restaurant, and she was out of ideas. The eyes still glared as she fumbled in her brain for a way out.

'I'm so sorry, Mr Porter,' she gabbled, the words losing their focus as they stumbled from her lipstick-stricken mouth into the thick air of the room. 'It was quite accidental, I assure you.'

'Really? That's a shame,' he said, finally averting his stare and looking back down at his wine glass. Donna could not be certain, but was that a hint of a smirk at the outer edges of his lips? And if it was, what the hell did it mean? Maybe he was toying with her, exploiting his position to manipulate her into humiliation. Well, he'd certainly managed that all right. Or had he, too, experienced the flicker of electricity that she had felt as skin brushed on cotton? What was going on behind those lush eyelashes?

Donna headed for the door.

'I'll see how your main course is coming along,' she blurted, and dashed outside.

She headed straight for the emergency exit at the rear of the kitchen. If you can't stand the heat, she thought, as she crashed through the stainless-steel jungle of Guillermo's kingdom, ignoring solicitous questions from the sous-chef. I need air.

Thumping back the pushbar, she launched herself out into the night, gulping in the cool summer evening. She realised she was perspiring but couldn't tell if it was simple nerves or a huge burst of adrenalin from the encounter in the private dining room. Without thinking, she drew a sleeve across her moistened forehead, then looked down in horror. Smeared across her arm was a pale streak of make-up. Fan-bloody-tastic, she thought. That's just what I need on a night like this. Now what?

As she teetered slowly along the alleyway behind the restaurant, her polished high heels dragging her down, she knew she was doomed. It didn't matter how good Guillermo's food was, or how sumptuous the surroundings. A good review rested on the whole package, and they were just two parts of the jigsaw. If service and a desire to please were missing, it was just as lethal to her review as anything else not on the menu.

She stopped and stared at the moon, clear and full and neatly framed between the two buildings at the end of the alley. As her feet stopped, her mind ticked on. The moon smiled sympathetically at her, as if it understood. Service and a desire to please. Service – she could do that, couldn't she? A desire to please? Oh, she desired all right. This was it. This was all or nothing. Here were no crossroads, no choices to be made. There had to be only one outcome: a stunning review. And if pleasing Mr Porter was what it took to get it, then that was what she was bloody well going to do. Whatever he pleased.

Turning on her heel, her long hair flowing determinedly in the moonlight, she marched back into the kitchen.

'Harriet, give me your blouse,' she ordered. The girl was stunned. 'Don't just stand there, do it! Come with me.' Donna grabbed the girl's arm and steered her forcefully towards the staff toilets. Flinging aside the two doors, she was unbuttoning her own blouse before they'd even reached the privacy of the ladies'. She hurled the stained item at Harriet, who paused only long enough to see the thunder in Donna's face before hurrying to follow suit. 'Now get back out there and give me the best night's work of your life,' Donna said, the threat all too obvious.

When she was alone, she allowed herself a moment to regroup. Standing in front of the wall-to-wall mirror above the basin, she looked hard at her own reflection. In her black lace bra, her breasts were pushed up into a pleasing cleavage and she nodded approvingly at the image before her. Still glowing a little, she had to admit, but for all that, she knew she had the ability to turn heads. She lifted her chin and smoothed the skin underneath it with the back of one hand before realising that the other still held Harriet's blouse. She looked down at it and hesitated. She hadn't even noticed what Harriet was wearing when she demanded the shirt from her back – all she knew was that they were roughly the same size. Now that she came to look at it, she felt a surge of apprehension. The blouse had a crossover front to it with a daringly low neckline and, unlike her own heavy cotton shirt, was thin and diaphanous. She'd been able to get away with her bra under the heavy cotton, but there was no way she could parade about the restaurant with black underwear clearly visible through this flimsy garment.

With a deft movement, she unclasped the bra and slipped out of it. Uncertain, she stopped for a moment as she caught a glimpse of her firm, round breasts in the mirror, but when she pulled her shoulders back to lift them up, they looked decidedly pert. She allowed herself a smile, then wrapped them in Harriet's blouse. She sighed resignedly as she looked at the same round breasts, staring blatantly back at her under the sheen of the fabric. It would be excruciatingly embarrassing, being on display like this, but still better than showing off the black lace. And in any case, she would be telling the girls to look after the front of house while she tended to her special guest in private.

Standing in front of the private-room door, warm plate in hand, Donna drew a long, steady breath, then blew it out slowly. Her heart was racing, the pounding causing a visible tremor in the soft folds of the blouse. She turned the handle and entered, leaning against the inside of the door to close it behind her and silently turning the key with her free hand.

He sat there still, as if nothing had happened. She waited.

After a few moments she wondered if he was all right. His head was bowed and his hands were out of sight below the table. Then he looked up.

This time, Donna was sure she caught an unmistakable expression. Mr Porter was surprised at her appearance. There was no question that in that first moment he had taken in the full extent of the fine fare before him. The food looked pretty good, too.

Almost immediately, the expression was gone. Mr Porter was grim-faced again.

'Put it down, then,' he said simply.

The brusque instruction had a strange effect on Donna. She'd never let herself be ordered about by anyone, but she found the strictness of the voice oddly exciting. She made her way across the carpet, trying not to let her free-range breasts get too close to those of the chicken on the plate she was holding. But even as she moved, she felt the fabric of the blouse caressing her unconstrained nipples and the thrill returned. By the time she reached the table, they were as hard as little pebbles and, as she bent over to set down the plate, her breasts rocked eagerly in Mr Porter's direction.

She misjudged the height of the table and let go too soon. As the plate dropped onto the starched cloth, the sauce that was bathing the chicken breast sloshed energetically off the side and joined the lobster on Mr Porter's tie.

Donna was mortified. She gaped at the tie in disbelief and felt her legs start to go. A knot welled up in her throat and she fought back the urge to scream and stamp her feet.

Mr Porter didn't flinch. Instead, he calmly reached up to

his neck, loosened the tie and lifted it over his head. 'I don't seem to be having much luck with that,' he said.

Donna found her voice. 'Mr Porter, I can't apologise enough. I think I've got some making up to do.'

'You're damn right there,' he replied, the curtness taking her a little by surprise. 'You can start by picking up my napkin for me. I dropped it under the table.'

Donna fell to her knees in an instant. Service – that's what he needs to see, she thought. I'm not too proud to go crawling round under the table looking for his dropped napkin. Anything to please. Anything.

She expected to see the napkin as soon as she lifted the tablecloth and peered underneath. When she didn't, she leaned forwards on all fours and crept under the cloth to look closer. Mystified, she lifted her head and looked towards the top of the impeccable trousers, wondering if it was perhaps caught on his knee. And there, nestled among the folds of the material, was a firm, handsome prick, naked and ready for action. A few dark hairs shrouded the base of the shaft, where it emerged from the zipper, but otherwise it was unclothed and displayed in all its raw glory.

Donna almost concussed herself on the underside of the table as she threw her head back in shock.

'Mr Porter!' she exploded, trying to shuffle out backwards.

She felt a rigid hand grip her right shoulder tightly and she stopped where she was, her bottom hanging out from under the tablecloth, her breasts swinging madly below her, her head poised at the level of his two outspread knees.

'Now, now,' he said, quieter than before but just as strict. 'Didn't you just say you had some making up to do?'

Donna tried to lift herself up from the cramped huddle she found herself in, but the only way she could move was either by wriggling out from under the table – which his strong grip would not allow – or by putting her left hand on his right knee to adjust her position. As soon as she did, his other hand was grasping her wrist, and the loop of his tie was lassoed over it and yanked tight.

'Ouch!' she squealed as the tie bit into her flesh, pulling her arm at an awkward angle up towards him. She clenched her fist, then released it again as she realised the effect this whole situation was having on her. The thrill was back, her heart was pounding more than ever, and her nipples were simply overjoyed.

He spoke again. 'I think the least you could do is offer me some form of recompense,' he said, the public schoolboy emerging again. 'Some might even say you deserve a little punishment for the way you've treated me.'

Donna felt a lurch in her chest of dazzling excitement and let her hand be pulled by the tie lasso. She pretended briefly to offer some resistance as he steered her towards his crotch, but by now she was as eager to have him in her hand as he was to be there. The first touch was electrifying, made all the more thrilling by the sheer naughtiness of her position. A desire to please? My God, she had never even realised she had this much desire to please. She clutched his cock as best she could under his control, and began massaging it with her fingers. He obviously knew exactly what he was doing and manoeuvred her hand diligently with the tie, now pumping her hard, now easing off for a more caressing touch. Donna wondered if he would want her to take him in her mouth, and she tried to examine the prick to see if she would be able to accommodate it. But he didn't seem too interested and kept on shifting her hand this way and that, squirming occasionally in his seat.

Donna felt hot, really hot. Her hair was a mess, constantly mangled against the table. Her neck was flushed, her breasts were rocking out of control under the thin chemise and her bottom was stuck bluntly out into the room, where the split in her skirt, she knew, was riding high up her thigh, exposing all the intimacies of her stocking tops and suspenders to the firm Mr Porter beyond the tablecloth.

Donna was loving every moment of it.

She felt him move, differently now from the twitching she was experiencing under her willing palm. The tie drew her hand away from him and she felt the knot slacken. Uncertain what to do, she shifted backwards slightly, starting to move out from under the table. His grip on her shoulder was lighter now, and she realised he was letting her move. But when she wriggled herself round in an ungainly manoeuvre so that her bottom was nearer his side of the table, she felt a new controlling hand come into scorching contact with her rump.

She was stunned into immobility again. He had just smacked her bottom. And it was electrifying.

'Stay exactly where you are,' he ordered, the strictness leaving no room for argument.

Donna waited what seemed like an eternity for what was to come next. Half terrified, half exhilaratingly expectant, she wondered what more she would be prepared to do for this damned review.

Then his hand was clamped against her right thigh, just above the knee on the skirt's hemline. She could feel the power in his palm and willingly surrendered to the strength of his touch. The hand ran slowly up the thigh, picking up the skirt as it went, and moved enticingly up her leg. When it reached the top of her stocking, she drew in a sharp breath of excitement. His hand rose higher, the fingers brushing the lacy tops of the hosiery before finally, deliciously, making contact with her flesh. Donna felt her pussy give a huge surge of anticipation and she forced her knees wider to open herself up.

But the hand didn't move round to the front, where her belly and groin were aching for his touch. Instead, it continued up the thigh, lifting the skirt higher and higher until her whole rump was uncovered, the pink flesh offset by her tiny black thong. Donna nervously pictured the view in her own mind, wondering how much of her bottom was visible to him from his angle and where his fingers might be headed next. Then the contact was gone and his hand had left her smooth skin.

She was momentarily bemused. Until the sting came.

How could she be so stupid, she wondered through the pain. She'd only just been spanked over the skirt, so why the hell hadn't she realised that exposing her buttocks was a precursor to a proper punishment? She was furious, outraged and utterly thrilled. She had never been spanked before by anyone, but the added scandal of a stranger administering the blows was almost too much to bear. Donna knew she ought to leap to her feet, throw his wine in his face and demand he get out of her restaurant immediately.

She didn't move.

Tears pricked her eyes, now buried in both hands against the floor under the table, as he rained his smacks on her buttocks. This was no playful game, but a real, hard, painful spanking, his palms flattened into beaters to whip against her flesh. The fullness of the contact and the whipping action of his arm and wrist reinforced the agony and Donna clenched her left fist and stuck it in her mouth to prevent herself from crying out. Taking her weight on that forearm, she freed her other hand and put it to use. She groped for her left breast and pressed her palm hard against it, relishing the rock-hard nipple and twitching as a new spasm of electricity flowed through her. She let her hand move further down her body, feeling the fabric of the thin blouse brush against her skin. As her fingers reached the top of the thong, she let her hand come to rest on the smoothness of her soft belly. She knew that as soon as she touched her pussy she'd be ready to come, and she didn't want that. Not yet. Instead, she reached behind her and waited for the next smack.

Her lightning reaction obviously took him by surprise.

Her grasp was firm, too, and she had the advantage of a plan. Gripping his wrist forcefully, she levered herself against his body weight to slip deftly out from under the table and simultaneously yank him towards her on his bench seat, away from the confines of the furniture. Now they were almost facing each other: Donna tousled and on her knees with her skirt round her waist; Mr Porter off-guard and exposed, his prick quivering brazenly in front of her.

She waited no longer. Lunging forwards, she clamped her mouth round him and began sucking furiously. Her tongue flicked eagerly round the tip as she first held him a little away, then she opened up her throat and sank deep onto the shaft. Her left hand grappled for his balls, fumbling to reach inside the trousers, but she never stopped pumping him with her mouth, slavering over the stiff cock. With her right hand, she finally gave in to her groaning pussy, running her agile fingers quickly through her hair, enjoying the tingle of anticipation until, at last, she found her warm, wet, welcoming lips.

It was almost instantaneous – for both of them.

Donna felt the creamy juice welling up through the shaft of his prick a second or two before it exploded into her mouth, the sweetness and acidity mingling beautifully as she gulped it down. In the same moment, she felt the surge rising in her own groin, the waves of intensity erupting in spasms as her expert fingers massaged in perfect harmony with his climax.

She was still coming as she felt his prick start to slacken, and the movement on her tongue gave her one final wave of delight. She shuddered involuntarily and released him from her mouth, easing her hand regretfully away from her pussy at the same time. Without looking at him, she delicately wiped the corner of her mouth with a single finger, then smoothed her skirt back down from around her waist, tossing her head back to free the hair from her face. Elegantly, she got up from her kneeling position, made a slight adjustment to the way her blouse hung over the glorious breasts, then picked up the napkin from the floor and draped it calmly across his still exposed prick.

Neither Donna nor Mr Porter spoke another word until he was leaving.

Silently, she had removed his main course plate and returned with dessert, then coffee and brandy a little later. She had brought him no bill to pay, and he had asked for none, so there was nothing to say when he stood up to leave. She opened the door to the private dining room for him and allowed him to pass by in the doorway, her nipples almost reaching out to touch him as he brushed past, but still nothing was said. They crossed the crowded restaurant in silence, Donna absolutely convinced that every single pair of eyes in the place was fixed firmly upon them.

When at last he reached the front door, he turned back to her and smiled. 'Thank you for that,' he said, peering over his glasses at her. 'That was truly an experience.'

She returned the smile and followed him out onto the shingle path that led down to the gate. She watched him hold open the gate for a little bald man coming the other way and then, without another glance back, he was gone.

Donna sighed, her breasts heaving under the blouse, her nipples firm again in the cool night air. She looked up at the stars and offered a silent prayer that, for what he had just received, may Mr Porter be truly thankful. Then she brought her gaze back down to earth and gave her best smile to the little bald man approaching up the shingle path.

'Good evening, sir, and welcome to La Prima Donna,' she said, holding out a hand to be shaken.

The little bald man took the cue readily. 'Good evening,' he replied. 'Ronald Brookman, the *Good Food Guide*.'

Midnight Feast Primula Bond

The zip snags reluctantly up my back, closing my dress little by little. Oh, where is a man when you need one? I turn sideways to watch myself in the mirror between the long windows. With the curtains open and darkness outside, I can see three of myself, window, mirror, window. But then so can the neighbours. Not three of me. What they can see is my crystal Venetian chandelier sending diamond darts of light over one mad woman with her elbows out like wings, twirling stiffly about like a Cecil Beaton mannequin.

I know that because my previous lodger, who kept all hours and no wonder when she turned out to be a French escort, told me so.

'How on earth do you know what the people at number fourteen can see?' I once asked her. As usual I was coming home, she was just going out. I liked to come home to an empty house but I was also secretly fascinated each day to see what she'd be wearing, and there she was, tiny green ra-ra skirt flirting at eye level, endless legs zigzagging down the stairs towards me. 'There's a great big fig tree in the way.'

'Because I visit Signor Sanchez there on Tuesdays,' she replied, opening her Beatrice Dalle lips and painting them pillar-box red. Without a mirror. Without taking her eyes off me. 'Or at least that's the name he gives me.'

'But number fourteen's a bed and breakfast.' I tried to look away, but her eyes are so huge, black, with lashes like thick spider's legs, ready to catch you. 'Why go there?'

'Because that's where he lives while he looks for some-where permanent. And I go where the clients go. You say in the trade I service him.' Her tongue ran across her teeth. 'But really he wants to live in a beautiful house like this. Everyone in the street would like to live in this house.'

My fingers pluck awkwardly between my shoulder blades. It's stuck. Shit. The zip is stuck. There's no one to help. I'm going to be late.

'You'll have to leave, Veronique,' I had told her, when the penny dropped. When she'd stood in the hallway, telling me exactly what she did to poor, lonely Signor Sanchez and how much he paid her. 'I can't have a hooker living here.'

She stepped behind me, helped me as I struggled out of my jacket. The armholes felt too tight. Everything felt too tight when she was living here.

'I have to make extra somehow. How else to pay the rent you charge?'

'You could have asked me –'

'You'll miss my choux, Fey. My millefeuilles,' she cooed. Have you noticed with French people how they always sound as if they have their mouths full? You can't say 'millefeuilles' without curling your lips, saliva gathering to devour some delicacy. She lifted my hair away from my collar, reading my mind. 'You love to nibble even when I'm out. Admit the pleasure my pastries give you. See how your skin shivers to think of it –'

'Your pastry makes me fat.' The relief of getting my jacket off was exquisite. But she didn't move away. Just gave a pantomime Gallic sigh.

'Starving people are always so uptight. You're most beautiful when you're eating. It's a treat for you. If only you could see it in that mirror of yours. How your eyes light up, your cheeks! Food makes you horny. Remember that time I kissed you after the Cointreau? You loved it.' Her whispered breath was moist against my ear. Cointreau is another French word which you can't pronounce without looking as if you're either kissing something or sucking it. Sure I remembered that time. Our drunken laughter as we watched yet another cooking programme, then her lips so moist against mine, slicked as they were with the lightest of lemon syllabubs, which she'd spiked with the liqueur. Lips that could suck the chrome bumper off a Dodge truck. 'But it's not just my food you need, Fey. It's sex. Hear it. Sex. And I could help you find it –'

'I'm sorry, Veronique.' I flinched away. She was close enough to kiss me again, to flick her tongue over the tip of mine again. 'I like you. A lot. But not like that. And this is a respectable neighbourhood. I need respectable lodgers.'

I tried to sound businesslike, but I was invaded by the sudden graphic vision of her red mouth wrapped round an erect Latin penis. Her cheeks hollowing as she sucked, like his member was a spoon dripping with chocolate fondant. My cheeks burning as I thought of it.

'*Je comprends.*'

I skittered across the hall to let her past.

'I mean, your clients could be anyone. They might come here, you know, make trouble –'

'Not Signor Sanchez. He's handsome, but very shy. Very quiet. Maybe *un peu* kinky.' Her eyelids drooped sensuously. 'He likes to watch you. Even when I'm with him, can you believe? You turn him on. Maybe he should pay *you*!'

'A peeping Tom! That's all we need.' I shuddered, making her laugh even more, but something slipped and turned inside me. 'I could be in danger.'

She shook her head wildly. 'He's a pussy cat. He likes to do it by the window. He can see you best in the winter. When the leaves are off the fig tree.'

My limbs went loose to think of the majestic Veronique stripping, gyrating in front of him, her big breasts thrust invitingly, licking her lips, opening her legs for him. And all the time a pair of black Spanish eyes staring past her, through the branches of the fig tree at me.

So I still do it. I'm doing it now. It's my cheap thrill. Twirling in front of the window, that is, with the curtains open. Trying to zip up my dress.

'He peeps while we fuck, but mostly he practises his cooking. And he cooks like a dream! But still too quiet for me.' My French lodger had shrugged. 'Not like my best client. Lord Robert, that's his car coming down the street, he takes me to parties in Paris and he's hung like a –'

'So two weeks' notice, OK?' I said, rousing myself. 'No hard feelings?'

She flung open the front door and kicked her leg out like a racehorse. She'd told me when she applied for the room that she was a dancer.

'I will go, sure, but who else will feed you?' She flew down the steps to the grey Lamborghini vibrating with rock music. A hairy wrist weighted by a vast Rolex rested on the steering wheel. 'Next time, get a man.'

I've not seen her since. She's never even collected her stuff. When I went to clean her room for the next lodger it was a tip, clothes everywhere, shoes, knickers, expensive silk and lace – nothing to indicate that she got laid for a living. In fact the dress I'm trying to do up now is hers. It's elegant, far too short and fits like a glove. I thought it would be perfect for the office party tonight. But the zip is broken.

She's right, I do miss her. The occasions when we collided in my kitchen at odd times of day or night. She made amazing pastry, taught at the knee of some rustic French aunt. There were always tins, plates, trays, piled with croissants, brioche, tarts, vol-au-vents stuffed with chicken, sweet pastries, savoury, tiny, enormous, that flaked down your chin and dribbled chocolate and custard and creamy cheese.

And the next day I'd rush in from work, foraging for more, but the trays, tins and plates would all be gone, the crumbs swept, the droplets of cream mopped.

There's the taxi, rumbling by the pavement, and I'm stuck. I can't get the zip up, nor down. Sweat is curling up my hair as I struggle.

'*Merde.*' Where is a French lodger when you need one?

The doorbell goes. Must be the taxi driver. I rush into the hallway, still trapped in my half-cocked dress.

'I'm not ready,' I screech. 'Just keep the engine running, would you?'

All I can see through the peephole is a dancing bottle of champagne. Why is he waving a bottle of champagne?

'Apologies for being late, but I was doing the lap of honour.'

I wrench open the door. 'Lap of honour?'

The taxi driver is so tall that all I can see are the buttons on his neat striped shirt. His Adam's apple jumps as he swallows. There is sweat along his upper lip. His lower lip is full, and he's biting on it.

'Chef has to do the rounds of the tables, you know, after service. We opened today, but only for lunch, because I was meeting you tonight.' He shoves the bottle at me so that it nudges in between my breasts. The cold shears through the dress. 'The restaurant's going to be a winner. It'll pay the rent, you'll be glad to know.'

'Meeting me? Rent? I don't understand.' As I fold my arms crossly, the bottle rubs absently across one nipple, making me gasp. 'I ordered a taxi. Are you a taxi? I mean –'

'No. That's my van. It's refrigerated, but I'll have to unload my leftovers, if that's all right?' He bends down to peer at me. He could look like a lean Antonio Banderas if he wasn't so pale, his hair so neat. His eyes are very dark, with shadows smeared across his pale cheeks. There's the summery smell of strawberries wafting off him. 'You look blank, Fey. I phoned about the room? I'm Jonny.'

The room. The clean room, ready for my new lodger. *Next time, get a man.* A tall, pale man with black hair combed neatly to one side, trying to shake my hand.

'Look, I've got to go out. I'm late. Can't deal with this now.'

'Not a good time, then.' He turns to go. That's when I see the suitcase and what looks like a picnic box on the doorstep. 'It's my fault.'

'Hang on. Where will you go?'

'I'm so tired it doesn't matter.' He flattens his hand over his hair. There is dark stubble peppering his cheeks. 'I can sleep at the restaurant.'

'I'm being rude.' An icy draught whistles sideways down my bare back. 'Come on in, Jonny.'

He follows me inside just as the actual taxi arrives, honking. As I spin about to wave at it, I feel hands on my shoulders.

'Wait,' he says. His fingers are delicate, brushing the top of my spine. My hair is up, and my skin shivers. The last person to touch me there, touch me anywhere, was Veronique. I should shake him off, but I do wait. 'Your dress,' he adds.

Jonny pinches the edges together, pulling me about as if he's dressing a child, first forwards, then rocking me back against him. His body is warm. Then the zip slides easily up. Not much further, as it happens, just above my bra strap. The dress is very low cut. We stand still for a moment. My shoulders have been forced back, and my breasts push against the velvet. My skin yearns for another touch.

But he's busy now, heaving the box and the case through the door, heading straight for the kitchen as if he knows the way. Jumping down the steps, just as Veronique did, to bring more boxes out of his van.

'I have to go,' I say. But now I'm following him. He sets the cold boxes down on my gleaming counters then opens them slowly. I can't wait. He delves inside, and pulls out slabs of bloody steak, muddy vegetables, all green, fruit, all red, industrial-sized pots of cream, whole golden cheeses, silver-wrapped bars of chocolate. 'Duty calls.'

My stomach groans.

'I'm sure I can find my way around, if you have to go.' He's pulling a thick knife out of a leather case. Other knives are lined up like surgical instruments. The fingers that stroked my spine earlier, that dressed me, run along the sharp blade, then finger the pearly interior of a scallop shell. He's murmuring to himself. '*Coquilles san Jacques*, I think.'

'You're very quiet for a chef. Very tidy. I thought they were all –'

'Dynamic and sexy, like Gordon Ramsay?' His sudden smile wipes the exhaustion from his face. I can just see his white teeth. 'With hair that goes wild when he swears, and an obsession with his own bollocks?'

My face goes redder, but he's so right. Veronique and I fancied Gordon Ramsay like crazy. She used to wriggle about on the kitchen counter, watching the TV, practically creaming herself when he stripped off to put on his starched white chef's jacket.

I reach round Jonny to finger a baby leek. Its ends are frilled, the surface smooth. He takes the leek. My kitchen is tiny, so his sleeve scrapes my arm as he mercilessly starts to chop, releasing the garlicky aroma. Veronique used to describe what Gordon Ramsay would be like in bed. Those strong footballer's buttocks flexing between her dancer's legs . . .

But Jonny's hands are right here, in my kitchen, not on TV, flying over the wooden board, taming the vegetables. I can imagine them smothering me in warm butter. Flipping me over like a pancake.

'Your room is across the landing, on the left. Next to mine.'

'Have a good time.' He glances up. His eyes look less tired now, brighter. He rolls up his sleeves and reaches into a punnet to dangle a strawberry by its frail green leaf. 'I'll get you my references tomorrow.'

'Is that what you made for your special lunch? A strawberry pudding?'

My stomach twists as he nods and balances the plump fruit on the end of his finger before piercing it with his teeth. 'My pièce de résistance. How did you guess?'

'Your smell. You smell of strawberries. Sharp, but sweet.' I can hardly breathe.

He hands me a strawberry, too. 'Here's summer in a basket. You can just smell the freshly mown grass, can't you, as you spread out the picnic? Feel the sun on your legs as you lie back afterwards on the rug, dozy with wine.'

I stop examining the strawberry and find him leaning close, staring at me. His eyes burn like coals. I lick the bumpy surface then find myself opening my mouth very slowly to take in the strawberry.

'Go on, eat.' He extends one finger under my chin. 'Careful it doesn't drip –'

'Too late.' I smile as juice dribbles over my bottom lip and onto his finger. He wipes the finger across my mouth again so that my lips yield under it. My tongue just tastes the mixture of clean skin, leek and strawberry and it's all I can do not to suck his finger right into my mouth. My eyelids are actually fluttering with the rush of desire this simple touch has aroused. 'I should be going.'

He nods, turning away. But I lean against the fridge as he turns on the gas and brushes olive oil onto my griddle. The fridge hums against my back. I've never noticed that before. He lays out two steaks and starts to bash them.

'But it's winter,' I say, still thinking of the way he loved those strawberries. 'What about a winter fruit?'

'That's easy. Figs.' He pulls an old-fashioned brown-paper bag towards him, and out roll some green and purple ovals. He picks one up, makes a crisscross over one end, then squeezes the other end. The green skin of the fruit puckers and rips slightly, and there's the sudden, wet redness of the innards, fleshy and studded with tiny seeds, oozing through the crack. 'These Greek ones are in season now.'

He holds it up in the air between us, not offering it to me this time. The griddle starts to smoke. As I stare at the plump fruit, he slowly squeezes it harder so that the flesh and juice and seeds spurt onto the palm of his hand.

'I lace the figs with honey, maybe some mascarpone. So sweet,' he says, scooping the mixture out of its skin with his fingers and letting it ooze between them. 'And my other secret ingredient.'

Then he stuffs it all into his mouth, grinning, as I practically whimper with greed.

The doorbell rings, long and loud.

He wipes his mouth, clean as a whistle once again. 'You don't mind if I prepare some dishes for the restaurant while you're out?'

I push myself away from the fridge. I can't help my hips swaying in the tight dress. I straighten my spine, like I did when he zipped me up, but I'm dizzy with hunger now. My thighs above the stockings kiss each other damply as I walk towards the hall.

'So long as you promise to feed me when I come home.' My voice is husky with lust, but I'm hoping he won't notice. 'Although I don't know when that will be – after midnight, probably.'

'With pleasure,' he replies behind me, measuring out some flour. 'I've been wanting to feed you for months.'

I whirl round. He looks away and picks up the steaks with a pair of tongs and flips them onto the griddle. They sizzle urgently, smoke and steam rising into his face and turning my kitchen into a heavenly hell.

And through the steam I see that the effort of bashing and chopping has fired him up. Glossy strands of black hair have fallen over his eyebrows. He swipes at the sweat with his forearm, but the hair just falls back chaotically and now I can see how this work makes a man of him.

So he continues, muscles twitching under the striped shirt, bent over in that earnest, coiled way chefs have, fingers deftly avoiding the knife's advance and reducing leaves of watercress to flecks.

'We've only just met!' I remember I'm supposed to be challenging his last remark.

'Whenever I see you, you look hungry.' He looks up, pointing the knife at me, then looks quickly down again. From nowhere two chicken breasts have appeared, and he's making incisions in the gleaming fillets. 'I mean, too many bones showing when I did up your dress. Some more flesh is what you need.'

'What do you mean, see me?'

'Oh, you know, around.'

'And what are you doing now?'

He starts to push some mixture from yet another bowl into the cavity, his fingers so gentle. He closes the skin back over the stuffing then starts on the other one. 'Truffles and herbs. Orgasmic when it's roasted. It has to go in deep, see? But push it in like you're making love to the bird. Never fuck it.'

My fanny responds with a convulsive twitch of excitement. And before I can press him further about his 'seeing me', the door knocker rattles irritably and I stalk off to answer it, clapping my hand over my mouth to stop me squealing out loud. *It's not just your food I need.*

It's literally the stroke of midnight when I return. I was late for the party, and by the time I got there only dry snacks like peanuts and crisps were left. I might have eaten something if there'd been Veronique's gilded pastries there, overflowing with prawns or goats' cheese, but breadsticks? The mooted idea was to go out afterwards, try out a new South American joint, but although my new dress was admired and my glass liberally filled, all I could think about was how the watercress jus would look drizzled over the fillet steaks burgeoning on my hob at home.

The delicate barbecue smell greets me as I open the door and the lights are on, but the kitchen is dark. I dither on my doormat, kicking off a pair of Veronique's shoes she left behind, my ears pricked for any sound.

I can see that Jonny has settled in because his bedroom door is firmly closed. I picture him lying on his bed, the striped shirt unbuttoned to his narrow waist, no sign of the French girl up there now, his masculine belongings, jeans, jackets, wooden spoons, colanders, steamers, scat-

tered all over the floor in place of the dresses and knickers
I stole.

I'm so restless. My stomach is gnawing at me now. One
strawberry, that's all I've had all day. I wander into the
sitting room and the fire is flickering, the lights turned low,
and there, spread out on the coffee table, is a feast. The
bottle of champagne is in a bucket. There are two plates,
each with a steaming steak lying inside a star shape of
leeks and drenched in a pale-green sauce. A square stack of
chips is on a separate plate, glittering with salt.

I lean over the table and snatch up a handful of chips.
Jonny said I needed more flesh on me, so here goes. I stuff
the fried wedges into my mouth, making a snuffling noise
like a pig, which makes me giggle. The golden potato skins
burst against my teeth to give me the buttery, fluffy
centres. I sit down, hitching the tight dress up round my
thighs, and cut into the steak, letting the watercress sauce
linger on my tongue with each mouthful until the plateful
is gone. I'm about to start on the second plate when I
realise that mine was perfectly warm.

I jump up. I'm like Goldilocks, except this is *my* house.
I'm about to dart into the kitchen, call up the stairs, when
the chandelier sheds its diamonds of light over me. My
reflection dances in the long mirror. It's smiling. The cheeks
are pink, the hair is falling out of its pins, and I can see
right up my white thighs to my black knickers. I turn
sideways. My stomach is bulging softly against the velvet.
I reach behind me, try the zip, and the dress strokes me as
it glides easily off.

I glance outside. The fig tree is bare, but one branch is
pointing at a bowl of figs he's left on the table by the
window. They are all cut open and glistening. He's laced
them with honey, like he said.

'So, Signor Sanchez,' I say, quite loudly, picking up one
of the figs and squeezing its flesh out of the wound just as
Jonny did. 'Want an eyeful?'

The branches lurch and shiver eagerly. I start to sway,

right there in front of the window. My legs look longer in the stockings, the expensive lace bra lifts my breasts like muffins rising in the oven. More food would make them bigger. More food would add a curve to these hips. I gyrate so that the hips jut from side to side. Then I bite hard into the tender pink fruit, tangling it between my teeth, deliberately letting juice run down my throat.

I imagine Signor Sanchez gasping across the garden wall, panting for me at his window. Who's he getting to pleasure him, now that Veronique and her obscene lips are busy working on Lord Robert? Perhaps our poor Signor is all alone, turned on by watching me. I want him to watch me.

So what shall I show him first? What shall I do to myself first? The sweet fruit is delicious in my mouth, dribbling over my lips. I swig straight from the champagne bottle. For a moment the coldness clamps itself round my head. I wonder if that's the correct temperature it should be, but it bubbles and mixes in my mouth with the fruit. I drink again. I feel so greedy. I let droplets fall down my throat, over my breasts. A little more, directly over my nipples so that they burn hot, poking through the flimsy lace.

I lower the bottle so that it's between my naked thighs. The long shape is hard as I dance with it, levering it up and down, press it up against my fanny, letting the sex lips grab and nibble around it.

My fingers are sticky from the honey, and I trail my free hand over my breasts. My nipples perk up instantly. My throat swells in a moan. My head is spinning now, all inhibitions gone. My hands move over me more urgently, juice and honey on my skin, moving downwards as if drawn by the promise of a warm fire and the stickiness just feels so decadent. My fingers are drawn into my knickers and I hook them away, the silk agitating the little hairs, tugging them from my pubes. I smooth the curls down over the soft lips and one finger slips into the warm wet crack hiding there.

'Hey, Signor Sanchez,' I mew, relishing the sensation as I play with myself, spreading my legs as if for an audience. 'Wanna come over and fool around a little?'

'He can't see you.'

In mid-grope, there in the mirror is Jonny, standing right behind me. His hair is wet from the bath, beautifully dishevelled. His stubble is even darker than before. He's got my baby-pink towel slung round his waist and I was right. It's a very slim waist, but a line of dark hair marches down from his navel, down towards his groin, down under the girly towel, but the face I can see is that of a Mexican bandit.

'How do you know about Signor Sanchez?'

His hands are warm and heavy on my shoulder blades again, fingers tripping down my spine, but this time they find the bra strap and snap it open. My breasts fall forwards, swollen from the honey and champagne and fig juice and delight. The dark nipples point at where Signor Sanchez should be, like arrow tips.

'I know that he got tired of watching.'

Jonny's big steak-bashing hands come up and cradle my breasts, pushing them together, and my whole body is aching now, full of food, dizzy with champagne. He kneads my breasts as if he's shaping dough, rubbing the nipples until they're sore, while my fingers return to their trail, down my stomach, into my knickers, down towards my sex. It's throbbing. I prod the warm slit and it crackles like a mini firework.

'You haven't finished eating yet,' he says, his voice deeper than before, and I realise why. As he presses up against me I lean back, yielding to the pleasure radiating from my swollen breasts, and I feel the champagne shape of his big erection, bulging through my towel. He picks up another fig and rubs it across my mouth. 'And nor have I.'

I groan for an answer. I so want to let go. In the mirror my lips part as I watch one of his hands leave my breasts to rip at my knickers, tearing the threaded seams so that the garment disintegrates and falls in silky strips to the floor. I grab his hand and plunge it into the soft fur of my pussy.

'I want cream for my figs,' I gasp, making no sense. He's pushing me towards the table in front of the window, and then he bends me across it so that my breasts are squashing into the bowl of open, bleeding figs. They seem to yearn up towards me, sticking themselves to me with their honey and with the fragrance of Jonny's secret ingredient wafting off them and filling my head.

'On its way,' he replies. So quiet. His voice is always so quiet, but instead of shy he sounds sexy.

I reach behind me. It's my turn to rip at him. The towel falls away and there's his cock, stiff in my hand and ready to jab at me. A delicious spicy sausage. I grasp it and feel it grow harder in my fingers. Veronique would suck it, wouldn't she? But electric charges are streaking down me now, down to my empty, waiting sex.

His hands slide down my sides, bumping over my ribs, my skin alive under his touch. I wonder if he's counting the bones. He bends me over further, so that my buttocks are in the air and I'm wallowing in the bowl of figs right there in front of the window, for all the world to see.

'And the secret ingredient. What's that?' I ask again, my head really spinning now. My body is on fire. I've never felt this horny, not even when I was a teenager. Everything that touches me sears. His fingers. The edge of the table jabbing in my stomach. The figs squashing and squirting, my breasts like extra fruit.

'A horny woman is the only ingredient I need.'

'You smoothie –'

'And a little help from my secret potion, to make her relax. Make her want to dance in front of the window, just like this.'

I can just make out our outlines in the dark glass. The quiet voice is talking so dirty now, and I'm giggling and shaking with desire. If he touches me there, if I rub on the table, I'll come. He parts my buttocks, and I tense deliciously, waiting for his cock to come in after, fuck me, satisfy me, but instead he's reaching round me, taking another fig out of the bowl, crushing it into his hand, then there's a cool wet sensation as he smears the fruit up my thighs, over my pussy, the scent merging with my own scent of excitement.

'Now, let me taste you.'

I can barely hear him, he's so quiet, but he's on his knees behind me, his warm hands holding my cheeks open, and suddenly there's his tongue, swiping up warm and wet, licking at the dripping fig juice, tantalising the aching clit which has popped out of hibernation. I push the bowl so hard that it falls and smashes on the floor, but that's *tant pis* and I lie flat on the table because I can't support my weight any more, while he laps and guzzles and darts of pleasure grow and threaten to overwhelm me.

'No. Just fuck me!' I hear myself, wanton and hungry. He's obedient, that's for sure. He laughs softly, then stands up again. At last his cock goes where his mouth went, finding its way in. It is rock hard, just like the champagne bottle, and hot. Jonny's turned into a gigolo. A gypsy gigolo who cooks like a dream and lives in my house.

It's easy, so easy. I tilt my pussy and in he slides, the length of him, sliding into place. I'm spread across the table like a feast, my legs still in Veronique's stockings but nothing else, his hands grasping my hips and pulling me against him so that his cock enters then waits just on the edge. I can feel my sex wanting to grab and swallow him, but this isn't the quiet, tired chef any more. He moves slowly, edging that rigid length, luxuriously, further inside me. I should have known he would do this gradually, just as he unwound and became gradually more of a man in the kitchen.

I grip the table for balance, my breasts nestled, warm and soaked in fig juice, still searching for my invisible audience outside. He's right inside me now, all the way to the hilt. I want him to ram it now, I'm so ready, it's so lovely not to be hungry any more and to feel the solid length of a real man's rampant penis inside me, come on, please, go for it.

I hear myself moaning, pleading out loud and he gives a little nod as if answering not my signal but someone else's, which I can just see in the window, then he's ramming it, ramming up me, pulling me into his body so that I feel as if he's going to explode through the top of my head.

Now at last he's groaning, too, and bending a little so that we are moving as one and his warm torso is against my cold spine, keeping out the draught, and now I'm moaning and tossing my head, wishing Signor Sanchez could see me. No, not just him. Veronique, too. I want her to see that I can eat and have sex and have pleasure, wearing her clothes, maybe, but so what if it works?

And me and my lodger, Jonny, we have a rhythm and Veronique didn't teach me that. He's with me, slithering me back and forth in the fig juice, pulling his own hips back, waiting when I wait, but the desire to obliterate years of starvation is overwhelming me. I grind up and down his shaft, trying to ease the frantic urge to come. My body grabs to keep him inside, and his cock hardens with each thrust. In the glass I see his eyes blazing at me.

Then we're moving faster, his head above mine, rocking with mine in the window. The fig twigs scratch at the glass, but now my eyes are closing as the ecstasy reaches its peak, the orgasm hovering so close, the hot pleasure gathering to shoot through us. I'm already thinking, my God, he lives here, we can do this again and again, in the kitchen next time, in the bedroom . . .

And here it is, coming to the boil, then exploding into the silent night.

He rests on top of me for a moment, then reaches past me to close the curtains. They haven't been closed for months. He leaves me sprawled and walks to the other window, shuts the curtains there.

'Veronique told me it would be better than watching,' he says. From nowhere he produces a pile of meringue and cream, topped with strawberries.

'What's the name?' I lick my lips greedily, not really listening to him, opening my mouth like a baby bird to be fed. 'For your special pudding?'

He breaks a piece off the top and pushes it into my mouth. 'Strawberries Sanchez.'

Dinner Service Monica Belle

'What *do* men like, Keon?'

'What men like, girl, is pussy, 'cept for guys like me, who like a big, hard . . .'

'There's no need to be crude, Keon.'

'I ain't being crude, Honey, just telling it like it is. Guys like pussy, and tits, and ass.'

I grimaced, knowing he was probably right, at least in part. That couldn't be the whole story, because if James had been the sort of grunting caveman Keon was depicting he'd have picked me over Caroline de Lacy-Hamilton. *Miss* Caroline de Lacy-Hamilton as it had to be, always making sure I knew she was boss. And to think I hadn't minded at first, to think I'd looked up to her, even had a bit of a crush on her maybe.

Not any more, not after what she'd done, and it just wasn't fair! I was taller than her, slimmer than her, just about, and definitely had a better bust and a nicer bum. At least, everyone at Grosvenor's Bank said so, all my friends, but as she was the bitch boss from hell nobody was going to be nice about her anyway. Except James. And me, before she'd started to show an interest in him.

James seemed to think she walked on water. Always, he was going on about how well she dressed, how stylish she was, how she always wore the best. It never seemed to occur to him that maybe I would have liked to wear Prada and Loro Piana and Stephanie Kelian, but on the miserable pittance she paid me as her PA I just couldn't afford to.

He had started to confide in me about how much he liked her, and that was bad, seriously bad. Soon he'd be telling me I was his friend and asking me advice on what to buy for her birthday. She'd go for it too, not because she fancied him so much, but because then I couldn't have him. I could already imagine her smug little remarks, the casual drops of acid to make me feel small, as if I should never have aspired to him in the first place. Why, oh why, had I admitted to her that I liked him?

I didn't want to be his friend, I wanted to be his lover, but I just couldn't compete. If he went out with her it would be unbearable. I'd even admitted to him I occasionally fantasised about other women, which had really turned him on. If he told her . . .

It didn't bear thinking about. I had do something, but what? She had all the advantages. At least I had Keon, safely gay and so the only male friend I could possibly confide in. He was also a friend of James, but he wasn't being a lot of help, so far.

'OK, Keon, never mind the caveman stuff. What does James like? What can I possibly do to make him take notice of me over Caroline?'

'Forget it, Honey. The guy's not for you.'

'Yes he is! He's my God!'

He shook his head. 'No, he ain't. James is . . . James is kinda weird, for a nice girl like you.'

'No, he's not! He's a really sweet guy, he just . . . just . . . it's not him, it's Caroline. She's been throwing herself at him ever since I admitted I liked him, and I just can't compete, especially the way she bosses me around in front of him, and puts me down.'

'Like I said, girl, he's kinda weird. Don't get down about it, any man's got to pick you over her, normally. Find some nice, safe guy, like Dave from accounts, he likes . . .'

'Playing stupid war games and pretending he's some sort of action hero. I couldn't, not ever. So what's weird about James? I thought you were his friend?'

'I am. Maybe weird's wrong. I'm just saying he's not the man for you, doll.'

He'd gone into one of his impressions, Humphrey

Bogart, and I knew that meant I wouldn't get anything serious out of him. I drew a sigh. He was wrong. James was a nice guy, just easily led, a bit like a puppy really, and Caroline could always offer him better treats than I could. She was the sort to keep him guessing, too, always offering but never giving, and he fell for it. Not me. I liked sex too much. I'd gone with him on the first night. Big mistake.

'Maybe if I hadn't slept with him?'

'That ain't so, doll. I tell you, the guy's just strange.'

'Keon, stop it! Why are you putting him down?'

To my relief he reverted to his normal voice. 'He ain't for you, Honey, and I hate to see you get hurt, that's all.'

'I already am hurt, but I'm not giving up. If you want to help, tell me what to do to get his attention.'

He shrugged.

'OK, but don't say I didn't warn you.'

Working as Caroline's PA, and with Keon in the catering department, I didn't see him for the rest of the week. I knew he'd been out drinking with James, and I was desperate to know what had been said, but my chance didn't come until the Saturday, when he phoned to say he'd meet me at the Ring.

It was a gay pub, and I felt a little uneasy as I went in, but to my relief I wasn't the only woman there and nobody stared. Keon was at the bar, talking to a man every bit as muscular as him, only white, and with tattoos decorating his bare, brawny arms. Not for the first time I wondered why all the fittest guys seem to be gay.

Keon greeted me with a smile and a friendly arm around my shoulder as I joined him, giving me a squeeze as he introduced me.

'This is Honey, my baby sis'. Honey, meet Doug, and don't be scared of the way he looks. He's a pussy underneath.'

'Hi, Doug.'

I smiled as I answered, not at all afraid of him, rather intrigued, if a little disappointed, but I reminded myself that I wanted to be with James, so it didn't matter how many other cute guys were gay or not. I bought a round of drinks and Keon began to steer me to a quiet corner, excusing himself to Doug. He was in an up mood, and I was hoping that meant things had gone well, but his voice was unusually serious as he sat me down in an alcove and leaned close to speak.

'There's good, and there's bad.'

'Oh.'

'The good is that James is well into you, and I mean, well in.'

'Great! What's the bad news then?'

He grimaced and hesitated before he answered. 'I didn't want to say this, 'cause it might hurt you, but James is kinda kinky.'

'Kinky? How do you mean?'

'Nothing too weird, nothing heavy. James is an all right guy, just kinda kinky.'

'Tell me. I'm not a nun, Keon.'

'Thing is, he likes to have his girls helpless, you know, tied up and that.'

I swallowed, shocked, but immediately thinking how it would feel to be tied by James, completely at his mercy. Then I had another thought. 'I can't see Caroline going for that!'

Keon laughed. 'Dead right! Now that's where you're in, if you're up for it?'

I bit my lip, still doubtful. Sex shouldn't really happen that way, arranged in advance, but if it meant I'd be with James ...

'OK, but what did he have in mind? Couldn't we just have a date and see how it goes or something?'

'No, no, he's coming to dinner at your place, Saturday

next, and you just leave it all up to Keon, because when it comes to dinner, I am the man. I'll explain.'

'Are you sure this is going to work, Keon?'

'Trust me. I've got the guy's number. You'll blow his mind.'

I couldn't help but grimace. It had seemed a good idea at the time, over several glasses of white wine in the Ring, only now I wasn't so sure.

'Maybe it would be better just to have the dinner?'

'Don't you turn yellow on me, Honey. Now off with those clothes and into the shower with you while I start getting things ready.'

Still I hesitated, but I couldn't very well back out, not when Keon had gone to so much effort for me, and James would be arriving in a couple of hours, so there was no time to waste. There was time to get drunk though, because I'd need to be, and I grabbed a bottle of the Aussie Chardonnay Keon had brought as I made for the shower.

One glass just wasn't enough. Two and I was feeling a bit better about it. Three and I wanted a fourth. Four and I was sure I was as ready as I'd ever be. I had a fifth while I dried myself and made-up, just for good measure, which left so little in the bottle it seemed silly not to finish it off.

Maybe Keon was gay, but I still felt self-conscious as I went down stairs in nothing but a towel. He was going to see everything, bits of me even James hadn't seen, or any other boyfriend. Even if he wasn't interested, he was still a man, and what woman doesn't feel at least a bit uneasy going bare in front of any man other than her lover?

James at least I didn't mind. James I wanted to see, and to take full advantage, so he'd be completely smitten, just as Keon had assured me he would be. Like he said, what red-blooded male could resist such an offer? I just hoped he was right, or it would be the most embarrassing moment of my life.

I could smell the food as I opened the kitchen door,

honey and mustard dressing, which Keon was making at the stove, his dark face set in concentration as he stirred the grain mustard into the mixture. Blushing hot, I felt I had to say something, if only to put off the moment when I'd have to drop my towel.

'You, er . . . you like cooking, don't you?'

'When it comes to cooking, I am the man. We have just the sweetest Jersey Royal potatoes, fresh from the ground, red and yellow pepper, just a little bit of endive, all on a bed of rocket, but that, my girl, is just for decoration. For the *pièce de résistance*, we have . . .'

'I know, but what are we actually going to eat?'

He winked at me. 'I know what he's going to eat, Honey. He's going to eat cat, pussy cat . . . poor pussy cat . . .'

He'd begun to sing the Right Said Fred song, complete with all the motions, his muscles rippling beneath the deep-brown skin of his bare arms. Not for the first time I found myself wishing he wasn't gay. He did look good, and he made me laugh too, playing the fool and showing off all the time. Suddenly, it wasn't so hard to let my towel go.

'Quit mucking about, Keon, we've haven't got time. How do you want me?'

To answer me, he gave an elaborate flourish and begun to speak in a phoney French accent.

'Ah yes, for mademoiselle, everything is in preparation, compliments of the Grosvenor's Bank catering department, not that they know. *Voilà!*' He gestured to a trolley he'd obviously pinched from work, on top of which he'd put a huge foil dish. 'If mademoiselle would care to climb on?'

Now was the moment. I began to let go of my towel, changed my mind, slipped, and it was around my ankles anyway, leaving me stark naked in front of him. He merely made another gesture, twiddling his fingers and bowing, like something out of *The Three Musketeers*. I couldn't help but laugh, though I was blushing too and as he took hold of the trolley to allow me to climb on, I realised that I was going to have to get in an incredibly rude position, kneeling with my bum stuck in the air and everything showing from behind.

I knelt facing him, even though he was going to see anyway, and I was reminding myself over and over again that he was gay and it didn't matter. Unfortunately, it did, and I was reacting despite myself and in a completely inappropriate way, flushing hot across my face and chest, between my legs too, while my nipples had suddenly grown embarrassingly stiff.

'Mademoiselle is very beautiful,' he remarked, and to my relief turned back to where the honey and mustard sauce was cooling on the stove.

He had everything set out, leaving me no time to feel ready and no excuses. With my heart hammering and my face so hot I was sure I'd be the colour of a beetroot, I bent forwards as he cut a length of kitchen string with my scissors. I swallowed at the thought of how helpless it would make me, how easily James would be able to take me. It was good, and it had to be done, for all my embarrassment.

Keon was acting again, pretending to be a doctor as he came to me with the string stretched taut between his big hands, his evil grin giving the lie to his soothing words as he spoke. 'If you would cross your wrists please, Miss Martins. This won't take a moment.'

I was smiling despite myself as I crossed my wrists, but it was impossible not to let my feelings build as he lashed them together and tied them off with a neat bow. With my wrists securely bound, he went behind me to do my ankles, my tummy fluttering desperately for the view I was giving him, and just inches away. He had me helpless, in bondage, something far, far kinkier than I'd ever imagined myself doing, and it was turning me on so much, my throat was tight, the warmth between my thighs growing by the moment.

That was all very well, but if James didn't respond . . .

'If this doesn't work, Keon, I'm going to have to kill you.'

Suddenly, he was the French chef again, lifting his chin in disdain for my doubt as he spoke. 'Mademoiselle, have you no faith? In Paris, I have practised my art, in Bruxelles also, *et* Lille, *et* Bordeaux, *et pour le président de la République lui-même! Moi, je suis un artiste! Et vous, vous êtes une barbarienne Anglais, un Rosbif!*'

He finished with a haughty sniff, and I was giggling despite myself as I answered. I certainly felt like roast beef.

'I'm not sure that's a real French word, Keon ... ow!'

He'd smacked my bottom, quite hard, leaving my cheek warm and tingling, enough to want to reach back and touch, but I couldn't, not any more. I was tied up.

'Don't take liberties, you, even if you are gay.'

It was hard to sound as if I meant it, and predictably he refused to take me seriously, turning back and pretending to twirl a non-existent moustache.

'I am not gay, mam'selle, merely *Parisienne*.'

'So why have you got a boyfriend then?'

He gave what was supposed to be a Gallic shrug and turned back to the food, pinching his fingers together and rubbing the tips in a gesture of exaggerated delight as he admired his own handiwork.

'I am a genius, *non*? And you, *mon petit choux*, you shall be my masterpiece!'

'Just hurry up, will you, or James will be here before you're finished.'

'*Du calme, mam'selle*, genius must never be rushed!'

I didn't answer, not wanting to encourage him, even though his banter was the only thing keeping my mind off just how exposed I felt. It got worse too, as he began to arrange the salad around me, not making the least effort to spare my modesty, but walking around me so that he got the full view of my open cheeks behind and every detail between. I was wet, I couldn't help myself, and I was sure he'd notice.

He said nothing, either to save my blushes or because he was simply unaware how an excited woman reacts, but continued to arrange the salad and poured a little sauce on top, again walking behind me. I thought of how I'd look, open and ready, completely exposed to him, as I would be to James. Only James, James would take out his lovely thick cock and pop himself in, maybe my mouth first, then properly, deep, deep inside me, the way I've longed for him to do every single night.

Keon spoke up again, now in his normal voice. 'Calm down, hun, not long now.'

I realised I'd moaned as I thought of how good it would feel when James took me and felt the blood rush to my face. Again, I was telling myself it didn't matter, that Keon was gay, but I was kneeling nude on a platter with my wrists and ankles tied and my body decorated with salad and dressing, a sight nobody but the most intimate of lovers should ever have been allowed to see. It was too late, he'd seen, every little detail. I'd closed my eyes to try to calm my raging feelings as he spoke again, now as the doctor. 'This may be a little warm, Miss Martins.'

My eyes popped open as he began to pour the sauce over me. It wasn't warm, it was hot, steaming hot, leaving me gasping and wriggling on the platter. Suddenly, he was French again. '*Non, non, non!* Do not move by an inch or you will ruin the effect, *méchante fille!*'

'It's hot, Keon! Ow!'

'Ha! That I must work in such conditions, me! *C'est le bordel!*'

He'd spanked me again, across both cheeks this time and even harder, leaving me tingling behind in a way that sent the heat straight to my sex.

'Please, don't, Keon, that's not funny.'

His voice changed again, to a ridiculous exaggeration of upper-class English. 'Nonsense, my dear, nothing like a little spanking to keep a girl on her toes, eh, what? Now do hold still, won't you?'

'Keon, please ... ow, ow, ow ...'

I shut my eyes, my teeth gritted as he began to pour the

sauce over my bottom, right between my cheeks, the hot, sticky fluid running down onto the most sensitive places to set me squirming and wriggling my toes in reaction, not sure if I was in pain or in ecstasy. More went on, over my cheeks, and I had a sudden vision of my bottom like a plum pudding I'd once seen on the cover for a video of *A Christmas Carol*, big and round and dripping with cream.

As the heat began fade, I was still gasping for breath. My body felt warm all over, my skin tingling, and the urge to push up my hips to accept a cock inside myself was close to overwhelming. As Keon walked back into the kitchen, I watched the hard, muscular eggs of his buttocks move beneath his Levis, and again wished he wasn't gay, only to immediately fill with guilt. I was for James, and James alone. It was completely wrong to be getting horny over my gay friend, silly too, because he couldn't possibly be interested, however much I wanted him to come behind me and slide the full length of what I was sure would be an enormous cock up into my body...

I shook myself, trying to get the disturbing thoughts out of my head, but it was no good. As I opened my eyes and looked up, it was on the tip of my tongue to ask if, maybe, just maybe, he wouldn't mind putting a knuckle to my sex, just to help me calm down a bit. It was such a shameful thing to ask a man, to masturbate me because I couldn't control myself, but I needed it so badly, so very badly...

The words wouldn't come, sticking in my throat as he walked towards me once again, now with a small red apple in his hand. I wasn't at all sure what he was going to do with it, but it was much too big to fit if he had any ideas about putting it inside me, and I was going to protest when he spoke, again in his calm, professional doctor's voice. 'Open wide, Miss Martins, this won't hurt a bit.'

It was going in my mouth.

'Keon, I...'

My cheeks bulged as he pushed the apple firmly between my jaws, rendering me speechless as well as helpless. Only then did I remember that it was what you do to a roast pig, but I was too far gone even to feel resentful. Not that I ever could with Keon, he was too much of a clown and, as I turned my face to him, he was once more pretending to preen a moustache he didn't have as he admired his handiwork, then gave his verdict. '*Magnifique! Parfait!* A work of genius! Indeed, you do look good enough to eat! In fact, just hold still, Honey. Don't mind if I collect a little fee, do you?'

He'd changed to his normal voice, but I didn't know what he was talking about anyway, not until he got behind me and I heard a soft rasp, a noise I was sure I'd heard before, but it couldn't be what I thought it was – his zip.

He was gay!

Not that gay. I looked round. He had his cock out, and it was hard, a long, thick shaft of smooth chocolate brown man-meat. He was going to fuck me, outrageous, utterly outrageous, but I'd never seen one so big. It was going inside me and there was nothing I could do about it, while I wanted it so badly ... no, I didn't, I was James's, and only James's, but it didn't matter anyway, because I was tied up and I couldn't even speak and he was right behind me pointing that enormous cock right at my sex ...

... and inside me, deep inside, all the way, as much as it would go, filling my body until I felt he was in me right up to the top of my head. It was what I wanted, what I'd always wanted, not James, but Keon, so big and so strong, always soothing me, always making me laugh, and now he had me, tied and helpless on a plate, his lovely cock in my body as he moved in me, in and out, in and out, slow but steady and so, so deep, bringing me high, and higher still, until I felt I would burst.

I did, as he curled his hand around my tummy to rub at me, something no man had ever done before. Just a couple of touches and I was there, a tight, sweet orgasm that stayed in my head as he rode me, still pushing in and out to that same firm rhythm, even as I shook and wriggled on his cock. It seemed to last for ever, on and on, as he manipulated me, with my utter helplessness the dominant thought in my head all the time. I only stopped when he did, gasping over the remains of the apple I'd crushed between my teeth, and at last I managed to speak.

'You bastard, Keon, you utter bastard! Go on, do it harder.'

He gave a soft knowing chuckle and begun to pump into me as he spoke again. 'That's what we boys call a reach round. Good, huh?'

I couldn't answer, his cock now working too fast and too deep to let me speak, or do anything other than pant out my feelings. He was going to come, right in me, filling my head with confusing images of making it with James and then presenting him with a little brown baby. I didn't care. I wanted it, only fortunately he had more self-control and pulled out at the last second, covering my bottom instead.

He gave a long, contented sigh as he stood back. My whole body ached and I could feel the sauce slowly trickling back down over my skin from the mess he'd made. James could hardly fail to notice, and he'd be turning up at any minute. I struggled to find my voice. 'Keon ... Keon, that was lovely, so lovely, but could you untie me, please? James will be here soon and...'

'Be cool, babe.'

He came around to untie my wrists, leaving me shaking my hands to get my circulation back. I felt confused, not at all sure what I wanted, why Keon had suddenly done something so completely out of character. He'd done it, and that only showed I didn't know him as well as I thought, but if he wanted me, what about James?

'Why, Keon? I mean, do you want to be with me, or...'

'Sh, calm down, Honey.'

He reached out to stroke my hair, such a soothing gesture it made me want to melt into his arms, but it didn't answer my question.

'Tell me, Keon. I need to know, before James arrives. I didn't know you felt that way about me. I didn't even know you liked girls!'

'Yeah, I like girls, but I like guys too. Not more, just the same, only it's easier with guys.'

'Easier?'

'Sure. Guys, I can have four, five in an evening, as many as I can handle, but girls, girls need work.'

'But ... but don't you have anyone special? That guy who sometimes picks you up after work, I thought he was your boyfriend?'

'Thomas? Yeah, he's my boyfriend, kind of, but more a friend, like you. Friends can fuck.'

I nodded, weakly, not really able to argue, not after what we'd just done. Maybe friends could fuck, which opened up all sorts of enticing possibilities. No, I wanted to be with James, and with James alone ... No, I couldn't, not after what Keon had done, not after the way he'd reached around under my tummy ... No, it was all wrong, awfully wrong ...

The doorbell rang.

'Shit!'

'Be cool, babe.'

He quickly tied my hands again, popped another apple in my mouth, wiped my bottom and poured some fresh sauce over me, leaving me as before, but with my emotions a bigger mess than ever. Only when he wheeled my trolley into the space behind the curtains of my bay window did he go for the door.

I caught the click of the latch, and James's voice. 'Keon? What are you doing here?'

He already knew. I could tell by his voice, filling me with fresh embarrassment as I wondered just how much they'd decided together. What was to be done with me maybe? Even that Keon should have me as some sort of kinky treat?

Keon's answer might have come straight from Jeeves and Wooster, not one I'd heard him do before.

'Good evening, sir. I am your butler for this evening.'

'Jolly good show!'

There was laughter in James's voice, and I heard him smack his hands together as Keon shut the door. It was a familiar gesture, the one he'd made as I first lay down on his bed and beckoned him to come to me. Now it sent a jolt right through me and, again, I wondered just how much he knew.

I heard them come into the room, my sense of anticipation rising until I could hardly bear it, yet I was securely bound and could do nothing, not even speak because of the apple in my mouth. When Keon had told me James liked to tie girls up, I'd thought it was one of those odd things you sometimes have to put up with in men, but now it had been done to me I understood. It was so powerful, to be completely helpless, completely at his mercy, at the mercy of any man who chose to take me, Keon with his huge, smooth cock...

'Dinner is served, sir.'

The curtain was pulled back, suddenly. I started, and a shiver of reaction ran through me, so strong I felt faint as I was exposed to James's gaze, nude and trussed up on a plate, decorated with food and served to him like a suckling pig. He liked it too, his face immediately moving into the brightest of smiles, at which relief and arousal flooded through me. Again he clapped his hands.

'Splendid! Now that is what I call dinner service. Well done, that man!'

Keon was standing proudly to the side, holding the curtain back, and answered in a calm, even tone. 'Thank you, sir. One endeavours to give satisfaction.'

He took hold of the trolley, wheeling it out into the middle of the room and the full glare of the lights. James began to walk around me, grinning like a schoolboy as he admired my helpless, naked body. I already felt weak, and weaker still as he came behind me. A finger reached out to scoop up a little of the sauce where it had run down over the sides of my breasts. His touch was like an electric shock, and the lust in his eyes as he sucked his finger clean was enough to make me want to push my bottom up again.

A tiny voice inside my head was screaming at me not to be such a slut, that I'd enjoyed having Keon too much and that it was wrong to now want James as well. I didn't care, too far gone to think of the proprieties, which just seemed dull, pointless, stupid rules imposed by stuffy old fools and crackpots. My body wanted it, and I was going to get it.

That wasn't all. I'd expected Keon to leave the room, but he hadn't, instead propping himself up against the wall, still pretending to be a butler, but looking on with unashamed pleasure. He was going to watch, everything. First it had been by him, now in front of him, but there was nothing I could do but wriggle and wink, of which he took not the slightest notice, standing as still as a statue.

I was glad I was tied up, because who could blame me for being so dirty when I had no choice? But to be had in front of another man, and so rudely, bound and gagged and served for sex, it was ... was just so good and, as James's tongue touched the sensitive skin at the nape of my neck, my eyes closed in bliss and I surrendered completely.

James began to lick, lapping up the sauce from my body, nice and slowly, my neck, my back, my waist, tickling, but oh so nicely. Just that had my breathing deep and even and my need to be entered again too high to resist. Even before he began to lick the sauce from my bottom cheeks, I was pushing myself up for entry and, when he went between, I just lost control, wriggling myself into his face and pushing out, no longer rational, no longer bound by all the taboos and mores of society, but reacting with my sheer animal lust alone, like a she-cat on heat.

He was so cool about it too, taking his time as his tongue tip flicked between my bottom cheeks, sparing no detail, and lower still, to lap up the sauce from my sex and where it mattered most of all, right at the heart, bringing me up to within an instant of my climax when he stopped. I forced the apple out, gasping for breath before I could speak.

'Please, James, don't stop ... do that again, please?'

His answer was soft, a little chiding. 'Patience, Honey, darling, we'll get you there.'

I'd opened my eyes and looked around, to find that he had his cock sticking out from his open fly like a flagpole, fully erect and ready for me. Because of that, it took me a moment to register what he'd said.

'What do you mean "we"?'

He just chuckled, and it wasn't me he spoke to. 'Keon, perhaps you would care to indulge Honey from the front while I take advantage of her delightful rear?'

Keon gave a polite inclination of his head. 'It would be my pleasure, sir.'

I made to speak as Keon stepped towards me, but all that came out was a gasp as James pushed himself into me with a single, firm shove. His hands closed on my hips and, as he began to move inside me, my mouth came open by instinct, ready to take Keon in as he offered his big black cock. I'd thought of it, sometimes, having a man take me from each end, but only in my rudest fantasies.

Now it was real, my helpless body rocking between two gorgeous men, my sex and my mouth full of cock at the same time, so good, good enough to make me come if James would only do what Keon had done and reach around under my tummy to touch me. And he did, his fingers doing wonderful things as he slid his cock in and out and I sucked on Keon with ever greater eagerness, making him swell in my mouth. I wanted us to come together, but I couldn't help it, my pleasure rising higher and higher still until I felt my body start to lock ...

... and James stopped, and spoke. 'So, what do you think? Is she good enough?'

'Yeah, she's good enough. Let's go for it.'

I tried to look up, wondering what they were going to do to me, but Keon had his hand in my hair, holding me firmly onto his cock, and the best I could manage was a mumble. He laughed to see the state they'd put me in and withdrew, leaving me still dizzy with need, let down at the last moment for the second time. James spoke. 'Do you like this, Honey?'

'Yes. Now take me there, please, James ... please, both of you. Don't tease.'

He eased himself deep into me, drawing a moan from my lips as he replied. 'When we were together, the second time, you said you liked other girls. Is that true?'

'Oh God, James! You bastard, you ...'

Again he pushed into me, this time a single hard thrust, making me gasp.

'Is it true?'

'Yes. Yes, it's true! What ... do you want me to say what I like in front of Keon or something?'

'Just answer me. Would you really go to bed with another woman?'

'I ... I don't know ...'

I was lying, but to have to admit it in front of both of them was almost too much, almost.

'... for you, yes, I would.'

'Really?'

'Yes! I said so, I would, I would, any way you liked!'

'Will you?'

'Will I? Oh God, you haven't ... yes, you have, you bastard ... you bastard ... you bastard!'

He'd begun to move inside me again, faster now, setting me gasping and wriggling against him, and his fingers were moving on my sex once more. They meant it. I heard the door open as Keon took my hair and fed his cock back into my mouth, now rock solid once again. She was there, cool and poised in a sheath of black and red silk, no doubt from one of the top designers, her spiky heels to match, and her make-up, looking like a real bitch-queen – Miss Caroline de Lacy-Hamilton.

'Welcome to the Grosvenor's Bank swinging club, Honey.'

Chocolate Delight
A Colorado Woman

A long-legged university student breezed into Chocolate & Espresso Shoppe. 'Dusty,' she said, sliding into the booth, 'check the slut across the street in leopard-print capris. Extreme gauche.'

'Don't go there, Mary,' replied her girlfriend with burgundy-tinted sleek, straight hair. 'Dishing unconscious members of the populace generates karmic effect.'

A laugh and a smirk. 'You're lusting the pastry chef again. I hear your pussy slurp.'

Dusty rimmed the coffee cup with a crimson-painted fingernail like it was the head of a penis. 'Lusting is non-judgemental,' she retorted, 'What would be your rationale for a cease and desist order? Talk up, girl.'

The raven-haired beauty's butt shifted in the booth and she delivered a crosspoint sting. 'If you must know, his mom, Mrs Ayero, and my aunt are friends – name's Bob – and, by the way, don't stain the upholstery.'

'Quiet, he'll notice,' Dusty retaliated.

Mary reached for her girly purse. 'Since when are you Miss Manners? With half a notion, I'd abandon you to folly.'

'No "p" as in problem,' Dusty retorted. 'I have errands to run anyway.'

Salmon painted fingernails tapped the table. 'Rumour has it,' Mary whispered conspiratorially, 'he dropped out of a seminary to marry his childhood sweetheart who dumped him shortly thereafter.'

The out-of-the-blue revelation intrigued Dusty. 'Then

what happened?' she asked – she had read of a monastery in Italy where silent monks concocted exquisite chocolate Easter eggs.

'His mother had a nervous breakdown and he assumed management. Auntie says she'll never recover and Bob won't return to his studies.' Mary shrugged her shoulders and rolled her eyes as if their dialogue had reached an inarguable conclusion.

'You better be telling me God's honest truth.'

'Easy girl, raging hormones and former seminarians make for a frustrating combo. Auntie says he's straight-forward and partakes in Chamber of Commerce nonsense. Hey!' she exclaimed and reached for her purse again. 'I'm over this. How about we cruise and seek to satisfy luxuriant sex needs?'

Dusty exhaled and leaned against the upholstered booth. 'Sex is *all* you ever think about.'

'*You*, with the hot-box award of the year?' Mary chided. '*You* who never wears a bra? *You* who has enough love juice to drench a nine-hole golf course?' Mary finished her tirade and realised her humour was not appreciated. 'All right,' she said, 'you win. What *shall* we talk about?'

'How do you melt chocolate?'

'It's an involved, sticky process that burns fingers.'

Dusty grabbed her backpack, left money for the tab, and raised from the bench. 'Do without me. I have to go shopping.' Mary followed her out the door. In a publicly displayed ritual, the two kissed on the mouth, rubbed titties and slapped palms. Dusty boarded the mall bus.

Inseparable best friends, the two women shared lives like a pair of close-knit sisters, until that hot, sultry August. Both appeared younger than their 22 years and, at first glance, resembled indulged, high-school brats – jailbait. They weren't on either account. Both were serious students eager to graduate next spring with bachelor degrees who happened to relish edgy modes of dress and behaviour – like swapping boyfriends – if the dudes were cool enough.

Not even the onset of chilly autumn air dampened the constant heat emanating from between their thighs. Being turned-on all the time was just a hard-wired fact about their bodies' metabolisms. There were plenty of well-endowed willing squeezes in their circle of friends.

Favoured attire included tight skirts or jeans fitted comfortably below jewelled belly buttons and Celtic knots tattooed on the small of their backs. If absolutely necessary, they covered with rhinestoned sweatshirts or shrunken jackets. A plethora of silver bangles decorated their ears while high-powered brains churned between.

Local ale, syrupy liqueurs and foamed cappuccino topped their list of beverages. Preferred activities involved bold young men of intelligence who danced dirty and indulged in the wild thing. Sexual adventures were to be embarked upon and examined in the name of empirical research.

Each enjoyed a private studio apartment, and they slept-over often – sometimes with company and sometimes relaxingly alone. Neither ever wore anything so plebian as pyjamas: clingy T-shirts, G-strings, and crank the heat in the event of inclement weather.

Every morning, no matter how the night developed or ended, they met at the coffee shop cross-corner from the market and midway between their flats. The ultra-hip and groovy downtown environ saturated with jazz was close enough to the university to walk to classes or hop a bus to the shopping mall.

For a week, the woman with the burgundy-tinted hair, dark-purple eyeliner and red lipstick arrived a few moments earlier. If pressured, she wouldn't have been able to explain exactly that a new employee – some kind of pastry chef – fascinated her beyond infatuation.

Her pussy stirred at the sight of the man decked in crisp white trousers and side-buttoned jacket. Standing behind the glass enclosure, he exuded an enigmatic élan that conjured delicious, albeit nasty, abstractions. Chiselled bone structure bespoke nobility and blond hair wisped around ears bespoke golden treasures hidden behind starched pleats.

Hands irrevocably attracted her attention. Once, an article in a trendy women's magazine reported that, just as the sort of shoes a person wears predicts personality types, the size and shape of a man's fingers prophesied the size and shape of his penis. His long, narrow fingers tapered to a flattish curve at the end – the way she liked her men.

Holding by the stem end, the pastry chef dipped firm strawberries into a stainless-steel pan of melted white chocolate. Excess syrup dripped into the reservoir before he placed the mouth-watering morsels on parchment-lined baking sheets. Totally focused, his eyes never lifted; it was obvious he cherished the task.

Dusty longed to morph into a berry and enjoy his loving, meticulous ministrations. Sensual lips seemed to bless each piece of fruit double-dipped in dark and white chocolate. He gently peeled the fruit from the parchment and arranged them in waxed paper wraps ready for individual sales.

So far, she hadn't established eye contact. She was certain his were blue. But then again, any colour was all right by her – just keep flexing those fingers and maintaining total concentration. He never appeared to do anything else. Always, strong hands encased in skintight gloves and, always, the damnable white jacket covered his crotch and his ass.

He never uttered a word. Not even when touristy kind of people gawked and asked stupid questions over the glass enclosure. 'How hot is the chocolate?' and 'Doesn't the fruit get mushy?' He ignored inquiries and kept to himself.

Conceptually, Dusty's bell curve extended beyond shy dudes. What? Go to a movie or do a nature hike? No way.

She liked fast cars and smoky clubs. The man's innocence magnified her horniness to the point of obsession. The situation was an anomaly that called for action. She formulated a plan, which hinged on the HELP WANTED sign in the Shoppe's window.

The bus stopped. Dusty disembarked and entered a department store. Scents of perfumes and cosmetics permeated the aisles and made her dizzy. Back-to-school marketing banners sported Ivy League sweater-and-slack sets. Ceiling speakers blared top-40 garbage music. She trekked the escalator to the women's casual wear.

'Disgusting clothing,' she muttered under her breath. Soft pastels the colour of setting suns and burnished leaves pledged parental approval, yearbook inclusion, homecoming fiascos and victorious networking. Dusty frugally rationalised spending money on a conservative, job-interview outfit as a future investment.

'May I help you,' asked a chirpy clerk, who made no attempt to hide her disdain for the black-tube-skirted customer.

'Show me what nice girls wear,' Dusty demanded, with gothic nonchalance. After minimal deliberation, she charged a hyacinth-blue, knee-length skirt, a lavender hoody, a pair of brown boot shoes with pointed toes and a pair of stockings.

A bus transported her back to her quaint flat in the upper storey of a Victorian mansion with a private entrance. Originally designed for a live-in nanny, a rooftop garden flashed remnants of late-blooming roses and pansies. The deck was most awesome when a full moon flooded the skylights.

Dusty skipped the stairs two at a time, unlocked the door, and flung the shopping bags on the fold-out couch. She shimmied out of her normal clothes and high-heel boots. Naked behind fourth-storey windows, she arranged the newly purchased ensemble on hangers as painstakingly as he positioned fruit on parchment paper.

Finding the garter belt required steadfast and resourceful rummaging. She didn't mind looking straight on the outside, but she'd be damned if she had to look that way under the preppy, sweet, nice, job-interview outfit.

Shower cranked full blast, she entered the etched glass bathtub enclosure. Water ran over her head and burgundy dye rinsed down the drain. Thanks to a soft cloth and make-up remover, purple liner and mascara dissolved from eyelids and lashes. In like manner, she nudged the stains of red, red lipstick from her lips. She shaved her legs and trimmed stray hairs from her heart-shaped snatch.

Wiping the mirror with the towel, she cringed at the sight of naturally curly, strawberry-blonde hair, transparent skin, green eyes and white eyelashes. 'You are pretty in the Irish sort of way,' her mother used to say. She barely recognised herself. Never in a zillion years would Mr Bob Ayero recognise her as the cappuccino and biscotti customer who hid erotica between study notes.

Compulsive thoughts of the handsome pastry chef escalated the fervour and the urgency of her crotch. She lay back on silk-covered pillows. By habit, her cheeks snuggled into the soft comforter and her fingers knowingly tickled their way down her abdomen to the golden-red delta of curls.

Imagining his whatever-coloured eyes and his strong hand, sans gloves, dip strawberries into her pussy instead of the chocolate, she fantasised him sucking her love juices into his mouth. Her fingers slid in and out of velvet walls, her tongue tasted sweet, and she moaned a certain sigh of relief, wonder, and fulfilment.

For a lark, she dabbed a bit of her personal perfume behind her ears and hooked the garter belt around her hips. The stockings were high quality, sheer but durable. The fluffy skirt had a drawstring waist and the hoody fitted like a dream – dressing nice had some merit. She shrugged into a sweater and set off to apply for a candy-making job.

Just as she suspected, he was not behind the counter. She asked a tired-looking clerk about the HELP WANTED sign in the window. 'Fill in the papers, the boss will see you for an interview,' she said. Dusty quick-scribbled particulars on the application and paced until she heard her name called.

The door to an office stood ajar and she entered. 'Mr Ayero?' she asked. His blonde lashes lifted and their eyes regarded each other. His were the blue of the high-country lakes.

'Call me Bob,' he said. Long slender fingers wrapped around a handball, squeezed, released, and squeezed again.

'OK. Bob,' she said. 'I'm interested in working you – I mean *for* you. In between classes, that is. May I have the job?'

His eyes scrolled the application. 'You have no experience,' he said with finality, stood and turned to the window. White trousers stretched across taut ass muscles, which she was certain were frontally balanced.

'I'm a quick learner,' she blurted. 'I'll do anything you ask.'

He raised an eyebrow and asked if she could handle the early pastry shift. Mornings are my least favourite, she thought. This semester she managed to forgo eight o'clock classes. Goals required sacrifice, as did the leaping, demanding pussy screaming to him.

'Yes, when?' she asked.

'Tomorrow. Be here at five o'clock.'

'A. m.?'

'A. m.'

'Yes, sir, I mean, Bob.'

Thanks to double alarm clocks, Dusty made every single shift. Lazy autumn days progressed to the end of September with Bob rarely speaking to her – let alone hitting on her.

Convinced his shyness prevented him from responding to her flirtations, she fine-tuned her characterisation of a sweet girl and spaced her interactions appropriately.

'Excuse me,' she would say, and pass her tits ever so closely to Bob's industrious hands. 'A customer ordered a mango delight.' Or, standing ever so closely to his trouser-encased legs, she would inquire, 'May I help you wash your counter top?'

One bright sunny day, her infectious good mood found her twirling in the aisle behind the glass enclosure and her butt rubbed against his ass. 'Oh, Bob, I didn't mean to bump into you,' she giggled, knowing full well she did.

Silently, he tolerated her antics and appeared to think she was genuinely and charmingly clumsy. She considered writing a term paper about the latent mating habits of shy men. By holiday, she gauged, she'd break his tender shell.

Sexual tension mounted within her and, alone at night, nestled on her fold-out bed, she imagined herself to be him and have a rigid cock inside her pants all day. How difficult it would be to hide. The only trace left by dripping pussies were faint sticky streaks on inner thighs.

Mary considered her totally nuts and told her so. 'The end does not justify the means,' she said. 'Hell, plenty of dudes would dress in a chef costume and feed you strawberries.'

'You fail to understand my investment,' Dusty said aloud. What she could not share with her best girlfriend was that her obsession for the pastry chef was out of control and driving her recklessly closer and closer to melting point.

'Midterms are coming up,' Mary said. 'Quit the job. Study if you need a diversion.'

Dusty did study – Bob's habits and patterns. She came to know where it was safest from prying eyes to accidentally sidle into him and cover with a twinkle and a bat of her eyelashes – so naïve, she believed.

The end happened quickly on a Saturday morning just

before opening. Balancing three hours worth of work, Bob activated the foot pedal that opened the refrigerator door. Dusty sidestepped by him and the tray of double-dipped fruit dropped to the floor.

'That's it,' he cried. 'Go home. From now on, you work the afternoon shift. Am I clear?'

Tears stung her eyes. He yelled but his eyes were full of compassion. She hung her head, untied her apron, and replied, 'Yes, sir.' He made no move to correct the way she had addressed him.

On the way home after classes, she ducked into the corner market and bought a pint of fudge ice crème. Her apartment still showed signs of a recent cleaning binge, which was a good thing. She straightaway ran bathwater. A message from Mary invited her to party. She couldn't, her craving for Bob engulfed her. He was not available when she called and quit.

She extended the couch into a bed, fluffed the pillows and flipped on the radio. Strains of Cassandra Wilson's 'Travelling' danced the edges of the room and convinced her that after graduation, she'd leave town forever.

Leaving the ice crème on the counter to soften, she stepped out of her clothes and reached for her stash of amaretto. She swallowed a healthy measure, slid under the canopy of bubbles, and nearly fell asleep. Bleary eyed and chilled, she pulled the stopper with her toe, ate half the ice crème, and downed another couple of shots of liqueur.

Sitting on the commode, she brushed her teeth and fell exhausted onto the bed. Lonely pussy and neglected titties yearned for solace, but her funk was too great to comply. She drifted to that place between dreams and consciousness.

The telephone, programmed to play 'Shiny, Happy People' by R.E.M., woke her ungodly early. Ignoring the digital clock, she reached for the receiver and checked caller ID. It read 'Chocolate & Espresso Shoppe'. 'What's up?' she asked groggily.

'This is Bob,' the caller said shyly. 'I know it's a long shot – may I serve you breakfast?'

Breakfast is for kids, she thought. 'Aren't you working?' she asked. Remorse for sounding rude did not enter her mind space.

'Sundays are play days. How do you spend yours?'

'Sleeping.' A huge yawn escaped and a tingly feeling between her legs travelled to her nipples. She shivered. He must be near. 'Where are you?' she blurted.

'Parked below your apartment,' he replied just as quickly.

Access to my employment records, she deduced, and scanned the apartment. Not bad, she thought. Squiggling from the bed, she nudged the G-string into place and pulled the T-shirt over her belly. She padded to the bathroom. 'Would you pick up a newspaper at the market and give me time to dress?'

'I'd rather not.' His voice was soft and sensual – and bold.

'So, knock already.' She hung up and flushed the toilet. Inside of two minutes, the brass knocker sounded.

Dusty unlocked the deadbolt and swung the panelled oak door wide. Paper grocery bags stared her in the face. 'Morning,' said a muffled voice. 'Are you decent?'

'Sort of. Come in, let's talk,' she said. Thoughts of an employee reprimand session sent a ripple of nausea through her amaretto-drenched system.

Bob crossed the threshold and placed the bags on the counter. Soulful blue eyes the colour of high mountain lakes held her mesmerised. 'No talking,' he said, 'until you partake of my breakfast offering.'

An impromptu smile broke and she peeked in the brimming bags. With both hands, he grasped her waist and tenderly pressed her against the closed door. Raising one of her legs, he ever so lightly tickled her nearly naked bottom with his fingers and locked the door. 'Would you care to partake in an experience of culinary delight?'

Dusty nearly swooned and nodded her head in consent. Like a magician, he deftly produced from the tallest bag what appeared to be a length of batik-dyed silk. His wrist flicked and the material separated into two pieces. 'Costumes first,' he said, with an impish grin, and tied the fuchsia-pink slash of silk around her hips. 'Sarongs overlap in the front. I'll wear one, too.'

Effortlessly, he turned, kicked his loafers under the table and dropped his pants. No underwear, only a bikini-line tan like a swimmer. A bead of sweat gleamed at the base of his spine – at the uppermost end of the crack between his buttocks. She inhaled and watched him tie the sarong around his hips, fold his clothes neatly, and place them on the antique trunk in the hall.

Firmed, toned and fabulous, she thought – and mannerly. He turned to her and she saw the front of his skirt bulge. Would his sex be as she imagined? Her pussy cried a tear of frustration at the flimsy material preventing empirical evidence.

The next instant, the same strong, fruit-caressing fingers tugged her T-shirt over her head and he unabashedly admired the magnificent figure with a slender long torso. Her breasts tilted saucily upwards and her hardened nipples stretched to meet his lingering hands. He bent and nuzzled each breast. 'Not yet, my darlings.'

Leaving her bare-chested, he peeked under the sarong and smiled at the G-string valiantly protecting the heart-shaped pubic hair. Thumbs traced the tuck in her butt and he kissed the silk sarong. 'Little pussy, I shall return to you later,' he promised.

Moving upwards, he tracked her belly button. 'Perfect,' he murmured. Without warning and with staccato speed, he clapped his hands. 'Let the festivities begin!' he exclaimed, and produced a thermos of coffee and a pint of brandy from the smaller bag.

The blond-haired Adonis commandeered the kitchen as though it was a natural habitat. Minus starched, side-buttoned whites, his body moved like an athlete, more comfortable nude than clothed. Spilling nary a drop, he poured two insulated coffee mugs one-third full of thick coffee and split the difference with equal parts brandy and aerated whipped cream. 'Indulge,' he said simply.

Dusty tilted her head back and drank. Frothy foam coated her lips. 'Allow me,' he whispered. Like a cat, he licked the white film from her lips. Holding her at arm's length, he searched her eyes. 'Multifaceted women turn me on: I adore you painted in sexy make-up and I adore you squeaky clean.'

Dusty gasped. 'You knew?'

'That you remodelled yourself to attract me?'

She began to explain and defend her motives and stammered. His forefinger touched her lips and his eyes begged patience. 'No doubt your girlfriend spoon-fed you the seminary rumour.'

Pale-green eyes widened further. His shoulders shrugged. 'The scenario,' he continued, 'was mother's fantasy. There was no fiancée. In reality I was formally trained as a chef and worked luxury cruise lines the last few years. Let me share with you my recipe for slow, tasty love.'

Gone was the shy man and the one who stood in his place – the one with the sexy body wrapped in a batik-dyed sarong – appealed to her more than the innocent man she lusted. 'You are the first course – the appetiser,' he said slowly and with emphasis. 'Remain still. Pretend your very survival depends on immobility.'

Dusty, imagining sticky sheets, stood rooted. He swung the cane-backed chair into the centre of the kitchen and swooped his arm, indicating her throne. She sat.

'Perfect,' he reiterated. 'Hold that pose.' From the taller bag, he brought out a white box engraved with the Shoppe's logo. Delicate tissue paper nested an array of double-chocolate-dipped fruit and candy wafers.

Holding a strawberry by the stem end, he dangled it in front of her vision. Her nose crinkled at the delicate bouquet of mixed chocolates. Without warning, her lips parted and her tongue darted towards the dessert. He held the berry firmly. Pearl-white teeth sank into pink flesh. Ever so sweetly, he cleaned a tiny black seed from the corner of her mouth.

'Dusty reveres treats,' he said. Kneeling on the floor in front of her, he gently grasped her ankles and placed her bare feet squarely to the sides of the chair legs. The split on her sarong widened. Love juices smeared the chair under her cheeks.

'Luscious thighs earn a reward, too.' He spaced ice-cold wafers of pure white chocolate from the hem of the skirt to her knees. Tiny goosebumps erupted and her soft downy hair stood on end. 'If you stay still, body heat overcomes the deepest chills,' he said and proceeded to adorn each nipple with a dollop of whipped cream.

Without mussing the artistic creation, his hands reached under the silk sarong and expertly tested the increasing temperature between her thighs. A curious finger dipped inside for a visit. Responsive honey laced his palm. She squirmed and blushed.

For the next agonisingly slow minutes, he pumped her pussy and licked her breasts clean. So matched were their rhythms, not one of the wafers fell from her legs to the floor. With great aplomb, he transferred them to the coffee mugs. Sucking on a truffle cigar, they toasted to the end of the first course.

Thus unencumbered by delectable accoutrements and on the verge of explosion, Dusty sprang from the chair. 'It is *my* turn to be the confectioner extraordinaire – only no more lap dancing – I want you in my bed.'

Wrapped and entangled limbs fell onto the down comforter and the silken pillows. Ravenous fingers explored and slid into openings. Swollen lips nibbled and sought each other. He cupped her butt and pulled her to him with an ever so consensual force.

'Untie that silly skirt,' she exclaimed, and pushed him to the side. 'What kind of dude wears a skirt?'

Backside to her, he sat on the edge of the bed. 'One who is sure of himself and the woman he desires,' came the reply. The piece of material sailed across the room and he lay prone.

Sunlight drifted into the fourth storey windows and the skylights. His eyes invited her to feast upon his fantastic gift to her that morning. She raised to her knees, breathed the sight of his body, and worshipped the object of *her* desire.

Ringlets tickled his thighs. Holding himself still, he leaned on his elbows to watch and give. Her lips parted and she touched the tip of his sex with her tongue and sampled his first offering. Playfully, she licked like a child with a lollipop – and even smacked her lips. If they could, they would have laughed but the taste was too real and ardour parched their throats.

'Please make love to me,' she panted. He raised above. Smooth skin met smooth skin. Her knees fell to the side and she bloomed. Fevered sex lips expanded. He lowered and her breasts willingly crushed beneath him. She tightened her inner muscles around his hardness. He gasped and ventured his flattish curved penis to where resistance reverted. In response, she lifted her hips, moaned, and met his dance.

Second course completed, the Sunday morning lovers imbibed fresh drinks and fed each other chocolate treats. By and by, lust knocked again and the two bodies joined to assuage tension. She mounted him and her lovely spine arched to receive his rigid length.

Heads tilted forwards, dilated green met dilated blue. Hungry for flesh and hungry for skin, sweat mingled with scrumptious aftertastes of brandy and coffee. They stuck to each other and laughed deep throaty laughs of abandon.

'Dusty,' he murmured sleepily, 'permit me a comment.'

'Yes, Mr Bob.'

'Working behind a candy counter is not your forte. What is your degree?'

She agreed, laughed, and answered his question, 'Cultural anthropology.'

'Ah yes, the study of man. I predict great success.'

Ginger Tart Fiona Locke

It was exquisite – the perfect blend of sugar and spice. The burn of the crystallised ginger made Haley's mouth tingle and she closed her eyes, savouring the sensation. She had to restrain herself from stealing any more. There would be plenty for her later. No one would miss it. Nor would anyone miss the wine.

Haley adjusted her cap. The hateful little white doily always ruined her carefully tousled pixie cut. She checked herself, making sure her uniform was in order. Mr Bathurst was always pestering her about her apron being crooked or her top button being undone. As if anyone would notice. To the elite who dined at Asquith Hall she was nothing but a pair of hands that set fancy meals in front of them and took the empty plates away when they were done.

Her apron was definitely straight, but she wondered if he'd notice that she'd shortened her skirt yet another inch. Probably. The man could spot an irregularity from the next county. His pernickety nature was the thing Haley hated most about her job. Mr Bathurst prowled the hotel like a fussy Victorian butler, looking for things to criticise and people to scold.

Haley was too young to be hiding her assets under such an unflattering uniform. If her boss was so concerned about attracting gentlemen to Asquith Hall, he should realise the opportunity she presented. A flash of leg, a glimpse of cleavage and they'd be loyal patrons. What man didn't fantasise about a sexy French maid? Well, besides Mr Bathurst. Really, it was a crime that someone so good-looking should be so strait-laced.

Authority figures had always been her biggest turn-on,

but Mr Bathurst seemed blind to the possibilities. He was quick enough to reprimand her for every little mistake, but he was immune to her playful insinuations. Such a waste.

She sighed and stole a peek out into the dining hall. It was almost time to serve the soup. It was a small affair this afternoon – a birthday celebration for Sir Peter Somethingorother. Marissa had told her that he was a friend of Lord Asquith's. It explained why Mr Bathurst was at his punctilious best. The Man Himself was here.

Lord Asquith's portrait hung above the fireplace in the oak-panelled hotel lobby. He was dressed for the hunt, standing beside a magnificent white horse. His dark hair was combed back and there were flecks of silver at his temples. He held a riding crop by his side, as though he was about to tap it against his thigh. Lord Asquith had been invading her fantasies since the day she saw it. She could evoke his image with photographic clarity: his imposing stature, his aristocratic nose, his compelling black eyes.

But it was the riding crop that fascinated her most of all. Her bottom would tingle with unfulfilled need every time she passed the portrait. And when she confided her feelings to her boyfriend Matt, he incorporated the peer into the kinky threesome fantasies he whispered to her in the mornings as he fondled her awake.

Haley had only met Lord Asquith once, six months before. And it had been disastrous. He had held a huge New Year's party for his friends in the Great Hall. And he had generously let the hotel staff use one of the smaller rooms for their own party.

Haley was there with Matt, who was almost as eager as she was to see him in the flesh. They were both rather tipsy and Matt wanted Haley to sneak off to one of the hotel rooms with him.

'You're insane!' she giggled. 'Do you want me to lose my job?'

'Come on, no one'll see.'

Haley scanned the room and, sure enough, there was

Mr Bathurst, standing near the bar. 'Uh-uh. Bathurst's got ESP. He'll know.'

Matt looked thoughtful for a moment. Then he grinned devilishly. 'So offer him some favours in exchange for looking the other way. As long as I get to watch.'

Haley nearly choked on her champagne. Matt was a voyeur of the highest order, but he still sometimes surprised her.

'You're right,' Matt continued, scrutinising her boss. 'He *would* make a good Mr Darcy.'

Haley shook her head sadly. 'He may be gorgeous, but I'm no Elizabeth Bennet. He's completely un-seduceable.'

Matt shrugged. 'Too bad. It's his loss. We'll just have to take our chances.' He took Haley's arm and made as if to drag her off.

'Stop it, Matt! It's not worth the risk.' She pulled away.

Matt affected an exaggerated pout, looking so boyish and adorable that she was tempted.

'Very well,' he said. 'But your prudery has a price.'

'Oh, yeah?'

He arched an eyebrow. 'Two prices, in fact.'

'What's the first?'

'We crash the fancy party.'

A naughty grin spread across Haley's face. 'Oh, yes,' she purred.

The Great Hall was as festive as Haley had ever seen it, but the party was nowhere near as raucous as the staff's one. Garlands hung from the portraits of staid, dour-faced old men. Balloons with trailing streamers bumped against the great hammer-beams above them. But the guests were polite and restrained. Dressed in tasteful finery, they glided through the party with patrician grace. There would definitely be no photocopying of bottoms here.

'Real class,' Haley said admiringly.

'Yeah.'

She scanned the room for Lord Asquith, but she couldn't see him anywhere.

Matt cleared his throat. 'Now for the second price.'

'Which is?'

'Your knickers. Give them to me.'

She squirmed. 'OK. Just let me go to the loo and –'

He caught her by the arm. 'No. Right here.'

Her eyes widened and her cheeks flooded with warmth. 'Everyone will see!'

'Yes, I expect they will.'

Astonished at his boldness, Haley's body nonetheless responded to the idea. But there was no way she could do it *here*. Not in front of the wealthy and titled guests of Lord Asquith.

'No,' she said firmly. 'Forget it.'

'I suppose I'll have to take them off myself, then.'

His hand crept up under the hem of her short red dress and Haley shrieked in surprise, making everyone nearby turn to look at them. She dissolved into gales of embarrassed laughter. The onlookers turned away with disdain, no doubt lamenting the lack of discipline in schools today.

'They should bring back the birch,' muttered one prim dowager.

'Come on,' Matt said, leading her deeper into the room.

Nervously, Haley allowed herself to be led, wondering if he would really go through with it. The thought thrilled her and she imagined herself after a few more glasses of champagne, stripping off and dancing on the tabletops.

Matt pinned her against the Jacobean panelling and slipped his hand under her skirt again, cupping her cheeks and making her moan. He drew his hands around her thighs and gently rubbed his knuckles up and down the damp gusset of her panties. Haley shivered. Then he slid his hand under the elastic and peeled the flimsy red lace down below her skirt. French knickers. Matt's favourite. With a whisper, they slipped down her legs and she stepped out of them.

Matt held out his hand expectantly.

Haley was emboldened by the exhibitionistic thrill of being bare underneath her dress. It brought out the mischief-maker in her. She picked up her panties and dangled them in front of Matt. Then, when he reached for them, she pulled them away, hiding her hand behind her back.

'Oh no,' she said with a teasing smile. 'You'll have to catch me first.' And she raced for the nearest door, her high heels clicking on the waxed oak boards.

When she reached the door, she glanced back over her shoulder. She didn't see Matt anywhere. He must have gone out through one of the main doors at the other end, intending to cut her off.

The funhouse thrill of being chased excited Haley even more. She didn't know where the door led, but she didn't stop to worry about it. The room she found herself in was sophisticated and elegant, with dark antique furniture and heavy velvet curtains. A faded Persian rug sprawled beneath her feet and a fire crackled in the hearth. She paled as she realised where she was: she'd stumbled into one of the family's private rooms.

Terrified of being caught, she whirled round to run for the door. And crashed headlong into someone. Champagne splashed all over the man's dinner jacket and Haley babbled an apology, frantically brushing at his lapels as though she could wipe away the champagne like so much dust.

'Oh my God, I'm so sorry! I didn't mean –' Haley froze.

It was Lord Asquith.

He didn't speak. But his quiet bearing intimidated her more than any rebuke. Champagne dripped from the base of his now-empty glass onto the rug. His jacket was probably ruined. But his expression was inscrutable. The bottomless black eyes betrayed no emotion. They simply regarded her, unblinking.

Spellbound, Haley couldn't look away. The silence stretched between them like a hangman's noose. Asquith held her with his penetrating gaze until her own eyes felt starved for moisture. Finally, she blinked, breaking the spell and the silence.

'I'm so sorry,' she repeated, shaking her head. 'I got lost and – I wasn't watching where I was going.' She winced at her inane words; he was well aware of that. But she had to say *something*. The silence was unbearable.

He wasn't looking at her, though. He was looking at something on the floor between them. He placed his glass on a nearby table and bent down to retrieve the scrap of material. Haley turned scarlet as he held her knickers up inquiringly, stretching them between his fingers like a scientist examining some new discovery. His eyes met hers again and still she could read nothing in his face.

Without a word he calmly used them to blot at his jacket. Haley could only stare at him in blank-faced astonishment. When he was finished, he tucked her wet knickers into his pocket. He eyed her impassively for a moment and then continued on his way, leaving her alone in the room.

When he had gone Haley, realised she was trembling. It was only when she found Matt again that she was able to shake off the moment.

'Aha, there you are!' he said, beaming like a kid with a secret to tell. 'You'll never guess who I just saw.'

Haley turned to him, ashen-faced. 'Lord Asquith.'

'That's right.'

'No. My knickers . . .'

'What about them?'

'They're – in his pocket.'

Matt looked doubtful. 'Are you taking the piss?'

Haley shook her head, bewildered. She hardly believed it herself.

Matt thought about it and then burst into laughter. 'Brilliant! Though you should have charged him a tenner at least. Those were expensive.'

Haley blushed and slugged him hard in the shoulder.

She felt exposed and vulnerable. But the thought that Lord Asquith had her panties in his pocket was delicious. A sweet violation.

'Are you nervous?' Marissa asked with disbelief.

Haley jumped. 'Of course not,' she said hurriedly. 'What makes you think I'm nervous?'

'Well, your hands don't usually shake like that.'

Wiping her clammy, unsteady palms on her apron, Haley fabricated an excuse. 'Oh, I just ... I didn't have breakfast. My hands get shaky when I don't eat.'

Marissa bought it. 'Well, try not to spill wine on the guests,' she offered with a sympathetic smile. 'Mr Bathurst will go postal.'

'Don't worry.'

The truth was that Haley was extremely nervous. And not just because she would see Lord Asquith again. She and Matt were planning to host their own little party the next night. And it was up to Haley to procure the refreshments.

The intimate gathering only required two waitresses and Haley tried to focus on her duties and avoid eye contact with the guests. Normally that wouldn't have been a problem. But she could feel Lord Asquith's eyes on her. Boring into her. As though he could read every thought in her dirty little mind.

While Marissa was clearing away after the first course, Haley lingered in the kitchen long enough to shove two bottles of wine into her rucksack. Then she heard Mr Bathurst coming and she scampered back out to join her co-worker.

Another course. Another bottle. And another near-interruption by Mr Bathurst. This was not as easy as Matt had said it would be.

The staff were meant to keep a record of how many bottles they opened for a party. It was some accountant's job to see that the figures matched. Sir Peter and his friends were putting it away like lads at a stag night and Haley was sure no one would question whether they'd drunk ten bottles or twenty.

'Haley? Are you sure you're OK?' Marissa asked. 'You're white as a sheet.'

'Yeah, I'm fine. It's just hot in here.' She mopped imaginary sweat off her face and hurried back out to the guests, doing her best to avoid Lord Asquith.

At last, it was time to serve the pudding. There was enough for everyone to have seconds. But they weren't as gluttonous with the ginger as they'd been with the wine. Reverting to well-trained public schoolboys, they ate the portions they were given and soon began to take their leave.

In the kitchen, Haley eyed the leftover ginger covetously. 'Marissa, do you mind letting me stay and clean up by myself? I could really use the extra money.'

'Sure, no problem.'

Marissa was a sweet girl, but hopelessly gullible.

When the guests had left, Marissa slipped away as well, leaving Haley on her own. Mr Bathurst was nowhere to be seen and Haley heaved a huge sigh of relief. Finally.

She wrapped the rest of the crystallised ginger in cling film. Then she stuffed it into the side pocket of her rucksack, along with another bottle of wine for good measure. Now that the hard part was over, it was time to clean up.

There was one open bottle of wine with about a glass left in it. She sniffed it. The wine smelled sweet and flowery. She was no connoisseur, but she could tell it was good stuff. Unable to resist, she held the bottle to her lips and treated herself to a taste. It was heavenly. She let the flavour dance on her tongue for nearly a minute before having another gulp.

'Just what do you think you're doing, young lady?'

Jolted, Haley whirled to face her accuser, spilling wine all down her front. 'Mr Bathurst!' she gasped, wiping pathetically at her apron. 'I . . . I didn't realise you were still here.'

'Obviously.' His sharp eyes swept the kitchen, taking in the empty ginger dish, the cling film and the bottle she'd been swigging from. His gaze came to rest on the bulging rucksack on the floor. The neck of a wine bottle jutted from it obscenely.

Haley began to tremble.

'A connoisseur of good wine, I see.' His tone made it clear he recognised the bottle.

She was busted; there was no point in lying. 'It's the first – the *only* time, Mr Bathurst, honest. I just thought no one would miss a couple of bottles.'

'A couple of bottles? Young lady, do you have any idea how much "a couple of bottles" of Château Ducru-Beaucaillou costs?'

Haley lowered her head. 'No.'

'About seventy pounds a bottle.'

Her mouth fell open.

'So how many bottles have we got here?'

With a shudder, she sank to her knees and reached inside the rucksack as though she expected the contents to bite her. One by one she took the bottles out, setting them carefully on the stone flags. One. Two. Three. Four.

Mr Bathurst watched her, his arms crossed imperiously across his chest. 'I trust you were planning to reimburse Lord Asquith?'

She opened her mouth and closed it again. What was she supposed to say?

'I'll take that as a no,' Mr Bathurst said. 'But you're going to pay for it one way or the other. Do you have that much money?'

Haley felt ill. 'No,' she whispered. She was really for it this time.

He walked the length of the kitchen, deep in thought.

'I'll work it off, Mr Bathurst,' Haley said in desperation.

'I don't think that quite meets the bill, young lady. Not for theft.'

She lowered her head. Theft. It was such an unfriendly word.

'You will stay here while I fetch Lord Asquith. We'll see how he wants to settle the matter.'

Horrified, Haley couldn't get up from the floor. She stared at the wine, marvelling that it could be so expensive. Bloody Matt. It was all his fault.

When she heard the second set of footsteps she felt as though the warders had come to escort her to the gallows. She remained where she was, kneeling like a penitent. Perhaps Lord Asquith would take pity on her in her wretched state.

A pair of knife-pleated black trousers stopped directly in front of her.

From behind, she heard Mr Bathurst's voice. 'Come on, girl. On your feet.'

Haley stumbled to her feet, unable to look up. She stared disconsolately at the floor.

'And so we meet again,' came the baritone voice of Lord Asquith.

'You know this girl, Your Lordship?' Mr Bathurst asked, surprised.

Asquith chuckled. 'Our paths have crossed before.'

Haley cringed. She prayed he wouldn't tell Mr Bathurst the circumstances.

'How poetic,' he said in a sporting tone. 'This time you're the one covered in wine.'

She glanced down. The bright-red stain on her apron might as well have been blood.

Asquith contemplated the row of bottles on the floor. Then he nudged the rucksack with his polished shoe. 'What else have you got in there, my girl?'

Again she couldn't read him. It was unnerving. His cut-glass accent made her squirm as authority always did. But no schoolteacher had ever stolen her knickers.

'Um, just some ginger, sir,' she mumbled, still too afraid to meet his eyes.

'Just?'

She felt tears prick her eyes. Why were they torturing her?

'Look at me when I'm speaking to you, please.' His gentlemanly phrasing only enhanced his authority.

Haley obeyed, fingering the edges of her wine-drenched apron.

'What is your name?'

Swallowing audibly, she raised her head. He was dressed less formally than last time, but he was just as striking. His black eyes seemed to look right through her. 'Haley Devlin, sir.'

'Haley,' he repeated. 'Tell me something, Haley. Are you wearing knickers this time?'

She blushed furiously and darted a glance at Mr Bathurst, but he merely raised his eyebrows.

'Well?'

'Of course, sir,' she said, realising the ridiculousness of her statement as she said it.

He chuckled at that. 'Of course.'

She burned with shame, but it was a delicious sort of shame. He was toying with her.

'Show me.'

Here it was. The gauntlet. There was only one way to reclaim some of her dignity. With a coquettish smile she raised her skirt to display the French knickers she was wearing. Just like the ones he had confiscated at the party.

Lord Asquith nodded his appreciation. 'Do they meet with your approval, Mr Bathurst?'

He inspected them with the same cold, appraising eye that scrutinised her cap and apron and always found fault.

'Acceptable,' he said. 'Just.'

His indifference astonished her. Then again, she *had* been shamelessly flirtatious with him when he'd first hired her. He knew she was a promiscuous little tart. He probably even knew the sort of games she and Matt got up to.

'So we come to the issue of atonement,' said Asquith calmly.

Haley gulped.

'Oh, you expected to walk away scot-free, did you, my girl?'

She shook her head.

'I'm sorry, I didn't hear that.'

Her cheeks burned. 'No, sir.' She glanced at the open door and then back at Lord Asquith. 'What . . . what are you going to do?' she asked in a quavering voice.

'I'm not sure yet,' Asquith said. 'What do you think, Mr Bathurst?'

'Personally, I think she needs a damned good thrashing.'

Haley thought she would faint. She squeezed her legs together in a vain attempt to still the throbbing between them.

Lord Asquith was nodding. 'Yes, that might do her good, mightn't it? Right, my girl. Remove your uniform, please.'

She blinked. 'S-sir?'

He smiled pleasantly and looked at Mr Bathurst. 'I'm certain she heard me.'

'Yes, she must have done,' Mr Bathurst responded, mirroring his smile.

Asquith raised his eyebrows expectantly. 'Haley? Are you going to remove your uniform or must I do it?'

Baffled, Haley glanced from one to the other. Both men were watching her expectantly. Sternly. She had no choice but to submit.

Her hands shook with uncertainty and anticipation as she untied her apron and slipped it off. Mr Bathurst held out his hand and she surrendered it. He folded it meticulously, placing it on the counter like a blood-stained exhibit in a murder trial.

Unbuttoning her uniform blouse was more difficult. Her nervous fingers could barely manage the buttons and the more she fumbled, the more awkward the moment became. At last she got it off and she handed it to Mr Bathurst as well. It joined her apron and she reached back to unzip her skirt.

'Just a moment, Haley,' Mr Bathurst said, narrowing his eyes. 'Have you shortened that skirt of yours?'

She bit her lip to keep from giggling. Suddenly she was back at school, caught by the headmaster for altering her uniform.

'Yes,' she said, grinning impishly. 'I thought the customers might like it.' She tried to meet his expression with cocky impertinence, but their scrutiny was too much to endure and she looked down at the floor again.

Lord Asquith sighed. 'Well, well,' was all he said.

She found the zip and stepped out of her skirt. Standing in the kitchen in her black bra and knickers, she felt exposed and aroused.

'Your underwear too,' Asquith said.

Haley glanced at the open door. 'But – someone might come in, sir,' she said plaintively.

Asquith didn't respond. His silence was a command.

The fear of getting caught was half the thrill, Haley reminded herself. She unhooked her bra, baring her pert breasts. The hard buds of her nipples advertised her excitement. She hesitated, then shyly slid her knickers down, looking over at the door once more before stepping out of them.

She gathered enough courage to draw herself up and hold them brazenly out to Lord Asquith. He took them from her, the corners of his eyes crinkling as he offered her the slightest of smiles. He held them to his nose and sniffed deeply.

Mortified, Haley buried her face in her hands. Asquith seemed determined to quash every shred of confidence she managed to muster.

There was sound and movement behind her, but she didn't dare look out from behind her hands. Mr Bathurst was opening drawers and rummaging through them. She heard the clink and clatter of knives and other cooking utensils.

'I think this will do,' Mr Bathurst said.

Asquith voiced his agreement.

Haley stubbornly resisted the urge to look.

'Right, my girl,' Asquith said in a maddeningly amiable voice. 'Up you get.'

She peeled her hands away from her face and saw him patting the large butcher's block in the centre of the kitchen. Mr Bathurst stood beside it. He was holding a long wooden spoon, smacking it lightly against his palm.

Filled with exhilarated trepidation, Haley climbed up onto the butcher's block. The wood was cool beneath her naked bottom and thighs. She could feel the scarred surface beneath her, the work of many knives.

'On your back,' Mr Bathurst ordered.

Her fear forced her to make light of the situation. 'If you're planning a virgin sacrifice, I should warn you . . .'

'Do we need to gag you?' Asquith asked.

Her eyes widened. 'No, sir,' she whispered.

He smiled then, a divinely wicked grin that turned her knees to water.

She lay back, crossing her arms over her breasts, her legs hanging over the edge of the block. She stared up at the array of pots and pans twirling lazily above her. The harsh lights of the kitchen made them glint with a clinical chill. She could hardly breathe.

'Legs up,' said Mr Bathurst.

Haley gasped. What were they going to do to her? She looked at him pleadingly.

Asquith tutted with disapproval. 'She isn't being very obedient. Perhaps we should restrain her.'

Heat engulfed her like a wave, threatening to drown her. There was something strangely liberating in the casual way they were discussing her. She had no say in what happened to her. The helplessness was intoxicating.

Mr Bathurst glanced around the kitchen. 'I doubt there's any rope in here.'

Asquith was looking off to Haley's left. 'What about ...'

He moved out of her line of sight and returned with the roll of cling film. Haley bit back a giggle. All they needed to do now was truss her up like a turkey and stuff her full of ...

'Legs up, girl!' Mr Bathurst commanded, giving her a sharp swat on the thigh with the wooden spoon.

She yipped and raised her legs up, an obedient little maid, if a rather wayward one. She was seeing her boss in a whole new light.

Asquith held the cling film up to her right leg. He wrapped it around her ankle several times, spooling it out to reach the rack where the pans hung above her. He wound the plastic around the rack and tied it off. Haley tugged at it, surprised at how strong it was.

He repeated the procedure with her left leg, pulling it to the side so that her legs were splayed. They would be able to see absolutely everything. She prayed they couldn't see how wet she was.

Asquith didn't stop there. He pulled her arms up over and behind her head. Then he wrapped her wrists together and secured them to the legs of the block. The position thrust her breasts up like an offering. Finally, he passed a wide strip of cling film over her waist, around and underneath the surface of the block, pinning her tightly to it. She tried to struggle in her bonds, but the plastic was much stronger than it looked.

'Jolly good stuff, this,' Asquith said with a chuckle.

'Just the thing,' Mr Bathurst agreed, tapping the wooden spoon against Haley's upraised backside.

She flinched, dreading the first smack. She'd been spanked before, but only as a prelude to sex. This promised to be far more intense.

'This is what happens to naughty maids who steal from their masters,' he said sternly.

Haley had fantasised about Mr Bathurst before. In her mind, he rebuked her for her cheekiness and punished her in childish ways. It was safe as a fantasy. Because then she was in control. Now she was completely at his mercy.

The spoon connected sharply with her bottom, delivering a potent sting. She yelped. Another stroke. Another sharp report of wood against flesh. Another cry of pain. She pictured the precise little red circles it must be leaving on her pale skin and she writhed on the butcher's block, unable to escape the stinging blows.

'Oh, please, sir,' she whimpered between strokes. 'Oww! I'm sorry, really ... I'm so ... Oww! ... Sorry!'

They ignored her.

Lord Asquith walked round the butcher's block, watching calmly as Mr Bathurst spanked her. He stopped directly behind her, placing his hands on her shoulders.

He held her down firmly while she tried to wriggle away from the wooden spoon. Then his hands crept slowly down her front until they were cupping her breasts.

Through the pain, Haley moaned and shivered at his touch.

His attentive thumbs brushed back and forth over her nipples, making them stiffen. He pinched them between thumb and forefinger.

Then the wooden spoon directed Haley's attention back to her burning backside. She howled with pain as Mr Bathurst increased the force and tempo, scolding her for her indolence, her impertinence, her indiscipline. She had forgotten all about the stark view she was presenting to him. She struggled against the cling film, causing the rack to shake. Above her the pots and pans clanged and clattered together in raucous accompaniment to her cries.

Asquith increased the pressure on her nipples, rolling them between his fingers. They stiffened fully, responding to his touch with aching compliance.

Gasping and panting for breath, Haley couldn't focus on

either the spanking or the fondling. The sensations began to blend into one.

Asquith commented favourably on her responsiveness, but Haley was in orbit. She was so intent on finding the balance between the pleasure of his touch and the pain of the spanking that his voice was only a fuzzy echo in the back of her mind.

She closed her eyes and drifted deeper into submission. She felt Asquith's warm breath on her throat and she arched invitingly, as though presenting herself for a vampire's kiss. His lips travelled down her neck, lingering above her left breast, making her yearn for his contact. His tongue found the hard bud of her nipple, circling it and teasing it. Haley gasped and the sound seemed to fill the cavernous kitchen. She realised that the spanking had stopped. Not daring to open her eyes, she waited for Mr Bathurst's touch as well.

And when his hand came to rest between her legs she arched her back as much as her position would allow, straining to meet his fingers.

Asquith's teeth closed softly on her nipple with just enough force to make her whimper. She knew her boss would be feeling the dew the action produced.

Mr Bathurst's fingers probed and stroked her sleek wetness, making her writhe and squirm. The fire of the spanking had subsided to a warm, pulsating glow. She felt herself climbing and her breathing quickened and grew shallow.

Asquith twisted a hand in her hair, pulling her head back to expose her throat even more. His lips and teeth caressed the vulnerable flesh there and she shuddered as gooseflesh rose on the back of her neck.

Mr Bathurst trailed his fingers over her sex, teasing her and making her grind her hips obscenely to get what she wanted. She was so close. He had to know it. Why didn't he finish her off? She wanted both of them. They could take turns with her. One could hold her down while the other . . .

'I think she's enjoying this far too much,' said Mr Bathurst.

The hand between her legs stopped and she groaned with frustration. Mr Bathurst patted her tender bottom, making her wince.

'Indeed,' Asquith said. 'Bad girls aren't meant to enjoy their punishment.'

Why not? Haley wanted to whine.

'Mr Bathurst, would you do the honours?' Lord Asquith was holding a long chef's knife out to him.

'Certainly, Your Lordship.'

Haley's eyes widened with terror. Mr Bathurst placed the knife between her breasts and pressed the tip of the cold blade against her skin. She forced herself to stay absolutely still as he drew it sensuously down along the length of her body, stopping at her navel. Then he slid the blade underneath the cling film and sliced through it, releasing her. He repeated the operation with her legs and her arms, though he left her wrists wrapped together.

Asquith stood her up and turned her around to face the block. 'Now, bend right over,' he said.

She obeyed, her legs weak from the bondage and the unfulfilled throbbing need. Surely now they meant to have their way with her. She stretched across the block, present-ing herself.

'There is a punishment Victorian governesses used to find most effective on naughty girls. I think it's especially appropriate for you, Haley.'

She had no idea what he was talking about.

Mr Bathurst was somewhere behind her and to the left. She thought she heard the refrigerator door open and close, but she paid it no mind. Haley closed her eyes and waited. She was their plaything, their slave. They could do any-thing they wanted.

Her reverie was interrupted by the intrusion of some-thing cold and slippery between her glowing cheeks, too high to reach her sex. At first she thought the hand had lost its way and she adjusted herself to assist.

'Be still,' Asquith said sharply.

The oily finger pressed gently against the little puckered rosebud and Haley cried out.

'No! No, please!'

'Hush. Do you want your bottom smacked again?'

Awash with shame, she shook her head frantically. She lowered her head to the butcher's block, mortified at the intrusion. The finger slipped inside her, greasing the passage not even Matt had explored. She was a virgin there. It was a bizarre sensation, but not entirely unpleasant. Still, she wished his hands would roam lower, to where she desperately needed attention.

Gradually, she became aware of a peculiar sound behind her. Some sort of scraping. For a moment she was afraid someone was at the door, but the invading finger was still moving inside her. Surely he would have stopped if someone came in. No, they were definitely alone.

But she couldn't puzzle out the scraping sound. Like the rasp of a knife against ... something.

Without warning, the finger withdrew. Haley heaved a sigh of relief and relaxed against the block. There was a clink as the knife was laid aside. Then Lord Asquith was in front of her. He took her cling-film-wrapped wrists in his hands, stretching her out across the block until she stood on tiptoe.

'Since you're so fond of ginger,' he said, the corners of his mouth turning up ominously.

Then Mr Bathurst was behind her and she flushed deeply. Now it was his turn. But the cold probe didn't feel like a finger and all at once it became clear. With an embarrassed cry she tried to pull away, but Asquith held her wrists firmly.

Mr Bathurst spread her cheeks apart with the fingers of one hand while inserting the ginger root with the other. It had a slightly coarse texture, but it didn't hurt. She made herself relax, surrendering to the penetration.

Suddenly she became aware of a distinct warmth. The ginger was making her tingle and she squirmed, waiting for the unfamiliar sensation to pass. But it didn't pass. The warmth developed into a sharp, piquant burning, like the effect of hot peppers on the tongue.

As the feeling built, Haley found herself writhing against the butcher's block, trying in vain to escape it.

'Oh, please,' she begged. 'It burns!'

One of her tormentors chuckled, but said nothing. It was clear they knew exactly the effect it would have.

Whimpering as the fire intensified even more, Haley struggled against Asquith, trying to pull away. She danced from foot to foot, inadvertently clenching her cheeks and intensifying the sting.

'Now, now,' he chided. 'None of that, my girl. You're going to take your medicine.'

Mr Bathurst was tearing off a long sheet of cling film, presumably to restrain her kicking feet. But instead, he wound it high around her legs and waist, pulling it tightly up between her cheeks like a transparent thong. It pressed the ginger further inside, holding it securely in place. Haley wailed in misery and wondered if it was possible to die of embarrassment.

The burning showed no sign of dissipating. The men exchanged a look and traded places. Mr Bathurst took firm hold of her wrists.

She closed her eyes, feeling faint.

Lord Asquith caressed her over the cling film, making her jump. The plastic retained the heat from her desire as well as the ginger, making the pressure of his touch even more agonising. The ginger continued to make her burn inside with each movement of Asquith's skilful fingers, and she whimpered with pain even as he pleasured her.

Then she was climbing again, quickly and steadily. Sensations shot through her like jolts of electricity and she uttered little gasps and sighs as she struggled both to escape and encourage them. Each time she tensed her muscles she felt the ginger burn.

At last she felt the rising swell of ecstasy and it overtook her with singular intensity as she arched her back, pressing herself into his fingers with breathless abandon. Her eyes squeezed shut, she imploded, as the surges of her climax battered her from within.

It lasted so long it was almost unbearable, but soon the throbbing began to subside and she collapsed over the block, panting and shaking and unable to straighten her legs. Mr Bathurst released her hands and she crumpled to her knees, trembling and spent.

It was a long time before she found the strength to stand. She hissed as her movement reawakened the spicy sting of the ginger. With a shaky hand she reached for the cling film at her waist, ready to unwind it and free herself.

Mr Bathurst smacked her hand smartly. 'And just what do you think you're doing, young lady?'

She stared at him, bewildered. 'I . . . I just . . .'

He was holding her uniform. 'Get dressed.'

Bewildered, Haley knew she must obey. But when she reached for her knickers, Lord Asquith plucked them away. 'I'll keep these,' he said, tucking them into his pocket.

Haley blushed and finished dressing, wincing at the unremitting burn. Relaxing her cheeks was impossible.

Mr Bathurst went to the cupboard and got her a fresh apron. 'Here. You can't very well wear yours.'

When she was dressed she stood before them for inspection. Did they intend to send her home with the ginger still inside? Oh, Matt would love that.

Mr Bathurst smiled. 'Mrs Marjoribanks's party is in the Wellington Room. They're expecting tea.'

Trencherman Nuala Deuel

I've never been able to eat much. Not because I put on the weight, or break out in acne, or suffer from acute flatulence. It's just an inability to feed well. I don't pig out. I don't snack. I don't graze. Maybe it's all down to a small stomach. I eat till I've had enough, and that's enough for me – I don't get hungry, so I must be doing all right. But I love *watching* people eat. I like to see hungry people demolishing plates piled high with steaming tucker. I hang around the food hall in Selfridge's watching businessmen swallowing oysters, or little old ladies ploughing resolutely through pies, or slim, well-dressed ladies-who-lunch nibbling on their *nasi goreng*. Watching people eat, well, I suppose it turns me on. Food and sex are happy bedfellows after all. I eat, I want sex. I have sex, I want to eat. It's no vicious circle in my eyes. I love it.

Because I don't hoover up food, my figure is pretty trim. I'm petite but athletic. 32B-22–32. My hair is black, short and cut in a choppy, almost boyish style. I've got large green eyes and a jaw that sticks out a little bit, like Reese Witherspoon. It makes me look cheeky, apparently. Provocative. Suits me.

I work as a sub-editor for a magazine whose title carries an exclamation mark. It deals with celebrities and ... well, that's about it, really. I spend my days trying to come up with witty headlines, standfirsts, captions. It's a good job, well paid, but by the end of the week, my enthusiasm is flagging. Pictures of Angelina at the beach with her boobs out? There are only so many you can look at.

I play squash three times a week with a colleague. I like to read edgy fiction by unheralded British writers. I listen to CDs by The Ink Spots or The Chordettes or Leadbelly. Old stuff. Comfort listening. I have a weakness for Jimmy Choo shoes. I love Kubrick's films. I live alone. That's me, all you need to know.

And the food thing. It's not that I'm obsessed by food. But I'll buy large fish suppers wrapped in paper and open them on a bench and just look at it all, inhaling the sharp vinegar fumes and wondering how so much food can fit inside such a small organ. I'll buy a double cheeseburger meal from the drive-through and stick it on the dashboard, watch the ketchup oozing as steam fogs the windscreen. I'll order a family pizza and take the hot cardboard box from the delivery boy, trying not to let him see the astonishment in my eyes at its insane radius.

I lie in bed at night slithering the glossy, purple-black tip of an aubergine across my pussy lips.

I don't know how the subject came up. It was probably Mike who mentioned it. He's interested in just how depraved human beings can get. He brings books to work with titles such as *The World's Unofficial Sex Records* ('Listen to this: "Swiss biologist Albrecht von Haller recorded the dimensions of a clitoris that was thirty and a half centimetres long."'), or *Atrocity!* ('Listen to this: "When the Egyptians conquered Libya in the thirteenth century, they harvested trophies: thirteen thousand, three hundred and twenty penises from the bodies of their vanquished foes."'), or *Porn Trauma* ('Listen to this: "Skin flick star John Dough could satisfy up to fifty-five women per day."').

Anyway, suddenly, everyone was talking about food, and competitions where you could win prizes for eating the most baked beans, or meat pies, or sheep brains in ten minutes. Gavin, the editor, decided to do a feature on celebrity eating, *for a change*, and took half a dozen of his writers off to the pub to brainstorm. It was a slow day and I'd only subbed a couple of pages of raw copy; my inbox was empty and we were waiting for the art department to start dumping batches of designed pages on the server. I typed the words 'food competition' into the search bar of my web browser. Nearly seventeen million matches. The first tranche of these were simple question and answer jobs – 'Send us the ingredients to a quiche lorraine and win a kitchen makeover!' – and contained nothing about scarfing down spare ribs against the clock.

I tried other combinations that were equally fruitless. That's the thing about the internet. It can be a great research tool as long as you punch in the correct data string first. Mike must have noticed my frustration, because he Quickmailed me:

sup?

I looked up at him and he arched his eyebrows. You're not supposed to fraternise during office hours and even though Gavin had left the building, his spies were everywhere. Quickmail was a godsend when you wanted to gossip during the slow parts of the day.

tryin to find out about those gross comps . . . you know.
eating hundred burgers in a minute . . .

trencherman

Now there's a word I'd never seen before.

que?

swat y'call those guzzlers . . . people who can eat and not
feel it touch the sides . . . like the guy in that film, diner

I lifted my head and mouthed the words 'thank you' to Mike. He winked at me and went back to his furtive reading of *Pearls on Film: A Visual History of the Money Shot*. I typed my new word into the search engine and voila.

I became instantly aroused.

'Are you OK?' Nesta, a fellow sub sitting at the workstation alongside mine was peering at me quizzically. My sex was pulsing. The redness that scatters across my chest and my neck during arousal was there now; a hot giveaway to what was happening to me. I was worried I might have leaked through my skirt, or that the smell of my sex might now be apparent to everybody.

'Fine,' I said, a little too breathily. 'I thought I was going to sneeze, but it wouldn't come.'

'Aw, Jeez. I hate it when that happens,' and she went back to her three-page spread on embarrassing bikinis.

The first website I'd landed on – hungryhogs.com – had been like the finger on my love button when I needed it most. They had a gallery of the greatest scoffers in the UK. Jeremy 'Fleshman' Talbot had once eaten 78 cheeseburgers in 8 minutes. 'Munching' Martin Mercer specialised in hard-boiled duck eggs and could manage 26 in the space of quarter of an hour. Edward 'Cookie Crumbler' Simpkins had mastered the art of cracker swallowing – without water – and could easily work his way through three packs in the time it took for some people to season their meals. But the man who caught my eye was someone called Johnny 'The Mouth' Lawton. He maintained, as odd as it sounds, a balanced diet, reckoning that by varying what he put in his mouth his interest level was retained and his health less likely to suffer than if he were to stuff kilo upon kilo of mussels down his gullet at one sitting. As such he tended to enter freestyle competitions. At a charity chompathon last year he had eaten – over a period of 24 hours – 100 sandwiches, 50 egg rolls, a gallon-tureen of onion soup, 50 cherry tarts, 5 gallons of tea, 12 bananas, 20 packs of dried apricots and 50 assorted tins and bottles of soft drinks. 'I was on a diet at the time,' he said, 'otherwise I'd have aimed for sixty cherry tarts.'

The website listed some of the forthcoming meets. There was one arranged for the weekend, in a village in the commuter belt to the north of London. I wrote the details down in my diary and closed the browser. I came to my senses and saw that I had been absently rubbing my left nipple with my thumb; it was as erect as a pen cap. I squeezed my thighs together on my moist V and didn't dare look up from my screen again for the rest of the day. I was convinced everyone had been watching me.

On the way home, I stopped off at the supermarket and sauntered up and down the aisles trying to summon the hunger that would enable me to eat some supper. I imagined what Johnny Lawton might be dining on this evening. Was he perpetually in training, having to eat prodigiously, and quickly? I wondered if he ever put anything other than food between those soft, bowed lips of his.

The photograph of him on the web page had stayed with me. He had blond hair that fussed around his face in that Robert Redford way that you knew was nowhere near as natural as they hoped it looked. His eyes had been downcast, fixed on the hot dog his jaws were sawing into. Apparently, the best technique for frankfurters was to gobble the sausage and then dunk the roll in water before you ate it. Otherwise the dry bread would swell in your stomach and make you feel full before you were ready. Clever folks, these trenchermen. I walked up and down the ranks of tins and boxes and packets, daydreaming about the face and the obscene way he ravaged the food that was put in front of him.

I put a tray of asparagus tips in my basket, along with a bunch of bananas, a whole cucumber and a pack of baby courgettes. A tin of treacle. And some popcorn. We had run an article – hadn't everybody? – in the magazine about how supermarkets were a hotbed of frenzied singles activity. I wasn't seeing much of it tonight. There was an old guy dithering over which Fray Bentos tin to take home with him and a woman and her two children loading up on shrieked-for sugar and fat. A power-dressed woman picking through the lo-cal ready meals and a plump guy in a tracksuit with a basket full of lettuce and wholemeal pasta.

Come on, I challenged the dead aisle I was walking along. Let's see a hunk turn that corner before I hit the sweetcorn.

I drew level with the Green Giant's niblets and a stocky guy in a blue T-shirt and jeans turned into my path. He had a couple of days' stubble on his face, longish hair, intense eyes and a deeply kissable mouth.

I thought, Hello.

He had this way of sticking the tip of his tongue out when he assessed the stacks of goods in front of him. I checked out his basket. Organic bread, milk, butter, tomatoes, eggs and chicken. One breast. I suddenly decided I wanted to up that count to three for him.

He saw me and gave me a nice non-committal smile that I liked. It was a kind of 'here we are shopping, isn't it a grind?' kind of smile that didn't carry any ambiguity at all. I liked how comfortable he seemed with his own body, the slow, pantherish steps he took, the deliberate way he picked up produce and turned it this way and that in his clean, elegant hands. I was suddenly desperate to see him palpate a loaf, or an avocado. Or me.

I followed him discreetly, mildly astonished by the relaxed, padding stealth of the man, the subtle swing of his broad shoulders. I liked the minuscule shift of the curls of his recently shampooed hair, the simple black thong tied around his neck. Suddenly the priapic veg in my basket seemed wanting.

I wanted to go to him, do something outrageous like show him my cucumber and ask if he had anything like it on his person. Or just press him back against the earthy new potatoes and grab his plums. But I didn't do any of it. I watched him select two bottles of wine and move to the cashier in that maddeningly laid-back fashion. He paid with a credit card and strolled to the exit. I dumped my basket and followed him. I felt panicky, uncertain, wild. I didn't know what I wanted, what I wanted to do, or why I wanted to do it.

He put his bags down at the bus stop and pulled out an iPod. I found myself frustrated that I didn't know what he was listening to. It suddenly became more important than anything else that I know what was pouring into his ears. All thoughts of Lawton, of work, of eating, went out of my head. I felt faint. I felt as though I was going to cry with the simple need of my situation. He was a guy I liked. He didn't know me. What next? I got on the bus that he boarded. I hadn't even bothered to check its destination. I didn't like the way I was behaving, but it was out of my control. I wasn't stalking him, I was giving in to the impulse of the moment. It was that or lose him for ever.

I sat a few seats back from him on the top deck. He checked me out as I walked past him and I felt the electrifying compulsion to just sit next to him, which I resisted. I couldn't tell from his expression if he remembered me from the supermarket. If he did, would he be curious that I didn't have the shopping with me that I had been collecting?

This is madness. These three words went through my mind all along the bus route until he got up from his seat. I was getting ready to follow him when he turned and approached me.

He said, 'I bought an extra bottle because it's a nice evening and you look like you've had a hard day at work. I hope you like Riesling.'

We reached that time of the night. He stood behind me and unzipped my dress, stroking my shoulders, the back of my neck, as I stepped out of it. He traced the white lace pattern across the curve of my bra, lingering at the imbroglio that shielded my nipples.

'I don't . . .' I said. 'I didn't . . .'

'Shhh,' he said. He unclipped me and looped the straps over my shoulders. The bra shivered against my breasts as it fell free. I liked the way he didn't reach immediately for my tits, but moved his focus to my belly, tickling the firm flesh as if it were the fabric of an expensive shirt he was testing before a purchase.

Dinner had been ... interesting. He was a confident cook, and had created a lightly spiced chicken dish with a tomatoey sauce and a crisp green side salad. The wine was good and I drank a lot of it. I was self-conscious over the paltry amount I ate, however. I just couldn't get more than three forkloads past my lips. He didn't seem to notice. Or if he did, it didn't bother him. I was glad about that too. I enjoyed the way he looked at my body. He was really drinking it in, almost as if he were studying it, *reading* it. I have quite pink, puffy nipples, they never go really erect, just kind of swollen, like a semi-inflated balloon that has its end squeezed. I could tell he liked that.

'Suck them,' I said, surprised by the desire in my voice. It made me sound drunk. There was a lot of spit in my mouth. He knelt before me. I was topless now, wearing only my white cotton thong. The light of a candle on the bedside table picked out the blonde furze leading down from my navel to the thin material of my underwear. He nuzzled it with his nose, kissed me on either side of my belly, where the nerves sweep down through the gully of my hips, and straightened his back until he was breathing hot air against my left tit. He took the nipple into his mouth and closed his eyes against its softness, its yield. He bit it gently, his tongue ceaselessly rolling around and against it, sometimes grinding hard against it, or fluttering around the tip. He took his mouth away from that nipple and paid some attention to its twin, sucking it in so far that it was almost lodged at the back of his throat. My hand sought the slick flesh of my left breast, my fingers sliding against its prodigious lubrication.

His hands slid up the backs of my thighs, nails scoring me gently, and cupped my small bottom. He squeezed and kneaded me, his thumbs wriggling underneath, finding a way into my gusset. He stroked the hair there, occasionally grazing against one of the labia, and I bit my lip, wanting to squat onto his fingers and have them all inside, until all my excitement puddled out of me and I was too weak to move. But I managed to stay upright, wanting him to retain the lead, only revealing my need for him through a series of soft moans or sighs. His fingers moved haltingly against the dry flesh there and it was only when he dipped deeper and met the fluid building at the neck of my sex that things got more slippery. I produce a lot of juice when I'm aroused and I could see in his eyes how astonishing it was for him. Soon his fingers were slurping and sucking in and out of my folds and the smell of my sex was heavy in the warm air of his bedroom.

At last he pulled the thong free and I stepped out of it, thrilled to see how the crotch of his jeans was packed out with the shape of his own desire. He raised a glistening hand to his nose and let it linger there before licking his fingers clean.

'Lie down,' he said. I did as I was told. He said, 'Close your eyes.'

I trusted him. I blocked out the light. I heard his clothes coming off. I wanted to look at his cock, see how big he was, see his shape and colour, but I remained blind, as he had asked. I felt him get on the bed beside me and gently part my thighs. I felt the tip of his prick glide between my pussy lips, and oh my, he was big. He was, fuck, he was huge. I shifted on my ass as he gently came on, trying to accommodate what was becoming a slightly uncomfortable girth. Then he stopped and gyrated against me a little, giving me time, before, impossibly, he drove further inside me.

'What ... How?' I said, confused and ecstatic, feeling his meat ironing out all my wrinkles, impaling me. I came almost without realising it. The sensation of him filling me up had concealed the rising tide of my climax. I stiffened and reached out for him, but he wasn't where he ought to be. I opened my eyes and he swam out of the gloom, sitting on the edge of the bed, smiling down at me.

I looked down and he was tenderly withdrawing a fat, foot-long cucumber from my dripping cooch. I was so shocked I didn't know what to say. Other than, 'Don't stop.'

'I saw your shopping basket,' he said. 'I had a feeling you might like a bit of phallic food.'

He fucked me for another ten minutes until my heat and wetness were beginning to cause the cucumber to droop.

'C'mere,' I said, woozily.

He shuffled onto the bed on his knees, his boxers straining. I let him loose and he sprang up and hit me on the chin. Nowhere near as big as the salad vegetable, but infinitely nicer. I stroked the underside of his cock with my nails, paying attention to his balls. I noticed he was shaved and liked the velvety feel of his heavy sac in my hands. I leaned over him and opened my mouth; a great wash of spit fell from my mouth, coating his head.

'Sorry,' I gasped, embarrassed.

'It's OK,' he soothed, stroking my hair. 'I like it. It feels nice.'

'It's drool saved up from all the meals I can't eat,' I said.

He chuckled, a nice, deep, sexy sound. 'Well, you can make up for it now,' he said.

I sucked on his tool for a long time, enjoying the glide of his super-smooth flesh against my tongue. There were no pubes to worry about, and it was thrilling to be able to see his meat disappearing between my lips, unobstructed. I pulled away when it seemed he might lose control, and spat some more onto his length. I slowly wanked him off, at the same time dragging him forwards so that he was poised above me. I touched his glans against my pussy and rubbed him up and down my wet slot.

'Doing anything tomorrow?' I asked him.

'Anything you want,' he said, breathily. He was straining, trying to push forwards, but my hand was blocking him out. I moved my hips against his head, swirling my bush around him, bouncing my swollen clit against the dewdrops seeping from his eye. There was so much moisture all over my mound that I thought he might just skid straight off me onto the floor.

'Come for a drive to the country,' I said. 'We'll grab a bite to eat.'

'Yes,' he said. 'Please.'

I removed my hand and he plunged in. I think we got a little sleep before sunrise. But I'm not too sure.

'My name's Eric, by the way,' he said.

I laughed and politely extended my hand. He shook it lightly, then kissed it. 'Sam,' I said.

'Well, I'm pleased to make your acquaintance.'

We were in his car, a red Citroën Xantia that was ageing well, nipping up the outside lane of the M1 on a clear blue morning. We'd breakfasted early (he wolfed down a bowl of cornflakes, All-bran and blueberries, toast and marmalade, coffee; I nibbled on a dried apricot) in a bid to beat the rush-hour traffic, a plan I put in jeopardy when I decided I needed to have him finger-fuck me a little more as he was unlocking the door to leave.

We managed to get out before we lost control, and I sat happily in the passenger seat, feeling my wet thighs slide against each other. Occasionally, he lifted his fingers to his nose and made mmm-ing noises. I liked how up front he was about his enjoyment of the more cloacal side of sex.

It took us about half an hour to make it to Little Frinley, just by the Buckinghamshire border. A large banner had been hung across the main road into the village. It read: WELCOME WOLFERS! UK TRENCHERMAN CHAMPIONSHIPS 2005

Eric gave me a funny look and I shrugged. 'Food,' I said. 'It's an interest of mine.'

'Don't I know it,' he said.

I told him about the magazine article but neglected to tell him of my intense reaction to seeing so many men gulping down stacks of pancakes or jawing their way through dozens of quarter-pounders. Just the thought of those facial muscles clenching over such a bizarre repast gave my pussy muscles another twitch. I wondered if I should get Eric to pull over in a secluded layby for ten minutes, but by then we were approaching the village green and I had to put my professional hat on.

I grabbed my reporter's notebook and checked that I had three or four working pens in my bag. Then I grabbed my digital camera and gestured for Eric to follow me into the scrum of stalls that were being erected all over the green.

People were sitting on deckchairs outside the small inn at one corner. We went to get a drink and stood watching as the TV crews set up their equipment in front of a large stage.

'This is weird,' Eric said, gesturing at the incongruity of the competition preparations against the bucolic restfulness of the countryside.

I put my hand on his bottom and stroked him. 'There's time to kill,' I said. 'Why don't I take you into the trees over there and practise my trencherman skills on your hot dog before the experts get going?'

We were about to ditch our drinks when I noticed Johnny Lawton limbering up by the stairs to the stage. I grabbed Eric's hand and excitedly pointed him out. And behind him stood the disconcertingly lanky Leonard 'Tiger Teeth' Keith. There had been a number of accusations levelled at Keith that he had had a bypass operation that sent food straight to his small intestine, enabling him to eat more.

'How does that work?'

'There are nerves in the stomach to tell you when you're full. Nothing like that in the small intestine.'

'Jesus,' Eric said. 'They take it that seriously?'

'There's big money in big eating,' I said. 'Sponsors will fly you all over the world to participate. This contest today has six-figure prize money at stake.'

'Where do I sign up?'

'What would be your speciality?'

'I'm not sure you could categorise it as food,' he said. 'Cannibalism, maybe. Of a kind.'

I poked him in the arm and we went down to the front of the stage.

I took some photographs of the competitors, and managed to get an interview with Magnus 'The Gannet' Callaghan. It became busy. The competitors lined up behind a table set with silver platters concealed by lids. Glamour models positioned themselves at the side of the contestants, holding flip-boards bearing numbers to show the audience how many items had been consumed. The MC strode onto the stage to a smattering of applause. I felt Eric nestle into the back of me. I clearly felt the shape of his cock delineated against my buttocks. He was getting hard. The crowds increased. It was astonishing to see how many partisan supporters there were. There were women with tight T-shirts bearing the legend: PUT ME ON YOUR MENU, JOHNNY! People had placards and banners and scarves. I was jostled on each side as spectators scrambled to get a better view. I felt Eric's hands sweep up my flanks and cup my breasts fleetingly, thrillingly. I felt his thumbs snag against my nipples. I wanted him with the force you sometimes get when you need to pee and there are no loos for miles.

The MC had finished introducing the contestants. There was a final limbering up: trenchermen breathing deeply, flexing their gut muscles, opening their mouths as wide as they could. The lids were removed.

I felt my cunt turn to honey. Apple pie. I loved watching people eat apple pie.

Johnny 'The Mouth' Lawton was grinning. This was his favourite foodstuff if a freestyle event wasn't on. He was the bookies' favourite now.

I had Eric's erect schlong snaking all over my arse.

I was in heaven.

The MC blew a whistle, the large LCD stopwatch clicked

from 10:00 to 09:59, and the gustatory orgy commenced. The pies were divided into quarters. Each segment counted as a hit. The number cards were already spinning, the glamour models' fingers working hard to keep up with all those powerful jaws as they pistoned through pastry and fruit as if it wasn't there. I kept my eye on Johnny Lawton. He cupped his wedges with the palm of his hand and mashed them into his mouth tip first. I almost groaned. I couldn't help but think of him doing that with me, his strong hand squeezing my bottom as he munched on my quim. I ground my backside against Eric's dick. Nobody could tell what I was doing. There were too many people around us and they were intent on what was happening on stage. Emboldened by that knowledge, I reached behind me and rubbed Eric's crotch slowly. He responded by kissing my nape. I hitched my dress up around my hips and pressed against him some more. I located his zip and unfastened him.

Johnny Lawton was on his eleventh wedge. He was just in the lead, with Leonard Keith on his tenth. Apple sauce was dripping down Johnny's chin, gleaming stickily in the hazy midday sunshine. That could be my pussy juices as he came up for air after a marathon plating session. I closed my eyes as Eric's teeth bit me softly on the shoulder. I reached inside his jeans and he was sans pants too. Nice. His cock was semi-erect, its moist tip nuzzling into my palm like the nose of a friendly dog. I led it out into the open air and he whispered my name, an admonishment, an approval, I couldn't tell and didn't care. He didn't try to put himself away, which was encouragement enough. I languidly tossed him off, peeling him back hard on the downstroke, really using his length to the full; his breath turned harsh in my ear. I fed his swelling bulb into the soft split between my cheeks. I had to get up on tiptoe to enable him to nuzzle his way into my hole. I craned my neck as far as possible and his lips clamped against mine, my tongue rolling against his. He rocked against me, into me, his slippery cock threatening to spring clear of my sex. The crowd jounced and jostled us, lending weird, new rhythms to our fucking. I watched Johnny Lawton move further ahead of the pack, his dirty apple-slurping technique showing the others how it should be done. There was no room for sophistication here. It was all plunge it in and swallow. I grabbed one of Eric's hands and planted it over my right tit. His other hand I guided beneath my skirt and onto my clit. I got him stroking me there, firm and fast. The moment was wondrous, but I wanted to come as soon as possible. It was animal need. Everything around me: the crowd's baying, the mannerless hoovering of food, it was all utterly alien to what I was used to. I was suddenly a fucking machine. Something that needed filling with hot come, something that was using someone else to get her orgasm nailed. It was ugly, brutal and beautiful all at the same time. I arched my back, lifting my rump so that Eric could hammer himself home with more ease. I no longer cared if we were seen by the other spectators. I noticed some of them enjoying the free show, and it seemed the most natural thing in the world.

The stopwatch was entering the final minute of the competition. I watched Lawton quickly check around him at the scoreboards. He had just finished off his fortieth slice of pie. 'Tiger Teeth' was ten behind him. Johnny had the competition in the bag. He started playing to the crowd, waving between bites. I felt my climax building somewhere in that delicious nexus of nerves somewhere north of my perineum. Johnny Lawton fixed his eyes on mine and sucked a drizzle of apple sauce off his finger. That was it for me, I was on my way.

I started yelling, strange formless shrieks of pleasure, as I rammed backwards against Eric's hard prick. I lifted my hands in the air and my blouse went with it, riding up over my breasts to show Eric's hand crushing my soft, pink boob as his own excitement reached a plateau. Johnny winked at me. I levered myself off Eric and turned around.

His face was simultaneously flushed and confused and aghast. I smiled at him, kissed him and dropped to my knees. I let him fuck my mouth as frantically as he needed to. I took his load, holding on to his legs when it seemed he must topple over, so strong was his orgasm. I swallowed, as I had seen Johnny swallow, and slurped and licked at the juice that pulsed from his end when the ejaculations had subsided. By the time I got back to my feet, Eric was hastily pulling his jeans up. The crowd was dispersing. The stage was empty, Johnny waving one more time, his hands filled with a glass bowl trophy.

I clung to Eric, my legs shaky. I felt something I hadn't felt for a long time.

'Do you know what I want now?' I asked, reaching down and cupping balls.

'Surely not,' he said. 'I'm done in.'

I smiled and pulled him close. 'I want ... apple pie.'

Over a Barrel Maya Hess

Blackcurrant, plum, sweet chutney and roasted ham. It was all there, drenching my nose with the initial draught of Christmas stocking-like gifts. I closed my eyes and absorbed the rewards on offer from the sample of St Émilion Grand Cru Classé. Beneath my eyelids, I sensed the fossil-littered limestone allowing the pervasive root of the vine to delve deep into the cool ground, rather like easing a finger into a coarse-sand beach. I imagined the plant, struggling against the imposed conditions, battling with its own genetic decision-maker: to grow or to reproduce. Such was the control exerted by the viticulturist, I could taste the agony endured by the vine. Do I spread my arms and reach for diversity or do I hang heavy with fruit and plunge into fertility? Such was *my* dilemma as I stared into the Frenchman's chocolate-glazed eyes.

'Can you smell the syrup of autumn, the drowsy end of the summer in here?'

Not bad for a foreigner, I thought, and took another lungful. He was right. It was sleepy. It was as dozy as half an hour after sex. It was warm and snug but dangerous too, like a stranger's embrace. With my eyes still closed, I brought the glass to my mouth and drew the wine between my lips. It seared the sides of my tongue like I had licked a burning log.

'Do you not see? Are you blind?' His English was abrupt but the clumsiness of it was perfect for discussing wine.

'I do see.' I opened my eyes. 'I'll take a dozen cases.'

There was a clicking sound, possibly his lips or fingers but it punctuated the end of that particular bottle. Several other buyers made notes and another ordered. I was watching my host select our next sample, analysing him intently as he moved behind the mahogany bar, as an entertainer would travel the width of a stage. Each time he passed me, my throat constricted. I told myself that it was the antici-pation of the bottle between his hands that merged my senses into a compost of eagerness and adrenalin, not the way his fingers entwined lovingly around the slim, jade neck. Nor, I had to convince myself, was it the ease with which he twisted the corkscrew and slid out the cork, smiling privately as the vapours touched his nose, that made my eyes narrow and my cheeks turn pink.

I was being stupid. I was caught up in wine-speak that I didn't understand.

'*Excusez-moi*, actually, can I make that *deux* dozen?'

There was a beat, a moment comparable to the first taste, while he sized up my request and ineptitude for French. His impatience was palpable as he ripped a page from the order book and rewrote my order.

'Sorry,' I offered, thinking I should have said '*pardon*'. 'It was just so nice.'

So nice? So nice?

I dug my thumbnail into my left palm and excused myself from the gathering. I glared at myself in the mirror of the ladies' restroom. My fire-red hair had come loose and I had plum-coloured circles under my eyes. Buying on a budget had meant driving rather than flying to Bordeaux in order to obtain the best for our restaurant and 36 hours without sleep had rendered my appearance less than its best.

Annoyed with myself, I splashed cold water on my face and returned to the group. I stumbled as my heel caught between two flagstones and only managed to stop myself falling completely by grabbing onto the bar.

'Mademoiselle has had too much already?' That private grin again, as if his accent allowed him to speak his mind without fear of insulting.

'Quite the opposite. Mademoiselle would like much

more.' I settled back on my stool and held out my glass for a taste of the vintage Bordeaux.

'Perhaps mademoiselle would like to know how to take my wine in the correct way?' The smile broadened and his eyes narrowed, fixing me as he walked around to my side of the bar. He was right. I hadn't a clue what I was doing. The feelings that had been stirred while tasting the St Émilion had clearly been kick-started by my French host's good looks, accent and snug jeans rather than me knowing what I was talking about.

'I would very much like to know,' I replied. 'I'm rather naïve.'

The Frenchman snorted, grinned and shook his tousled hair. 'You Englishwomen are all naïve,' he said. 'There is much I can teach you, if you are willing to learn.'

'Isn't that a bit of a generalisation?' I asked, immediately thinking of Gilly Goolden and Jancis Robinson. 'There are some fine female wine writers in England.'

'I was not talking about the wine.' And then he was next to me, visually tasting me as if I was one of his freshly corked bottles, with his eyes all serious and his lips slightly apart.

'Oh?' I croaked, wondering how my boss would react if I forgot to buy any wine at all. I sat up straight, took a deep breath and twirled the Bordeaux around my glass. Immediately, the wine sloshed onto my skirt, again showing my inexperience. The Frenchman moved swiftly and offered me a linen napkin doused with sparkling water. I hesitated, hoping he might mop up the stain for me. He didn't.

'My name is André Moreau.' He held out his hand instead and I wasn't sure whether to arrest the spreading wine or take his outstretched fingers.

'Milly Arnold.' I briefly went for the fingers before mopping at my skirt, creating an amorphous wet patch over the front of both thighs. 'Great,' I muttered to myself, wondering if I should slip back to my room to change. I hadn't even unpacked yet, let alone showered or freshened up from my long journey.

Twenty minutes ago, I had stumbled into the reception hall of the stunning chateau, quickly registered my pre-booked place on the wine buying tour that Gérard, my restaurant-owner boss, had demanded I attend, and literally dumped my suitcase on the four-poster bed.

I was about to excuse myself from the tasting to go and change but André had poured himself a sample of the Bordeaux and was evidently lost in its aroma. The Frenchman's eyes were closed and his dark eyebrows drew together. I could see tiny lines around his eyes and one or two grey streaks on his temples in his otherwise black, pulled-back hair. In fact, André was a picture of darkness – from his black cotton shirt, his deep indigo jeans to his burnt-umber skin. He was as beguiling as the St Émilion I had just tasted and I can only assume it was fatigue and unfamiliar surroundings that intrigued me.

'So, Miss Arnold, tell me your reasons for wanting to sample my wines.' André skilfully twirled the red wine around his bulbous glass until it skimmed the rim. He pushed his nose into the glass and breathed in deeply, again closing his eyes. I wasn't sure whether to reply or allow him to concentrate. '*Magnifique*,' he continued. 'Forest fruits and bonfires with wet oak or perhaps cedar.' André tipped his head sideways before drawing another lungful of the wine's aroma. '*Non*, it is definitely oak. And autumn rain too.'

'That's quite impressive,' I said. 'I'm here to buy wine for the restaurant I manage.'

'*Ici*,' he said. 'Let me show you how.' André's fingers were suddenly wrapped around mine on the stem of my glass. His hand began to move in small circles, gradually increasing until the wine was swirling in a dangerous whirlpool. I glanced at my cream skirt nervously. 'Don't worry. There will be no mess this time.' André's words were drenched in his heavy accent, adorned with skewed vowels and a low rasp from deep within his throat. It was utterly charming.

'Am I doing OK?' I grinned. He let go of my hand and I was swirling by myself.

'Wonderful,' he said. 'Now, stop and breathe in the wine. Close your eyes and let it fill your entire body.'

I did as I was told, only it wasn't the wine that I imagined in my body. 'Delicious. It reminds me of my mother's Sunday roasts,' I lied.

'*Bon*.' André was obviously pleased with me. 'What else do you sense?'

I paused and breathed in again. 'Plum jam and lamb with rosemary. Perhaps a log fire.' I opened my eyes and found that André had moved closer. 'Christmas. I can smell Christmas in this wine.' I didn't tell him that's also what I'd smelled in the first sample. To me, the two were pretty similar.

'Now drink and slurp some air also for the full flavour.' His expectation was palpable. He was desperate for me to appreciate all the seasons of love that had gone into his wine's production.

'Should I swallow?'

All colour drained instantly from my face, leaving me ashen and feeling ridiculous. Then, like a flash flood, my whole head burned scarlet from embarrassment. 'I mean the wine.'

André's skin remained the same earthy, sun-kissed tone. It was merely highlighted by a flash of white as he grinned. 'Of course!' he exclaimed. 'I would always advise swallowing. And besides, what else would you be referring to?'

I filled my mouth with wine so that I couldn't say anything else stupid. My tongue was bombarded with wild taste combinations. André mirrored me and took a noisy sip from his glass and when he finally swallowed, so did I.

'So, what do you think?' He paused to refill the glasses

of the other buyers and spoke a string of French to one, who began to scribble notes again.

'I'd like three cases of this one too, please.'

'*Non*, I will not allow that. Not until you fully understand this exquisite wine.'

'Full-bodied?' I offered hopefully. 'Without being offensive?' I'd heard Gérard say that about wine before. André nodded. 'And it has an aftertaste of moist fruitcake, like raisins and candied orange.' I was really trying.

'Good. Very good. This will be one of the wines served at dinner tonight.'

The mention of food reminded me just how hungry I was. It was unclear if it was the wine, my need for food or André's proximity that sent my head spinning as fast as the wine had chased around the glass. Either way, I wobbled when I stood, causing André to catch his arms tightly around my waist.

I couldn't eat another thing. The other six guests obviously felt the same as they either pushed back in their chairs or went to stand by the enormous fire that crackled and spat within the ornate ormolu fireplace. I was one of only two women present at dinner, the other being from Belgium and probably in her fifties. She sat to my left and at my right, at the head of the rosewood table, was André. He was the perfect host, entertaining all his paying guests with witty anecdotes of life as a *vinificateur* and how he came to learn his craft from his father and grandfather.

Since the entrée of wild chanterelles and port sauce, I had ordered another two dozen cases of André's fine wines. Gérard would be delighted. He was passionate about the reputation of his London restaurant and had entrusted me with the day-to-day running of the place while he concentrated on creating the best in French cuisine. I was honoured to be choosing wine to accompany his fine food.

With every new course, André uncorked the appropriate

bottle and I purchased more and more. Sampling the various wines was like making love to a stranger and I relished discovering unfamiliar tastes and smells and bodies. It was 11.30 when I realised that I was quite tipsy, although I didn't appear to be the only one. Earlier, André had told us that he didn't agree with spitting out the wine when tasting.

'Ingestion is part of the process. My wine wouldn't be complete if you didn't take it in your body and allow it to work on your mind. What it makes you think and how you behave is the final stage of winemaking.'

We were sitting on a leather chesterfield beside the fire, finishing the amber dessert wine that had accompanied the medley of forest fruits imprisoned in a mesh of caramel, when André took out his order book, tore off a page and handed it to me. Most of the other guests had retired, only the woman from Belgium and another man remaining. André glanced at the pair before shifting across the sofa so that his thigh was pressed against mine. He brought his mouth close to my ear.

'Your bill, mademoiselle.' He tucked the folded paper inside my hand and patted my wrist. His eyes narrowed into delighted slits as I frowned and unfolded my order. It was a fine selection and I knew that Gérard would be delighted with my choices. But then my eyes fixed on the scribbled total at the bottom of the page and all I could see was Gérard cursing and screaming and firing me when I explained what had happened.

'Fourteen thousand, eight hundred euros?' I put my hand to my forehead, hoping he would take pity. 'There's been a mistake, surely?'

'*Non*, it is correct.' André rose from the sofa and leaned against the fireplace. He was a fearsome sight with the orange flames reaching up the chimney behind him. 'Would you like a cognac? I have something very special for you to taste.' That glint again but nothing that alerted me to his plan.

'Really, I'd better quit now. If I buy anything else, Gérard will fire me for sure. As it is, I'll have to take many of these –' I paused, not wanting to upset him '– these fine wines off my order. Our budget simply won't stretch this far.' Before I could protest, André was thrusting a glass of brandy at me.

'You are not obliged to buy this one. My cousin produces this fine cognac about a hundred kilometres from here. I want you to enjoy it as if you are my personal guest.' He sat down again and I felt myself sliding towards him as the sofa dipped.

'But I'm not obliged to buy anything, surely? I'll have to cut my order right down as I only have five thousand euros to spend.' I laughed nervously and sipped the brandy, wincing as my throat was suddenly charged with fire.

'You misunderstand, mademoiselle. I have issued instructions to my staff and your wines will already have been moved from the *cave à vin*. I cannot possibly put them back among the undisturbed bottles now. It would be a disaster.' His hands exploded in a display of his vehemence, making me flinch. In my fuzzy, wine-numbed mind, which only wanted to relish in the otherwise enjoyable evening, I was beginning to think that I had a problem.

'You're saying that I *have* to buy the wine on this list?'

'Of course. It is in our contract.' André removed the paper from my hands and ran his forefinger underneath my signature. Indeed, I had signed at the bottom of the page but for what, I wasn't sure. Above my scrawl was a paragraph of indecipherable French.

'Oh,' I said and visualised myself washing dishes for Gérard. 'Is it final?' Perhaps he would take pity on me.

'How do you say –' he tipped back his head and then placed a hand on my shoulder '– set in stone, I think is the expression.' He grinned and then took the remainder of his cognac. I did the same but without grinning.

'*Bonsoir*, Monsieur Moreau.' The other two guests were

leaving and I was thankful for the reprieve as André said goodnight. I thought of climbing out of my bedroom window and slipping away into the night without paying my bill. I considered begging him on my knees, crying even, but my sluggish brain refused to allow me to do anything except help myself to another cognac.

André was suddenly behind me as I was putting the stopper back in the decanter. His hands rested lightly on my hips. 'There is one way we can sort out this mess,' he offered. He turned me round to face him and relief washed over my face.

'I knew we could –'

Then his mouth was on mine, his tongue pushing between my teeth as if he was searching for leftover wine. I pulled away but he gripped my waist harder so I stood like a stupid doll with my arms outstretched and my eyes wide open trying to focus on his close-up face. Finally, I escaped but sloshed some cognac down my front. André scowled.

'Don't waste it or you'll have to pay for that, too.' His eyes were sizzling as they dragged up and down my body, reflecting the flames along with something far more sinister. 'You can't deny that you've been desperate to kiss me all day.' André placed a finger on my wet mouth and trailed it down my throat and between my breasts, where the brandy was soaking into the fabric of my evening top.

'You're wrong,' I lied. 'I've been absorbed in the tastings.'

He laughed. 'And now you can't pay for what you have purchased.' He paced back and forth in front of the fire. 'But not to worry. This has happened to me many times before with you Englishwomen so I have developed a special repayment plan. You get the wine you ordered, I receive payment and we are all happy, *non*?'

Although still reeling from the shock of his kiss, I nodded. I would accept any terms to get out of this mess.

'*Bon*. Just sign here and everything will be fine.' He handed me a pen and virtually wrote my name for me as the paper slipped in and out of focus. Again, there was a page of unintelligible French but I relaxed, sure that Gérard would understand. Besides, a repayment plan seemed quite a shrewd business move and could only make my boss think more highly of my management skills. I was silly to worry so much.

'Now, come with me.' André snatched the brandy glass from my hand and virtually dragged me by the arm. In a moment, we were outside the chateau striding across the deserted courtyard. The chilled night air bit at my exposed legs and shoulders and revealed my breath as quick shots of frosted mist. André fumbled with some keys and then opened the huge wooden door to the medieval barn where we had been tasting wine earlier. 'Inside,' he hissed and pushed me into the darkness. I couldn't see a thing until he lit a candle.

'What are we –'

'Be quiet and do as you are told.' André led me through an arched door into a small room, stocked with barrels. He placed the candle on a table and locked the door. The air was steeped with the scent of rich fruit and fermentation. 'My own private collection,' he said. 'This is where I have very *special* tastings.' He took a glass from a cupboard and drew off some red wine from a barrel, this time not bothering to savour the aroma or comment on colour. André took a large swig.

'None for me?' I wanted him to kiss me again.

'Certainly not. You have a debt to repay.' He sat on a wooden chair. There was no trace of the wicked glint in his eyes or the flash of a grin to soften his angular features. He stared at me coldly, sizing me up. 'Take off your clothes.'

'My clothes?' I glanced at the door, which prompted André to jangle the keys. 'Shouldn't we kiss again first or something?' I laughed nervously.

'Get them off, now!' His voice echoed around the small chamber and I noticed his knuckles whiten around the stem of his glass. Very slowly, fearfully, although with an exciting tingle in the pit of my belly, I loosened the straps that held my sequinned top in place. I pushed them off my shoulders and allowed the flimsy garment to drop around my waist. I was wearing a strapless bra, which was fighting to contain my D-cup breasts. I unfastened my skirt so that both the top and skirt fell to my ankles. I stood in front of André in my bra, tiny pink knickers, stockings and high heels and although he tried to maintain a blank expression, his face briefly mirrored what he saw in the form of a tiny twitch at his jaw.

'And the rest,' he ordered, before taking a large mouthful of wine. 'You must be completely naked.' When I attempted to speak again, he slammed me with a string of French and banged his fist on a barrel. The candle beside him flickered and seconds later I felt a draught of freezing air around my ankles as if someone else had entered the main barn. 'Now!'

The urgency in his voice made me reach for the catch at my back. My black bra dropped forwards, as did my breasts, thankful to be released. I wasn't sure if it was the cold air, the wine or André's stare that made my nipples stick out like sugared almonds pressed into fresh dough, but they caught his eye.

'Take your panties off, too.' He could barely drag his gaze away from my cream-coloured, oversized bust to watch while I tentatively slipped a finger inside the strap wrapping around my hips. I wanted to enjoy the striptease but was finding it impossible. André was demanding something from me that I wasn't quite ready to give. I'd hoped he'd kiss me again, perhaps weave his fingers through my scarlet hair instead of firing orders at me. What choice had I but to obey?

I eased my knickers down my thighs and hooked them over both ankles. I heard André stifle a gasp as I leaned forwards to remove them. My stockings clung to my legs in a faint glimmer of decency and the high heels caused me to teeter in my wine-drenched world. Had fear not gripped me by the throat, I may have made advances on André as he sat on the chair, his slim legs slightly apart, his shoulders bent back and his head tilted to fully appreciate what I was offering. But I was choked by a feeling of apprehension, while André took a long draught of wine.

'You remind me of spring,' he said, 'when buds appear on trees and the world wakes for summer.' I mellowed when he said this, believing that I had misinterpreted his intentions. But then he stood up and lunged upon me, shoving me roughly against the stone wall. I felt the skin on my back graze as his mouth came down upon mine, although not in the desperate, searching way it had done before. This time André drove his tongue down my throat and sucked the life from me, while his hands took hold of my breasts and kneaded them as if I had no feeling. Within seconds of this, I felt my entire body moving across the room to another wall where he grabbed hold of my wrists and clenched them both in one hand. If I tried to speak, he silenced me with his lips. If I tried to writhe free, he confined me by placing a knee between my thighs. I was captive, completely unable to break free, while he secured my wrists over my head in cold, metal straps. My heart beat like a lion was about to rip the skin from my bones.

'What are you –'

'Silence!' he said, standing back to admire his work. I was virtually suspended from the wall by my wrists. I was like a living oil painting and André the artist. He walked away and refilled his wine glass. 'You must be quiet while I concentrate. It's not every day I have the luxury of sampling something this exquisite.'

I didn't dare speak. My breathing quickened, forcing my breasts to rise and fall. My arms already ached and I had to stand on tiptoe to give them some relief. André approached me with his glass of wine and, with one hand beneath my breasts, packing them together like they were stuffed into a cleavage bra, he poured his wine onto my chest. Immediately, a plum-coloured lake formed and

André dipped his face to my bosom and began to lap. He groaned with appreciation.

'You make my wine taste *magnifique*.' His face was close and his lips were burgundy. 'You have a beautiful bouquet.' He breathed in deeply before allowing the pool of wine to flow out of the channel and down my belly. I felt a tingling between my legs as the liquid drizzled into the little triangle of hair, searching for the capillary that led to my pussy. Then his mouth was clamped to my nipple, sucking and chewing as if he thought he could quench his thirst further.

'Hey,' I cried out and was about to protest at the way he was using his teeth but he jammed a hand over my mouth. All I could do was allow the stinging to transform into feelings of pleasure needling through my body. I wanted to push a hand between my legs, to ease the burning from the wine, but of course I couldn't. Strapped up against the wall, I was completely helpless and was beginning to delight in the fear of what André might do next.

I closed my eyes and waited while he lapped at one nipple then the other. Soft animal noises vibrated against my skin as he cleaned every drop of wine before dipping his head, following the trail of Bordeaux. I noticed a faint tang of liquorice mingled with the healthy zest of André's sweat and realised, as I felt bare skin brushing on my thighs, that he had removed his shirt. I was about to look at his body and was desperate to dig my nails into the hard line of his shoulders but reality was knocked from me when he prised apart my legs and began to eat my pussy as if he'd not had food for a week.

'You have the aroma of a wild animal, a touch of game and musk. And you taste of nutmeg and cream with the texture of velvet.' André's words were hard to understand because he continued to feast on me as he spoke. I was desperate to be released although I wasn't sure if I would flee or rip into his trousers.

'Please, let me down,' I said, but André ignored me. He

gripped my hips, sinking his fingers into my flesh, and worked his tongue high into me, making sure he guzzled every drop of wine and juice that had merged into what was obviously a delightful dessert, judging by his greed. Slowly and with the care of a skilled lover, he circled my clitoris with his thumb. Spasms of pleasure radiated through my womb, right up to my nipples, and when my body tensed, when my head lunged from side to side and my thoughts were consumed with crashing into orgasm, he stopped.

'Definitely one to be drunk young,' he said, wiping his hand across his mouth. I was barely aware that he had untied me from the straps and was hauling my body across the room towards the rows of barrels. Suddenly, I was leaning forwards over the rough wood of a cask, my breasts squashed onto the hard oak and not a drop of energy or desire to move was left in me.

'You have a large debt to repay,' André said, his words thick with accent. 'It may take some time.'

'I know, I know. It was awful of me to run up such a large bill and I'm sorry –' Instead of making excuses about my wine-buying ineptitude, my mouth was unexpectedly filled with André's freed cock. His trousers were pushed down to his knees and he appeared in front of the barrel as if he had done this a hundred times before. He took my head in his hands and eased himself between my teeth, gradually increasing the frequency of his thrusts until I tasted several salty beads erupt from the tip of his cock.

'Now it is your turn to taste yourself as I did.' Again, he was one step ahead of me due to my failing consciousness. The wine and the danger of my predicament had overridden reality. I was naked on a ghost train and at André's complete mercy. Again, I felt a burning between my legs and wetness spilling between my upturned buttocks as he poured more wine on my body. Then, without warning, I was stabbed from behind as André pressed his cock inside me. At first, it wasn't clear which part of me he had entered but, when his fingers teased my tight arse muscle and probed inside, I knew that his cock was working deep into my exposed pussy. But, as quickly as he had entered, he withdrew and once again he was pressing his erection into my face.

'Breathe in and tell me what you smell,' he ordered. 'Then I want you to taste the blend of your juices and my wine.'

I did as I was told and cupped his cock in one hand and cradled his cool balls with the other. My breasts ached as I see-sawed over the cask but that only enhanced my enjoyment of him.

'I can smell caramel and almonds, perhaps marzipan but there's something else too, like musk or the sea.'

'Kiss me,' André said and bowed his face to mine. He kissed me not as a lover would but in a scientific, analytical way as if discovering a new, rare substance. 'That is fascinating,' he said. 'I have never encountered this before. There is a definite aroma of ambergris in your mouth. An exceptional discovery!'

I was perplexed and my hazy mind wouldn't allow me to process what he was describing but he was obviously keen for more. André moved behind me and his entire face nuzzled between my buttocks and into the generous outer folds of my sex. It sounded like he was drowning and I could actually feel my juices flowing into his mouth. There was no wastage. Aware of the needles reaching up into my body once again, I shifted on the barrel so that I could position a couple of fingers at the top of my pussy lips. Within seconds, I was on the brink of coming on his face.

'André, you have to get inside me, I'm begging you.' I gripped the barrel, panting and trying to free my hips from his grasp because I didn't want it to end yet. I needed to grip his super-hard cock when I came, feel the weight of his body on my back and have his marinated lips biting my neck. 'Please!'

Finally, André retracted his face. 'I have never smelled

this aroma on a woman before. I could bottle and sell this aphrodisiac along with my wine.' He laughed and hitched my buttocks higher, positioning me for his entry. My skin was chilled again by a draught of night air – a door opening? – heightening my anticipation as André reinserted himself. The outside breeze had cooled his erection as its cold length tentatively searched my sex. With less urgency and a desire to pleasure me more, he slowly pulled in and out, nipping my sensitive pussy lips with each stroke. André dropped forwards and pressed his weight onto my back, although he wasn't as heavy as I'd imagined and his body was soft and brushed over me with a tenderness I hadn't expected. From his cruel games, a sensual lover had emerged, throwing my preconceptions into disarray. He was doing his utmost to keep me on edge; expect the unexpected.

Slender fingers wrapped around my face, covering my eyes, tracing my nose and lips and following a path down my breastbone and out to the pressed flesh of my breasts. The lightness of his touch was more painful than the harsh way he had treated me before. He swiped his lips across my back and up onto my neck, pushing away my long red hair, before licking my neck with a sensitivity that I had only experienced when doing it myself. Warm silky flesh slid across my spine as he pushed up on his toes to reach his cock higher inside me and a moan, unfamiliar and soft, was released inches from my ear.

Then again that roughness, but this time it was in my face. With immeasurable speed, André's cock was invading my mouth again but, but – I didn't understand – he was still inside me, gently teasing my sex with slow-motion strokes. I opened my eyes and took the familiar taste of him deep down my throat as my forehead pressed against his dark-haired belly. Yes, it was true – André was standing in front of me, so who was behind? I tried to turn but he fixed my head in place. My mind was bombarded with possibilities but instead of trying to work out my unusual situation, I relished the tender caresses my body was receiving from the rear, almost feminine in touch, as well as concentrating on André's urgent pumps in my mouth.

It was my unknown lover behind that tipped the balance. Those delicate, precise fingers worked beneath my hips and expertly tended to my needs.

'Whoever you are, don't stop now,' I begged. At this, André gripped the base of his cock and massaged his shaft right under my nose. I felt it start and there was nothing I could do to prevent my pussy contracting around the hardness inside me. Shock waves gripped me as I took André back in my mouth, right at the moment he flung back his head and pulled on my hair and jettisoned an irregular round of salty come onto my tongue. The probing behind slowed as aftershocks still raced through my sex. My unknown lover began to kiss my back and remained unusually hard inside me. A tongue wetted the entire length of my spine, pushing up into my hairline and around my ear.

'I'm André's accountant,' the voice said. 'I hear there's been a bad debt.' She sounded as sweet and soft as the delicious orgasm she had given me and her accent was even more alluring than André's. My sex pulsed around the ever-hard cock still inside me.

'I owe more than you can imagine,' I replied. 'I still have so much to repay.'

Finally, I was allowed to turn over and ease myself off the barrel. She was beautiful: slim and blonde with marshmallow breasts and a dildo fixed firmly around her hips.

'Meet Simone, my girlfriend and financial advisor.' André laughed and took the naked woman in his arms. 'She is very good at debt control, don't you think?'

'I understand you have signed a repayment plan, Miss Arnold. Under the terms and conditions set out, I have to insist your account is cleared.' Simone's features became serious for a moment before she relaxed into laughter.

'There are many ways this can be done.' She giggled as she unhitched the dildo and passed it to me.

'First though,' André interrupted, seeing my eyes widen at the offering, 'I think we need to drink a toast.' He poured three glasses of deep-plum wine and raised his glass. 'To full-bodied reds,' he said.

'And bad debts,' I added before swirling the wine in my glass just as I had been shown.

Sweet Chilli Dipping Sauce
Candy Wong

The ladyboys were at it again, drinking and dancing the night away in the room across the hallway, burning off the adrenaline that had fuelled another of their stage shows. She lay in her bed, curtains parted, watching the stars fade back into the sky and the sun rise over the ocean, staining the waters a vivid crimson. As the boys began to fall quiet, she would sink at last into slumber, swirls of pink and scarlet in her eyes, telling herself that it didn't matter, that she would sleep late, that that was what holidays were about. That there was nothing to get up for.

Holidays! she'd think when she wakened, late in the morning, a hollow feeling in her belly that she suspected any amount of hotel pastries wouldn't fill. Was this really a holiday, or had she run away, unable to deal with what was happening in her life? She shrugged on her bikini top, sat on the floor to slither into the bottoms, and then covered them with a bright sarong that she knotted at the waist. Pointless to try to analyse all that now. The fact was, she was here, on a trip born of a whim as she ate a Thai takeaway in front of the TV one night, and whatever the deep-seated reasons, she ought to just relax and enjoy herself. Read trashy novels and drink iced tea by the pool, leave all the problems at home. There'd be time enough for all that when she returned.

There were few people around the pool: the sun was at its high point by now, and the other guests had gone to seek shade in the beach café. A lone man, face down on a lounger, slowly sizzled like a strip of bacon in a pan. She sat down beneath a canopy and reached into her bag for her sun oil. Squeezing some into her palm, she slathered it onto her lightly tanned flesh as she contemplated her fellow guest and tried to decide whether to wake him.

Her train of thought was broken by a movement across the pool. It was the young man again, the one she'd seen from her balcony dredging the water in the morning before the guests arrived, clearing it of leaves. Now he was moving rapidly between the palm trees, scooping up coconuts and slipping them over his shoulder into a large wicker basket with deft movements. She let her eyes linger on his lithe limbs, trying to assess his age. He couldn't be out of his teens, eighteen or nineteen perhaps. An apprentice of some sort, she thought, doing all the jobs no one else wanted. A boy Friday.

She looked at the water winking invitingly in the sunlight, imagining the cool sweep of it over her. Almost unconsciously, she loosened her sarong, stepped out of it and moved towards the pool edge. Without testing the temperature, she dived in, body arced, sleek as a fish. She came up gasping, head cleared of the last vestiges of sleep by the rush of cool liquid.

Several lengths later, she came up out of the water and showered by the pool. The foolhardy sunbather had gone now, leaving a sweaty imprint on the beige canvas of the lounger, and she was alone. She sat on another lounger to towel herself off and apply some more oil, then lay back and closed her eyes, trying to think of nothing, nothing beyond the beat of the sun on her skin, the slow pulse of her blood in her veins, the feeling of just being *here, now.*

She woke with a start, possessed by the strange sensation that she was being watched, but the poolside was still deserted. Her mouth felt sticky, and she looked vainly towards the bar in the hope of glimpsing a waiter from whom she could order some juice. In the absence of any other bathers, they seemed all to have disappeared, probably to take refuge in the cool shadows of the dining room.

Compounding the sour taste in her mouth was the bitter certainty that she had dreamt of Jim again – Jim standing in the doorway with that terrible look in his eyes: hurt, blame and a sort of beseechment. His eyes were asking her what he should do, whether he should stay or leave, and she hadn't known how to answer. She had wanted neither, or both. She had been angry he'd seemed to have made the decision and then at the last moment devolved it to her merely by the expression on his face. Her burning rage was what kept her returning to the scene in her dreams. What if she had kept her calm? Would she have saved her marriage? Had it been worth saving?

The sun pressed her into sleep again: she let its heat penetrate her, dissolving the fury. A jumble of images floated across the white haze behind her eyelids: the porcine flesh of the man on the lounger, slowly roasting to a crisp, seemed to merge with Jim's skin, pink with exertion, filmed with sweat, as she and he had fucked for the last time; her husband's eyes rolling back in their sockets as he ejaculated became the glitter of another pair of eyes, this time fixed securely on hers.

She sat up with a stifled half-cry in her throat. There *was* someone watching her – the boy Friday, his arm propped against a rush broom, a cigarette burning away in the corner of his mouth, was regarding her coolly from the trees. She stared back, her natural self-consciousness curtailed by curiosity. The brazenness of his gaze both unnerved and fascinated her, especially in one so young. Perhaps, she mused, it wasn't taboo here. Perhaps it was a cultural thing.

Unable to hold the stare any longer, she risked a small, uncertain smile in the young man's direction. She was glad when he reciprocated, plucking his cigarette from between his teeth and tossing it to the ground. Then at last he

looked away, resuming his sweeping of the fronds fallen
from the trees.

She stood up, stretched. Guests were returning to the
pool now, casting off their shorts and kaftans and plunging
into the water or spreading out on their loungers, paper-
backs in hand. As they did so, a trio of waiters reappeared
at the bar, and she walked over to order a drink before the
cocktail hour got into full swing. After a long glass of iced
papaya juice, which she drank perched on a bar stool, she
decided to return to her room to shower and change before
dinner.

Upstairs, in the cool of her room, she slipped out of her
still-damp bikini top and looked at herself in the full-length
mirror on the back of the wardrobe door. After a few days
in the sun, her fair skin was turning a pleasing golden
colour, and a rash of freckles had appeared across her
throat. She brought one hand to her clavicle, let it drop to
her right breast, which felt firm as a barely ripe peach in
her palm. She enjoyed the look of her body, and felt sad
that it hadn't been a greater source of pleasure to her, or to
anyone else for that matter.

Was it Jim who was duff in bed, or her? Or had it simply
been a lack of chemistry between them? She couldn't know,
having nothing to compare it to. How she wished she'd
experimented a little beforehand, as her friends had. She'd
always thought it would be better to wait. She'd been
wrong.

She thought of the young man's eyes on her, blazing
into her, hotter than the sun. On an incontrollable impulse,
she thrust her free hand into her bikini bottoms, astonished
by the sudden wetness blooming there. Her fingertips slid
into the moist core of her almost of their own volition, as
if her own body was trying to swallow her up. She let go
of her breast, moved her other hand down and began
massaging her clitoris with her fingertips. Falling back onto
the bed, she listened to herself purr, wondering at the

pleasure she was able to give herself, wishing only that she'd known, long before, that this was possible.

She was late down for dinner, and the dining room was packed; normally she ate early and went up to read on her balcony when the place got busy. The manager greeted her with an apologetic smile, explaining that unless she was happy to wait for an hour or more, she would have to share a table.

She sighed, acquiesced unwillingly. She had succeeded until now in avoiding all but the most fleeting social contact with her fellow guests, and she really wasn't in the mood to make polite conversation. She was of half a mind to head back upstairs and order room service, but before she could speak the waiter had guided her across the room and was bending forwards to explain the situation to a middle-aged man seated at a corner table. The diner looked up at her, and smiled assent. She was relieved to be greeted by a friendly, open face. He looked like a genial, harmless uncle, the sort who could always be relied on to break the ice at family gatherings.

'Hermann,' he said as she took her place opposite him, shooting out a large hand.

'Jen,' she said, more timidly, as she shook it. 'Nice to meet you.'

'You're British?'

She nodded. 'I'm from London. How about you?'

'From Berlin.'

They smiled at one another again, and then she picked up the menu and made a show of reading it, though by now she knew its contents by heart. Hermann fell quiet for a moment, then leaned forwards slightly.

'If you don't mind – perhaps I could be so bold as to recommend something?'

She looked up at him in surprise. 'Well, I – it's just that I normally have the same thing.'

It was his turn to be taken aback. 'Isn't that a bit unadventurous?'

She shrugged, feeling a little pathetic. 'It's just, well – I found something I like, and I've stuck with it.'

'What do you have?'

'Satay chicken.'

The man chuckled. 'Well, I hate to say it but that really is the least interesting dish in the Thai repertoire.'

She smiled wanly. 'It sounds silly, but it honestly hadn't occurred to me to try anything else. It's what I always have at home, from the local Thai restaurant, with spring rolls to start with. I guess it's turned into a bit of a habit. Either that or I have one of the Western dishes.'

The man had leaned in closer to her, and she thought she saw something appraising in his soft brown eyes. 'Let me order for you,' he said. 'I promise you won't be disappointed.'

She gazed at him, took in his unruly salt-and-pepper hair, his slack jowls, the bushy moustache over his full, somewhat feminine lips. 'How can you be so sure?' she said.

'I'm a food writer,' he said. 'I specialise in southeast Asian cuisine. I know my stuff.'

She laughed. 'Then I place myself in your hands,' she said.

Afterwards, she agreed to share a nightcap in the bar.

'So be honest – you really did like it?' said Hermann as he took a seat.

'I *loved* it,' she reiterated. 'It was way spicier than what I'm used to, but after the first few mouthfuls I just wanted more. It's kind of addictive.'

'Some people do find chilli habit-forming,' he replied. 'That's how they get to eating hotter and hotter food. They desensitise their taste buds to the point where anything mild is a waste of time.'

'I don't think I'm in any danger of that. But I'll definitely try to be a bit more daring from now on.'

'Listen,' said Hermann, 'there's an outing tomorrow evening, to a night market. Why don't you book a place? It's a real eye-opener.'

'Is it instead of dinner?'

'Yes. I suppose the theory is that we eat at the market.'

'What kind of things do they sell?'

He smiled wryly. 'Why don't you wait and see?' he said, tapping the side of his nose with one finger.

After he settled the bill – he'd insisted on paying – she'd gone up to her room and, feeling at a loss, called down to the bar for another whisky to be brought up. She rarely drank, and especially not alone, but one drink with the German had given her a sudden thirst for more.

She consumed her drink slowly, sitting out on her balcony, thinking about the day, about the new experiences it had brought. And now this – boozing in her underwear. What was happening to her?

Savouring the slow burn of the whisky as it traced a line down through her, she stood up and looked down over the balcony. The boy Friday was still down there, only he wasn't working now – he was sprawled on one of the pale loungers, his skin gleaming darkly against it in the moonlight. He was wet, she realised, and clad only in an undergarment of some kind; she surmised that he'd risked a swim while the other staff were busy serving dinner.

In one seamless motion, as if he'd known she was there, he turned his head and looked directly up at her. He smiled, and she smiled back. Then her heart caught in her throat as she watched him peel down his pants and grasp his stiffening prick in one fist. He didn't move his hand, but seemed to be proffering her his member, almost stretching it up towards her. She felt a melting sensation between her thighs, even more powerful than earlier that afternoon, as if some kind of floodgate were about to burst. An excitement so acute welled up in her that she was almost afraid, as if it might be too much for her body to bear. At the same time, she knew what the young man was asking of her, and she was happy to accord it.

Reaching behind her, she pulled her chair up to the edge of the balcony and sat down. Slipping off her knickers, she opened her legs wide, checking that her positioning allowed him an unobstructed view through the railings. Holding herself open with one hand, she began to strum at herself with the fingers of the other. Her eyes strayed from his, which were fixed on her sex, to his prick. He was massaging it vigorously now, but his movements quickened further as she watched him.

Her climax took her by surprise, so sudden and violent was it, and she could still feel it rippling through her as she righted herself on her chair again, anxious not to miss his. She looked down again just in time to see a flash of white against the young man's flat brown stomach, and a pearlescent shimmer as his come coalesced there.

His orgasm broke the spell. She grabbed her knickers and hurried indoors, sliding the doors closed behind her and drawing the curtains. Her heart thudded almost painfully in her chest, like a trapped bird. What had she been thinking? Some unknown appetite had overwhelmed her and inspired what she could already see was an act of madness.

After a calming lavender-scented bath, she wrapped up snug in her fluffy bathrobe and, propped up against a mound of pillows with a glossy magazine to hand, tried to obliterate the incident from her mind. Instead she forced herself to focus on her conversation with Hermann, on the coming outing to the night market. Now that it meant getting away from the hotel, if only for an evening, she felt more enthused about it. But how would she get through the day? How would she face up to the young man? She closed her eyes and tried to sleep.

* * *

The minibus was almost full by the time she made it down to the reception, where Hermann was waiting for her.

'So glad you decided to come,' he greeted her, gently steering her across the lobby and through the revolving door. 'How was your day? I didn't see you by the pool at all.'

'No, I fancied the beach today,' she said quickly, climbing into the minibus and scanning the interior for two vacant seats. 'I've hardly been down there since I got here.' She settled into a window seat and looked up at Hermann, wondering if he would still be as friendly towards her if he knew what kind of a woman she really was, what she had done after leaving him in the bar the night before.

'I do love swimming in the ocean,' he replied, 'but I tend to go down there first thing in the morning, before anyone else is up.' He smiled, a faraway look in his eyes. 'Or sometimes even in the night. Then I can swim in all my glory.'

Jen felt a stab of excitement in her groin as a vision of a naked body walking out into the foaming waves sprang into her mind. As she tried to hold on to the image, she realised that the figure had the smooth, mahogany-brown flesh of the young man. She wished she was alone, her desire to masturbate was so sudden and so forceful. She trotted out a few platitudes about the beach in an attempt to quell it.

Within quarter of an hour, they arrived at the market and the other guests began piling out of the bus. Already, she could hear strident voices calling out their wares. Hermann stood up, a hand held out to help to her feet.

'I hope you're hungry,' he said.

'I am,' she said, smiling. She wondered why it couldn't be his body that she fantasised about.

Outside, the market had spilled out of its main covered square and into the streets radiating off it. Beneath the canopies, stalls overloaded with glossy baby aubergines, ripe papayas gently leaking their juice, and a number of other fruits and vegetables she couldn't identify were crammed up against stalls selling hot food cooked in front of the diners, who ate either standing right there, or seated at a makeshift dining area with a couple of rickety metal tables and chairs.

She was used to Hermann's hand at her elbow by now, lightly guiding her in the direction he wished to take her, and she submitted willingly, savouring the freedom from responsibility and choice, and the feeling of protection. She looked up at the German gratefully, but his eyes were scrutinising the surrounds.

'This way,' he said after a second. 'Let's start you off on something easy.' He ushered her to a stall at which a gnarled little old lady was stooped over a vast pot of soup, stirring it assiduously with a spoon that was almost as big as her. They watched her for a moment, and then Hermann gestured to her and she ladled them two bowls of the pale, fragrant liquid.

Jen sniffed at it. 'What's in it?'

'Lemongrass, shrimp paste, galangal, lemon juice, chilli, coriander,' he reeled off. He brought his mouth to the rim of the bowl and drank in the broth. He finished it in one slurp, smacking his lips together in pleasure. 'You'd pay a fortune for stuff this good in London or New York.'

She emulated him; the soup, studded with tiny shards of emerald-green chilli, made her mouth tingle but was wonderfully refreshing. She turned to Hermann, who was exchanging a palmful of *bhat* for a half-dozen little round dumplings, which he blew on before selecting one and popping it into her mouth. Its flaky fried shell gave way to the crunch of vegetables. She felt the sting of spices on her palate, gave herself to it fully. As with the whisky, as with her solitary climaxes at the hotel, it felt incredibly liberating.

Hermann was moving away, cradling the remaining dumplings in his hand, eyes fixed on something a few aisles away. She followed him, glad he was there as her guide. She would never have signed up for the outing had he not urged her, yet she was finding the colours and sounds and smells of the market intoxicating.

They stood in front of a small stall at which a bare-chested man was heaving a metal basket out of a bubbling vat of oil.

'What the hell's that?' she exclaimed, recoiling instinctively. The charred little bodies she had spied in the basket looked like the remains of some kind of rodent.

'Deep-fried baby sparrows,' said Hermann, and in his smile she read a provocation.

'Oh no,' she countered, taking a step back, flapping her hands in front of her as if waving away a bad smell.

'Or what about some of this?' he asked, turning to point at a heap of rubbery crimson tubes.

She grimaced.

'Only teasing,' he said. 'These are a bridge too far even for me, and I eat most stuff.' He grinned. 'They're chicken intestines,' he added, 'just for your information.'

They moved away to a tea stall, where they drained several small cups of a strong green brew while Hermann explained to her what was on sale at each of the stalls and named the exotic fruits for her. He talked to her, too, of his youth spent touring much of Asia and of his training in the kitchen of a five-star hotel in Bangkok.

'So you're a chef too?' she said. 'Wow.'

He nodded. 'I'm long retired from the kitchen, but I still whip up a mean *gai pad prik* if you're ever passing through Berlin.'

Their eyes locked briefly, and her breath failed her for a second. An image flashed up in her mind: the boy Friday again, prone, a white tide coating his stomach. She wanted to want this affable, interesting, slightly overweight German so much. Why did her brain keep sabotaging her wishes, switching him for the young man? Nothing could come of that, and the sooner the incident was forgotten the better.

Hermann was standing up, tapping his watch. 'We need to get back to the bus,' he said. 'I'd hoped to get you to sample some more things, but I lost track of the time.'

Inside the bus, he took out a little bound exercise book and began to jot down some notes. Jen worried that her lack of response to his loaded remark about Berlin had offended him, and cursed herself for allowing her weird new fantasy life to jeopardise their growing friendship. Several times she made to reignite the conversation, but Hermann seemed intent on writing down his impressions of the market and she didn't want to distract him.

Back at the hotel, they bade each other a muted goodnight in the lobby and then each made their way to their room. Immediately she had closed the door behind her, Jen rushed to open the balcony doors and stepped out into the night air. There was no sign of the boy Friday. The moon shone down on the still water, making a mirror of the pool. Turning away, unsure if she was disappointed or relieved, she went inside and lay down on the bed. She wanted to touch herself, but she resisted the urge, instead closing her eyes and resting her head on the pillow. She pictured the young man once more, watched his hand glide up and down his member, saw again his eyes fixed on the liquefying patch between her legs as she pleasured herself. The desire to thrust her hands between her legs intensified.

And then, suddenly, there he was, the German, spread invitingly on the lounger, his belly soft and doughlike but his dick hard in his fist as he worked at himself. Her eyes burst open; she sprang up, pushed her feet back into her flip-flops, trying to remember the number on his key fob. Thirty-four, had it been? No, 43, she was sure of it. She raced out of the room.

He answered almost immediately, and when she followed him back into the room, she saw the notebook open on the double bed, a laptop whirring beside it.

'I'm sorry,' she began, 'I'm disturbing you.'

'No, no,' he protested. 'It's nothing that can't wait.' He regarded her curiously. 'Why did you come?' he said at last.

She paused, looked hard back at him. 'I'm still hungry,' she said.

The waiter wheeled in a trolley laden with white porcelain and silver domes and waited as Hermann peeled a few banknotes from a wad, which he pulled out of his shorts pocket. Jen strode in from the balcony, taking another sip of chilled white wine.

'A traditional wedding feast,' said Hermann, waving a hand towards the spread and smiling at her. She noticed the way the skin around his eyes crinkled and wanted to run her fingertips over the delicate folds, bring her hands to the side of his face and pull it into hers.

He turned back to the trolley, lifted one of the domes and murmured in approval. She stepped towards him and surveyed the platter.

'*Tod man pla, tod man kao phod, ka nompang na goong,*' he said, pointing at each in turn. 'Fishcakes, corncakes, and prawn and sesame breads.' He picked up one of the golden fishcakes, dredged it through a fiery-looking red dip in a small pot in the middle of the plate, and brought it to her lips.

'Mmmmm,' she said, drawing the disc into her mouth. It was chewy but not unpleasantly so.

Hermann turned back to take another, but before he'd done so, she had climbed onto the bed and was stripping off her T-shirt and shorts. He looked down at her, a thoughtful expression on his face, turned to take something from the trolley behind him and moved towards the bed.

She brought herself up on her elbows to let him unhook her bra, then lay back down as he inspected her breasts. Her head fell back in a swoon. She closed her eyes, then opened them almost immediately: with the fingertips of both hands, he was smearing her nipples with some of the orangey-red chilli sauce. She watched as they tautened, then observed as Hermann brought his mouth to each breast in turn, moving his tongue around and over until no trace of the sauce remained. Then he drew his tongue along the vertical line running between her ribs, from her throat to her belly, raising her haunches with his hands and sliding off her knickers.

'How was that?' he said. 'Did it burn?'

She shook her head, then bent her knees and opened her legs to him. 'Here,' she said, touching the tender oyster flesh with her fingers. 'Try it here.'

He nodded, delved into the pot on the bedside table and began rubbing some of the chilli-flecked sauce over her labia. She let out a gasp, clutched at the side of his head and almost slammed his face down against her. Then she closed her eyes and concentrated on the cool flicker of his tongue on her, in every crevice of her. The flames died away but his tongue stayed on her, making exploratory little motions and, as it slowly wound its way up inside her, she felt another kind of fire begin to rage through her.

'Still hungry?'

She opened one eye, smiled at him languidly, and sank back into sleep, not to wake again 'til late morning. Hermann was taking a shower, and the remnants of the previous night's meal lay around her – they'd finished it in bed, ravenous from hours of foreplay and fucking and afterplay, and she'd stacked the crockery on the bedside table while he coated himself with the last of the chilli dipping sauce. She'd gone down on him for another hour then, slowly lapping at him until the heat of the sauce melded with the sour saltiness of his come.

When he stepped out of the bathroom, she was standing on the balcony. He came up behind her, wrapped his arms around her and nibbled at her bare shoulder. 'What are you looking at?' he asked.

'Nothing,' she said, turning to him with a half-smile.

Pushing him down onto the chair and pulling aside her bikini bottoms, she impaled herself on him, glancing over her shoulder every few minutes as he writhed and moaned below her.

Butter Fingers
Maddie Mackeown

Pristine. That's how he liked it. That's how he wanted it to be. With everything in its correct place. Lowry looked around the room. Neat, tidy, minimalist. A subtle atmosphere of tasteful space. The cool colours and sleek lines shouted 'style' in dignified and powerful undertones, reflecting Lowry's private opinion of his own personal charisma.

He stepped, with feet swathed in supple leather, across a designer's dream of wood-block flooring to the huge expanse of window that overlooked the Thames below, flowing tonight in a soft grey glide that moved in muted persuasion on its way to the Houses of Parliament just beyond the bend.

He was standing at the centre of a power base and basking in that awareness. Well, maybe he was a tad off centre but close enough, surely, for some of it to rub off onto him. He ran elegant fingers through recently trimmed hair, which was just beginning to show distinguished grey streaks at the temples.

He could hear Eva in the kitchen preparing for his guests. She was quietly busy as she was in all things to which she applied herself. Efficiency personified. She would not let him down, that he knew. He listened attentively, trying to make out her manoeuvres, but all he could make out was the odd clatter, bang or scrape. Oh well, he always left it to her capability and did not interfere. What went on behind the closed doors he could but guess. It didn't particularly intrigue him. He had a vague impression of gleaming steel shrouded in a mist of steam. As long as the results were stunning as usual, then he was satisfied. Eva was mistress of her domain.

He turned at the swish of the kitchen door and watched her go over to the table. She minutely realigned the perfection of cutlery and candles around the fresh flower arrangement that she now placed on the shiny glass surface, an epicentre of the night's proceedings.

'Is everything going OK?'

'Of course.' She spoke in a low pitch, husky with intimate resonance. Lowry was aware that she knew he'd asked the unnecessary question simply to hear her voice.

She turned the vase to an angle of better advantage. Late evening sunlight filtered through glass panes in the ceiling, lending a shimmering brilliance to the ambience, which enhanced the creamy richness of each separate lily. The petals held spattered droplets of moisture that glistened. Lowry thought that the white lily was an odd choice of flower for a table decoration as they made him think of death and funerals. He had to admit that they were elegantly beautiful with a wonderfully exotic perfume. She always chose lilies, God knows why, and she always used five. He studied them and she studied him. But he knew better than to comment.

'Will you wear the apron?'

She touched the ties at her waist and thought for a few seconds. 'Mm, I'm not sure; haven't decided yet.'

He watched her face for some sign of perplexity but there was none. She remained as unruffled as usual. He would love to go closer, maybe wipe off a smudge of cream or strawberry juice, but there was none. Her skin was clean and dewy fresh. His nerves tingled as he imagined her sweat-smeared. She was unbelievably calm and collected. It was almost as if she had sneaked in a takeaway but he knew this was not the case. He wanted to approach and smooth a loose strand of hair back into place but its luxurious abundance was neatly clipped back. How did she do it? Such a profusion of wayward curls all held by a single clasp and not making a bid for freedom.

'I think I'll keep it on.' Her words cut through his reverie.

'Yes.' Lowry nodded. Then changed his mind as he remembered the plans for the evening. 'No, take it off. It'll give the right impression for these two.'

'OK.' She checked her watch. 'They should be here in about half an hour. Shall I get you a drink?'

'Yes. Please.'

He turned back to the scene outside, where a barge was passing in a miasma of muffled music. Some other type of pleasure was in progress beneath its canopy, something to do with dancing and celebration. Lowry could hear very little of it thanks to highly effective triple glazing and the ultra-soft hum of the air conditioning.

'Here you are.' Eva handed him a glass of iced mineral water shot with lemon.

'Thanks.'

She went to light the musk-scented candles while Lowry sat on the sofa that was nearest to him, sinking into soft grey leather. She took a place opposite, relaxed but not languid, perched on the edge, poised for immediate action if necessary. Her swishy skirt draped around her knees, flowing in raspberry ripples, the fragile, clingy fabric strangely at odds with her organisational precision. It was just the right touch, thought Lowry, suggestive of the softly feminine in service to the male.

'Well?' She raised an eyebrow in question. 'Tell me about these guests.'

He crossed one long leg over the other. 'Barristers. Both successful. One divorced, the other unattached and ambitious. Both, therefore, always ready to accept dinner invitations. Of course, they work alongside some highly respected women and I think might like the idea of an attractive . . .' He was at a loss for the correct term.

'Waitress? Housekeeper?'

'Exactly.'

'Or maybe the au pair. That would make you a dad,' she teased.

He laughed. Eva smiled, a gentle change to an otherwise rather serious demeanour.

'Isn't there something you should be doing?' he said.

'No. Everything's under control.'

Of course it was. He held her gaze, hoping to find a sign of tension or worry or excitement in her face, but no. She appeared to be calm and untroubled. He lowered his eyes to the gentle rise and fall of her breasts as she breathed evenly. Her top was clingy but not overtly sexy. She was one of those women who managed to be alluring without having to try. Classy and sensual. She moved slightly and he was amused to see the outline of a nipple becoming erect. Yes! What was she thinking? he wondered. He almost wished that his guests were not about to disturb this moment.

And then they did. The buzzer sounded.

Eva turned to glance at the intercom then back to Lowry. 'Well, here we go.' Her lips parted slightly. Was that the suggestion of a blush? Maybe Madame La Chef was not quite as cool as the cucumber that she had diced earlier.

They both stood, each tuning in to the anticipation that sizzled silently between them. Then Eva turned to go back into the kitchen while Lowry crossed to the intercom.

'Hello?'

'Lowry, it's Blake,' came the disembodied voice.

'Blake! Come on up.' He pressed the door-release button. In fact it was Blake and Sebastian, arriving together. Lowry took a deep breath. Yes, here we go.

'Good to see you again, Lowry.' Three pairs of eyes surveyed all that lay before them. Introductions and niceties duly observed, the men had drifted to the window to look down upon their world. 'Lovely sunset.' Muttered agreement followed by a pause. 'Sebastian and I are eager to clinch the deal ASAP.'

'Gentlemen, let's get straight to the point. Might I suggest that we sign the papers straight away and then relax into the evening? What do you think?'

'Good idea.'

With contracts duly signed and deftly secreted into Lowry's briefcase, it seemed appropriate that the three men took a sofa each, as if mapping out their own territories.

Eva appeared centre stage with a tray of glasses and decanter.

The three pairs of eyes followed her every move. Lowry was momentarily mesmerised by the thin gold chain that now circled her ankle. She had removed her shoes and the toenails glowed with a polished redcurrant sheen that matched her top. His eyes crinkled at the edges as he smiled inwardly. She always did this, threw in a surprise for him, something off key.

'This is Eva, here to help me.'

'In the absence of your culinary skills, eh, Lowry? Good evening, Eva,' said Blake.

Sebastian greeted her and managed not to allow his eyes to travel over her body until she had turned away. A gentleman indeed. He will probably be the one to watch, thought Lowry.

He frowned. 'Eva, be careful. You've splashed drips on the tray. Wipe it, please.' The stopper slipped from her fingers and dropped to the floor with a small thud. She hastily retrieved it and disappeared back into the steamy world of 'kitchen'.

The conversation was genially challenging and flowed with the ease of whisky-lubricated tongues and the natural loquacity of all three men. There was the time-honoured rumble of undulating male voice as they analysed various aspects of the financial, commercial and sporting worlds.

The briefcase disappeared as Eva tidily removed it.

'It's nice and cool here. I was in chambers today. No air conditioning or none to speak of. Almost a sauna! Sweated buckets – and then went on to the gym. Sucker for punishment. Must be crazy.' Lowry smiled politely at Blake, appreciating the well-toned physique of his guest, and took a sip of his extremely diluted drink.

Sebastian's eyes had been slowly taking in all the aesthetic detail of their surroundings. 'Have you been here long, Lowry?'

'Oh, about eighteen months.'

'Nice place.'

That's not all you like the look of, thought Lowry. Eva had come from the kitchen with a salver of canapés, offering to Blake first. Lowry was amused. Was that a wink? But as Eva went to Sebastian her foot caught the edge of the sumptuous rug and a slip of crab and tomato landed on his thigh as the salver tilted mid-stumble.

Eva's cheeks flushed an almost match to the tomato. 'Excuse me, I'm so sorry.' She hurried to fetch a cloth. As she knelt before him and dabbed at Sebastian's thigh, it seemed that anger was not the prevalent emotion.

'Please, don't worry. Accidents happen. I hope you didn't twist your ankle or anything.'

Eva smiled her gratitude. 'No. I'm fine, thanks. Maybe I'll just leave these here,' she said, placing the salver on a small side table. She refilled the glasses, a mere drop into Lowry's, and escaped once again to the kitchen.

The sun had finally given up on the day, with blood-red streaks fading to salmon pink in the sky upriver. Lowry pressed a button and curtains slid smoothly to drape across the window, effectively shutting them away from the dusky world behind a barrier of peppermint-tinged voile. Another button and unobtrusive lighting glowed into luminescence at the room's perimeter with subtle invasions of the deepening shadows.

As the men took their places at the table, they moved into an area of fragrant candlelight, teasing the senses up a notch.

Lowry watched and bided his time. Voices were raised and laughter became louder.

'They don't accept blame, of course, but nonetheless agreed to . . .'

Eyes followed Eva each time that she served or cleared.

'. . . even though the main witness was out of the country. Diabolical!'

Emerald green of watercress soup was matched by the blackcurrant of richly red wine.

'. . . used to have an MG, real sporty little model . . .'

Fingers broke into softness through the crisp crust of recently baked rolls and creamy butter melted onto the warm freshness.

'. . . advised to buy shares in all things African or Olympian . . .'

'. . . a field day for construction companies!'

The bed of rice was bright with yellow, red, orange and sprinkled speckles of leafy green.

'Eva, more wine please.' Then in a whisper that could be overheard: 'Will you take more care of my guests! You are being lax.'

The two men politely covered any embarrassment with complimentary remarks about succulence and taste, admiring the tenderness of the stuffed pheasant that had been soaked in a complex marinade.

Meanwhile, Eva refilled the glasses, gliding silently from man to man.

'So what is it exactly that you do, Lowry?' Sebastian asked.

Blake was taking a mouthful of rice when the bottle slipped in Eva's fingers and caught the rim of the tall-stemmed goblet. The glass tipped over with a small crash, spilling wine in a trickle, which seemed to catch the vivid sunset. All four watched it in silence until Blake overlaid his napkin and stemmed the flow. 'Everything under control. Nothing broken.' He laughed, putting the goblet to rights again. 'A little mishap, that's all. Nothing to worry about.'

'I beg to differ,' said Lowry, his face stern. He looked at Eva. 'Come here.'

She went across and stood before him. 'I'm sorry, Lowry.'

'I'm not amused. You have embarrassed me enough in front of my guests.' He threw his napkin onto the table.

Silence and stillness seeped through the room as each person knew that something was about to happen. A flicker of unease rippled between the two guests. Or was it excitement? They glanced at each other but kept their silence, intrigued. Nerves of expectation began to bubble.

The man and woman held each other's gaze and neither backed down.

'Are you going to punish me?' Her voice was huskily soft with a slight tremor. 'I didn't mean to be disrespectful to your guests.'

'Nevertheless, you were disrespectful.'

Blake opened his mouth to speak then changed his mind and shut it again.

Lowry slid his chair back a little from the table. 'You must take more care and I intend to see that you will remember this in future.' There he paused. Neither of them looked to the two men nor spoke to them. It was almost as if the guests were no longer there; as if the two of them were alone, locked in a byplay of their own.

Then she moved, taking a small step towards Lowry. He took her wrist and pulled her across his knees. He did not need to be forceful; she was acquiescent, even willing.

It was obvious what was about to take place. Blake and Sebastian were shocked but didn't interfere. Their silence became a collusion that held them on the periphery. They were watchers, waiting for the inevitable moment when Lowry would pull up her skirt. Would he also pull down her knickers?

He did neither. He simply rested his hand in the small of her back and spanked her, hard enough for her to wriggle and gasp. Then he stopped abruptly with his hand left lying on the curve of her bottom. 'Gentlemen, do you think that I am being too lenient?'

They were instantly drawn further into this bizarre happening.

Blake shifted to make himself more comfortable but did not speak.

A pause followed that didn't last long but was filled to its brim with seething excitement. 'Maybe you should be a little more stern,' said Sebastian, catching his lower lip between his teeth.

Lowry smiled a private smile. Yes, they were hooked.

Without looking at the other two men, he slid his hand down her skirt then pulled it up, pinning it to her waist with his arm. He rested his hand on the strawberry-crush redness of her knickers, squeezing the plumpness gently. He was aware of a slight movement as Sebastian leaned forwards fractionally. He could feel the anticipation of his guests as they feasted their eyes.

The lightly scented air had suddenly become highly charged.

With deliberate slowness, Lowry began to pull down her knickers until they were halfway down her thighs, leaving the buttocks naked between the dual shocks of colour. The plumpness was firm and creamy, with a light garnish of pink finger marks. Lowry proceeded to spank her further. Eva began to squirm deliciously and then actually squealed, although it was a sound closer to delight than pain.

When he had finished, Lowry told her to get up. Eva slipped from his knees to stand before him. 'Hold up your skirt.' She did so, pulling it up to her waist and he felt two pairs of eyes searching greedily for a further glimpse. He was quick to pull up her knickers before they had a chance to see much, leaving them wanting more. 'Now maybe you will remember to take more care.' He slid his chair near to the table and continued eating.

'Yes, Lowry.' Eva turned and went back into the kitchen, rubbing her bottom as she went.

The two men were stunned. For a few moments they were speechless.

'Gentlemen, please, continue your meal,' said Lowry conversationally, as if the recent scenario was common-place instead of extraordinary. He smiled a challenge at them.

Blake spluttered a short laugh. 'Ha! Well ... you certainly have a way with women!'

'Don't I just!'

Sebastian kept his silence. There were the sounds of cutlery, as each man carried on with his meal. Appetites had certainly been whetted.

Talk turned into falsely quotidian conversation as minds were elsewhere.

Lowry watched for reaction. He peered through the glass top of the table, well aware that the other two men were extremely aroused but could do nothing about it. However surreptitious, any fumbling would be on full view through a glass darkly and so they remained horny but civilised. What a paradox! Well, gents, where do I take you from here?

He had promised his guests a bonus. What had they expected? he wondered: gambling, drugs, a blue movie? Maybe, but not Eva, a prize indeed, the cherry-topped icing on the cake.

He watched as they glanced around the room, unsure if the lights had dimmed or not. The atmosphere seemed to have become warmer, with softer lighting, red infused.

As Eva came to clear the plates he knew that each man was thinking of the pink-marked bottom. Was there a faintly accentuated wiggle to her walk? Eating suddenly became a serious business as the men concentrated on their meal.

Dessert arrived in the shape of baked Alaska, offering another paradoxical delight. The coolness of fruit and ice cream, trapped by the sudden heat of stiff white meringue.

Eat the message, gentlemen.

Eva hovered, ready to pour sweet dessert wine, very carefully, of course.

There was appreciative chat while the diners added a trickle of cream and hopefully awaited further mishap, which sadly did not happen.

Lowry allowed himself two mouthfuls before placing his spoon decisively onto his plate. 'This cream isn't fresh.'

There was silence as the men looked at him, spoons suspended mid-air. Then Blake spoke. 'No, I don't think there's anything wrong with it. Seems fine to me.' He gesticulated vaguely with his spoon.

'Actually, I agree with Lowry,' said Sebastian, also laying his spoon on the plate.

I knew you'd be the one to watch, thought Lowry.

Blake shifted in his seat. 'Well, now I think about it, maybe you're right.' He too put down his spoon.

Three pairs of eyes surveyed the woman beside them. She gently placed the bottle on the table and remained still.

Lowry allowed the tension to build a little then spoke. 'Fetch what I want, please.' They're practically drooling, he thought.

Eva disappeared briefly into the kitchen, to return moments later with a spatula in her hand. It was made of soft wood, quite small and very light.

She gave it to Lowry. He took it and patted it thoughtfully on his thigh. 'To chastise the cook with her own tool.' He raised an eyebrow in rhetorical question and looked at the men, pulling them into his game. 'Appropriate, don't you think?' They said nothing, did nothing.

He stood, pushing back his chair, then slowly slid his plate away to leave a space in front of him. He moved behind Eva and pulled up her skirt.

A thin sheen of sweat glistened on Blake's upper lip.

Sebastian remained cool.

She was calm, complacent. 'Pull down your knickers,'

Lowry demanded. She pulled them down to her knees. Her nipples were erect beneath the clingy fabric and her lips parted as her breathing came faster.

Blake looked at the top of her thighs, seemingly mesmerised by her shaven mound and the butterfly that had landed there in the form of a tattoo. He wanted to touch it, Lowry knew. The wings were outspread as if hovering, poised, ready to take flight.

Sebastian's eyes ran over her exposed body and the tip of his tongue passed across his lips. I know what you want to do, thought Lowry.

'Bend over,' Lowry said. Eva bent over the table where he had cleared it. He took the spatula firmly in his hand and lifted it, letting it hover for a moment. Then the sound of slapping cut through the air as he began to chastise her.

After a few slaps, Eva began to moan but it was not a cry of pain. She reached out her arms and gripped the edges of the table. Her lips were parted and her face was flushed. The soft smacks continued then Lowry stopped and dropped the spatula onto the table.

He stepped close to her, his belly pressing against her bottom and his knee pushing between her thighs in a stance that said, 'I am her master.' He reached to take the clip from her hair, which tumbled like a mane around her face. He buried a hand in the unruly curls, gripping and pulling up her head. Dipping a finger into the melting ice cream, he slid it between her lips. The men watched, fascinated, as she licked the finger.

'I offer you the final dish of the night, gentlemen. Not quite whipped cream.' He smiled, his fingers beginning to slide along her pouting lips, her tongue flicking the tips.

He released her, feeling the fizz around the table like bubbles in a champagne bottle about to explode. He stepped back, slipping his hand smoothly into his pocket.

There was no pretence that this was now anything but sexual. Lowry had given a clear message and the woman was obviously compliant. Blake was about to make a move.

At that moment, Lowry pressed 'Call' on the mobile in his pocket. A telephone rang. Eva stood, her skirt falling into place around her. Everyone was stilled.

After five rings Lowry went over to answer. 'Lowry here.' A pause. 'Hold the line please.' He replaced the receiver. 'Excuse me. This is a call I must take.' He walked over to a door. 'I'll be some minutes. Please, continue.' And he left them.

Closing the door, he pulled out the mobile and pressed 'End Call.' He turned back to the door which he opened fractionally. He heard Eva's soft voice but could not make out the words. Blake nodded and she lifted her skirt.

He saw Blake put his hands on her, pulling her towards him and touching the butterfly while reaching round to fondle her bottom.

Sebastian came up behind her and lifted her top to bare her breasts.

Lowry watched as the two pairs of hands felt her. Heat pulsed through his veins. His erection felt huge inside his trousers but he would wait. His staying power was tremendous.

Sebastian crouched and parted her buttocks, touching and tasting the delights that had lain hidden there. Lowry clenched his jaws.

They pushed her back to sit on the table. Sebastian pulled off her knickers and threw them onto the floor. She lay back. They blocked his view momentarily. Then he could see Blake feeling between her thighs and sliding a finger between her legs. There was a sharp intake of breath. Lowry imagined the warm smoothness.

Eva wriggled against the groping finger, which soon became two. Her legs were lifted and held open. The butterfly fluttered enticingly as she moved against the thrusting fingers. Sebastian pressed his mouth to the butterfly and his tongue slid downwards. The fingers were withdrawn and they parted the lips for his greedy tongue.

Lowry's face was expressionless as he looked from

beneath lowered lids. The men were hungry for the sight of her pink, spanked bottom. They lifted her from the table and bent her over.

Blake pulled her legs further apart to look at her. Sebastian stroked the pinkness as he undid his zip with his other hand and began to fondle himself. He glanced to the table and dipped his fingers into the butter, which was by now softened. Slowly, he spread some onto her bottom and began to rub it in, his hand smoothing firmly across the plumpness. Then he spread some on his own erection. His fingers slipped between her buttocks and slid easily into her.

The ice cream would have been cooler, thought Lowry, remembering the heat of her flesh as he had spanked her.

With trousers now undone, Blake stood, sliding her from the table and pulling her head towards him. He slipped his penis between her lips.

Her breasts hung free, swinging as they used her body.

Sebastian began to rub the tip of his penis across the slippery skin of her bottom. No direct penetration, thought Lowry. Don't come inside her. That's for me. He would wait and take her alone.

He closed his eyes. He closed the door, resting his forehead against the frame.

Some time later, in the dimness, supple leather shoes trod carefully on the wooden flooring towards Eva's bedroom door.

Lowry listened but could hear nothing. He pushed gently and went in.

A flickering candle added a delicate perfume to the warm air. The room was awash with muted light from a solitary lamp, which threw a spread of soft-hued radiance across the body of the woman on the bed and enhanced the creamy richness of her skin. She lay on her front with her face turned away from him, the duvet kicked down to below her feet. She was naked apart from the strawberry-red knickers, which rested mid-thigh and accentuated the flushed skin above. She was relaxed, although not asleep, Lowry knew. Her hips were raised slightly on a pillow.

He leaned over her to touch the anklet, then traced a finger along the fading pink marks on her bottom. She trembled slightly and spread her knees wider, tilting her hips to meet his stroking finger. He caressed downwards in inexorable slowness, tantalising, until he slid his finger into her vagina and felt the welcoming warm smoothness that gripped him delightfully. He imagined the butterfly, hidden from view, in readiness to take flight.

He sat on the edge of the bed and dipped into the dish that he held. Placing the flat of his hand on her bottom, he began to smear her skin with butter, now almost as fluid as oil. After a few strokes, she began to writhe in response. He bent his head so he could lick the marked flesh. She will have to shower later, he thought. Maybe I can help. Her hips rocked gently and she lifted her hands to squash the pillow beneath her head, snuggling her face into its depths.

He carried on, rhythmically massaging her plumpness. He held the dish above the candle to melt it further, then raised his fingers to drip warm oiliness along her spine. She moved against his hands as they moved downwards, unable to hold on to stillness. He smiled. Shifting, he knelt to straddle her body and proceeded to massage her back and shoulders. She reached down to place her hands on her bottom and held herself open for him. He dribbled the oil at the base of her spine in spattered droplets, waiting until they joined together and trickled tentatively between her buttocks. As the trickle reached her anus, she started to pant and lifted her hips, thrusting up in obvious demand. He ran a finger along the crevice and circled the anus before pushing deeply inside. She groaned into the pillow.

He could wait no longer. He wanted to force his penis into her.

He removed his finger and stood, already undoing the buttons of his shirt. He quickly stripped below the waist, allowing his penis to spring free at last. She was pulling down her knickers. He yanked them off her feet and knelt between her legs, which she opened wide for him. Lowering himself to her, he pressed his skin against hers, his penis pushing towards her raised hips and thrusting into her. There was a small cry.

They both lay still, feeling the moment.

Then he began to move slowly, burying his face in her hair and nibbling her neck. She turned her cheek towards him.

He had to know, even though it was like a punishment. 'Did they come inside you?'

'No.'

The surprise of relief rushed through him. He knew she told him the truth. 'Did they make you come?'

'Yes.'

He didn't like hearing it. 'Are you satisfied?'

'Yes, I'm satisfied. Especially now.'

A glow spread upwards from deep in his belly. His thrusting sped up. 'What next?'

Her voice drawled huskily. 'Mm. Musicians, I think, or maybe actors.' A small gasp escaped. 'Something . . . a little more . . . sensitive . . . moody . . . creative.'

He had a picture of himself hanging around stage doors ready to chat up the artistes: Excuse me, gents, would you like to do things to a woman while I watch? . . . Well, of course, darling! Is she gorgeous? . . . Oh, yes.

He couldn't hold off much longer. She whispered, 'Make me come again, Lowry.' Her hips were thrusting back in pace with him.

It was part of the game, to talk, delaying the moment until they could hold back no more. Think. Concentrate. Keep your mind off this glorious sensation.

. . . Maybe approach a woman. They had not tried that yet. But the thought of Eva with another woman only added to the present excitement.

Fortunately, she reached for his hand and squeezed it

down between her legs, fumbling with his fingers until they felt the spot. He rubbed at her clitoris. It didn't take long. She was already panting hard. He put the fingers of his other hand near her mouth and she bit on his hand as she came. He sank his teeth into her shoulder and her head jerked back. The pain of teeth and the pleasure of rippling muscles as they gripped inside her, both at once, a double whammy, was reward enough for the evening's work.

He slid his hands to her breasts as he worked his body on her. He licked at her skin, tasting the sweetness of butter and the salt of sweat. Or was it blood?

'Come on, Lowry, fuck me hard!' she breathed. It was a signal. He could come. He cried out at the moment of climax. He had her. She was his, at least for this moment. He had been kept on the brink, simmering for so long. His orgasm seemed to go on and on and at its end he was slaked at last; replete.

Their breathing slowed to normal though it took some time. Numbers on the bedside clock flicked to a new hour.

'Do you want me to stay?'

'No. Not tonight. I have an early meeting at The House tomorrow.'

He shifted his weight and reluctantly rolled from her.

'Maybe a mega session on Sunday? Just you and me.'

His sated appetite was stirred again. He could not get enough of her.

He got up and quietly dressed. He noticed a small glimmer on the sheet by her feet. The clasp of the anklet must have come loose. She seemed to be breathing now in a regular sleep-rhythm. He touched at her ankle and pocketed the chain, then gently pulled up the duvet and blew out the candle. Lifting the curls from her neck he kissed the teeth marks. No blood.

Switching off the light, he left the room and left the apartment, to be swallowed by the darkness of the night, to make his way back home through the city.

All About the Ratings
Sophie Mouette

It all started when he came backstage during her cooking show and stomped around. The walls were thin. The vibrations carried.

Caroline had been making a soufflé in front of a live studio audience.

OK, the audience hadn't been more than ten people – fifteen, tops – and had included her grandmother, her aunt, five desperately single men and three women she'd gone to high school with. But it was still embarrassing, and she was still certain that Drew had done it on purpose.

And then, to make matters worse, he started stealing her ratings.

Hers had been the highest-ranked cooking show on WPVL, Peaveyville's cable channel, until he'd come along. On her show she'd emphasised simple but elegant meals, the type you could serve on good china and light candles for, but which didn't involve complex recipes or hours of preparation.

Drew had breezed into town and offered up his own take: grilling, barbecuing and good old-fashioned home cooking. The station manager, desperate to fill a sudden scheduling hole left when septuagenarian Etta of *Etta's Gardening* had fallen in love (at her age!) and up and moved to Florida, had hired Drew, despite the fact that he and Caroline had similar shows.

Cooking with Caroline had had a wide audience. Busy career women recorded it. Stay-at-home moms swore by it. The local lesbians tuned in, and she suspected their interest wasn't always in the garnishing tips. She also had a variety of male viewers, both straight (for the same reason as the lesbians) and gay.

When *Warning: Man Cooking* came on the air, Caroline lost the gay men and a fair number of the straight women right off the bat. Fact was, Caroline could see why those segments of her audience had defected. Drew had a cheeky grin, a lock of black hair that tended to flop endearingly onto his forehead, and an ass you could bounce quarters off of. Plus he eschewed the traditional chef's jacket and baggy pants, preferring form-fitting T-shirts that showed off his biceps, and faded, tight jeans that showed off his impressive package.

Some of the hetero men switched to *Warning: Man Cooking*, too, because Drew was a non-threatening guy's guy who gave it to you straight.

Curse him!

Caroline had to rebuild her audience base. She had to grab back her ratings. And she was willing to do whatever it took.

Lee Remini, the station manager, called her into his office after she taped her latest show (shrimp kebabs, Thai noodles and cabbage salad). She'd had time to change into her usual outfit of mid-thigh, swishy skirt and high heels. Her one regret was that the cooking counter blocked a view of her legs, which she considered her best feature.

She was dismayed to find Drew already in Lee's office, lounging in a chair as if he owned the place, long jeans-clad legs stretched out in front of him.

The problem – the biggest, nastiest, most annoying facet of this whole rotten situation – was that Drew Benjamin made her panties wet.

Trying to ignore him, she slid into the other chair, searching Lee's face for some hint of what was to come. It couldn't be good.

Lee burbled about the popularity of both their shows

and how grateful he was about having them at his station. Caroline only half-listened. She was intensely aware of Drew next to her. She could smell his aftershave, musky and no doubt filled with illegal pheromones that people could smell through their TV screens. She was aware when he shifted in his seat, aware of his strong, long-fingered hand resting easily on the arm of the chair.

There were times, late at night, when the one thing that would bring her off was the thought of those hands on her body, tweaking her aching nipples, plunging into her wet sex until her hips rose off the bed and she panted out his name and . . .

'*Iron Chef*,' Lee said.

'What?' Caroline said at the same time Drew did. They glanced at each other, startled.

She saw his glance travel further down, consideringly, along the length of her bare legs.

Hmm . . .

'Hugely popular show,' Lee said. 'We want to try something similar here. Only it'll be an all-day thing. A team thing. Teams pitted against one another. A cook-off. Ratings through the roof.'

Drew leaned forwards, resting his elbows on his knees. 'You want us to compete?' he asked.

'Yes,' Lee said. 'No. Competition, yes. But not against each other.'

'Separately?' Caroline asked. Sometimes it was hard to get Lee to express a full idea, and you had to coax it out of him. She'd learned what kind of questions to ask to get a successful response. Mostly.

'No.'

This time when Caroline glanced at Drew, both their expressions conveyed their dismay. Then his changed to something more considering. His eyes narrowed thoughtfully.

This couldn't be good.

She uncrossed and recrossed her legs. Drew's gaze was riveted.

'As a team,' Lee said. 'You two against an amateur team. Found a couple, husband and wife. Real whizzes in the kitchen.'

'You want us to cook with amateurs?' Drew asked, breaking out of his reverie, obviously having missed part of the plan.

'Not with them. Against them. Two teams, competing.'

'I understand the idea of a competition, Lee,' Caroline said in her most placating voice, 'but wouldn't it make more sense to put us on opposing teams?'

Lee shook his balding head. 'Pros against amateurs. Plus demographics indicate viewers want to see both of you. Team thing. *Survivor*.'

Caroline doubted Lee had ever seen a single episode of *Survivor*. But she understood what he was getting at. Teams, but with the members still clashing.

Who would get voted out of the kitchen?

Drew muttered an invective under his breath, so low that Lee couldn't hear it. Caroline could, though, and, for the briefest moment, they were synchronised, in complete agreement.

It wouldn't last.

Soon, Caroline had a plan. It was a good plan, it was an evil plan and, if she pulled it off, she'd have her ratings back.

She put the plan into action the day before the actual show. Although they were going for an *Iron Chef* feel, with a studio-supplied surprise ingredient for each course, the teams were allowed to meet in advance to plan what other ingredients to bring.

Drew had suggested meeting at a café, but she'd proposed her apartment instead.

Her living room was already decorated with exotic, Middle Eastern-looking furnishings, plump pillows covered with soft sari silks, and lush, jewel-toned fabrics covering the walls. She made the room even more seductive for the occasion with scented candles and a bouquet of hypnotically perfumed stargazer lilies. Some low, sultry Middle Eastern music murmured and flowed through hidden speakers.

She dressed to suit the mood, in a silk camisole embroidered with shisha mirrors and bright patterns, a short black velvet skirt and stilettos. Not that she planned to seduce him, oh no. She just wanted him to start thinking about the possibility.

As soon as he showed up at her door, though, she realised the plan's fatal flaw: namely, she couldn't stop thinking about the possibilities either.

Drew seemed to fill the space. Every time she turned around, his long legs seemed to be in her way. His smell – not just aftershave but the underlying warm smell that was uniquely his – was inescapable. The candle flickering on a side table cast a shadowed light that accented his cheekbones and eyes.

Did she want to win or did she want to drag him to bed?

It was a shame it had to be an either–or question, but the parts of her that were voting for jumping him – and why bother getting as far as the bed – weren't the ones Caroline trusted to guide her career. There were always other men (although, as her body hastened to remind her, none recently that had the visceral appeal of Drew Benjamin). But there was only one cable station in Peaveyville.

And room for only one cooking show.

'Cucumbers,' she said suddenly, hoping to catch him off base. Judging from his expression, she succeeded. 'As one of our ingredients, I mean. I saw the most gorgeous cucumbers at the farmer's market today. Thick, firm, perfectly straight. I had to pick some up – just couldn't resist.' She gave what she hoped was a catlike smile.

'I've never been sure what to do with cukes.' Drew

realised what he was saying just too late to catch it. 'Other than pickles or salad,' he continued, evidently hoping that if he rooted the conversation firmly in recipes, he'd regain control. 'You can't grill them.'

Perfect. 'Leave the cucumbers to me, Drew. I know exactly what to do with a cucumber.' She leaned forwards as she said that, giving him a glimpse down the shadowy front of her camisole and a whiff of her warm amber perfume. 'I'll leave the figs to you.'

'Figs?' he echoed, his eyes fixed on the shadowed curves under the silk.

She pitched her voice at a purr. 'Don't you ever go anywhere but the meat market? It's fig season and I got us a case of soft ... plump ... juicy ones.' If he only knew how closely that described the condition of her own 'fig', they'd never get through the conversation.

As it was, he was leaning closer to her, looking like he was considering a kiss.

If Caroline let him, she'd lose everything. She sat back, crossing her ankles decorously in an attempt to remind herself to behave. 'I bet you could grill figs and make a relish with them,' she suggested. 'Maybe Middle Eastern spices and Aleppo pepper.'

They both thought of the implications of hot spicy figs at the same moment and looked away from each other.

Maybe this plan wasn't foolproof.

Drew stood up and stretched. She could see his muscles rippling under his tight T-shirt. Once the play of muscles stopped distracting her, Caroline could see why he was restless. The fly of his jeans looked uncomfortably tight, and she liked the look of what was outlined against the straining fabric.

Definitely not a foolproof plan, but if she could keep her cool while making him lose his, it could still work.

It had to work. This was war, not sex.

'Yeah,' he said too quickly, 'fig relish. And melons are in season too. I saw some nice casabas ...'

He looked at her cleavage again, turned red, and looked away. Caroline would be the first to admit her breasts were more the size of peaches, but the old joke was inescapable.

'Leave the meat to me,' he muttered. 'I can handle meat.'

'So can I,' she riposted.

Another long, breathless pause.

'Dessert?' he asked.

Oh, the places they could go with that thought! 'Peach tart.' She smiled as she said it. 'With cream.'

She couldn't be sure in the flickering candlelight, but it looked like he flushed.

The thick silence that followed that was broken by Drew adding, 'I think we've got a good start. I've got stuff to get into marinade, so, uh, maybe I should go.'

Oh, he was definitely riled up, all right. Caroline fell back on the overstuffed cushions and let out a long breath in her suddenly empty-feeling apartment.

The problem was, no matter how hard she tried to focus on saving her show, she kept coming around to the same issue: she was riled up, too.

Curse him!

Caroline arrived at the studio early the next morning dressed to kill. Her bright turquoise knit dress was short enough that anyone with blood flowing in their veins would wonder what colour her underwear was – or if she were wearing any. (She was, but the lace low-cut bikini did more to accent her ass than hide it.) The dress's halter top bared her shoulders, but was otherwise quite decorous – from the front.

The back view was another story. Her back was exposed to below the waist, low enough that if she moved just right, she flashed a hint of butt cleavage.

She always kept her strawberry-blonde hair pulled back in the kitchen. Usually she wore it in a ponytail, but today she'd gone for an updo, sophisticated, but with soft curls falling artfully out.

The viewers wouldn't see that it revealed the dragonflies tattooed on the back of her neck. At first glance, the tattoo was innocuous enough, pretty, delicate insects in shades of blue and green.

On second glance, you realised they were mating.

The audience couldn't see them ... but Drew would.

Her only regret was the shoes. Stilettos weren't practical when she was going to be on her feet all day. The flat Indian-style sandals decorated with turquoise and coral went well with the outfit, but they didn't work nearly as well as weaponry.

When she sashayed into the kitchen, though, it was pretty clear no one was looking at her shoes.

Drew leaned forwards for a closer look as she walked past him.

Their amateur opponents seemed just as fascinated. Ally and Stephen Jarvis could best be described as cute geeks. She was tall and angular, not conventionally pretty, but blessed with a charming smile and a perfect cocoa complexion. He was white, about six inches shorter and heavyset, with the air and fashion sense of someone who did something obscure with software. And both of them seemed to like what they were seeing a lot.

Good. Drew was her real concern here, not the amateurs, but distracting them was a bonus. If she and Drew won the contest *and* she made Drew look like a fool, all the better.

At 9.45 a.m., the opponents shook hands and took their places at opposite sides of the kitchen. Except her real opponent was on her side.

At 10 a.m., the cameras began to roll and a studio employee came in with the secret ingredient for the appetiser course: asparagus.

While the amateurs consulted frantically, Drew said, 'Prosciutto, asparagus, melon and figs. Classic. Only we grill the asparagus and figs.'

'I like my asparagus ... raw.' Caroline picked up a stalk

and began toying at the tip with her tongue, staring into his eyes.

'Are you trying to kill me?' he demanded sotto voce.

'What's that French expression? *La petite mort*?' She plunged the asparagus deep into her mouth, pursing her lips around it, then retrieved it, intact.

'Stop teasing me,' he said. Then he raised his voice to add, 'Start splitting the figs. The other's team's already cooking.'

'I bet I could get you cooking in no time, Drew,' she whispered. But one glance at the Jarvises confirmed that it was time to get to work.

Nevertheless, she made a point of applying walnut oil (to protect the fruit on the grill) with her fingers instead of a brush, leaving the pink flesh moist, shiny, and more suggestive than ever.

This cost them half a fig. When the camera was trained on the Jarvises' frantic preparations, Drew picked up one of the fruit halves and ran his tongue along it, his gaze never leaving hers.

Caroline clenched inside, imagining him doing that to her.

Dammit. Not only was he on to her game, he was playing back with her – and rather effectively. That would make things a bit more difficult, but she could handle it.

She could handle it. Think about *Cooking With Caroline*. Think about not being usurped.

Somehow, they managed to finish their appetiser course without too many more incidents, although they seemed to brush against each a lot. Caroline was doing it on purpose, but after a while she questioned whether she was doing it to distract Drew (who was fumbling the food quite a bit, although to his credit he hadn't yet dropped anything) or to enjoy the jolt of desire that zinged her whenever she touched him.

Purely an added benefit, that zing. She refused – refused! – to let it distract her.

The Jarvises had made an asparagus frittata. The judges pronounced it tasty, but it lost to the pros' offering partly on the grounds of visual appeal. The asparagus stalks were arranged poking into tunnels of pink prosciutto or laid out on top of gleaming, darker pink figs with heat-blackened skins, the plate accented with thin crescent moons of pale-green melon.

'Very sensual,' one judge proclaimed, winking at Caroline.

Lee grabbed Caroline before they headed back for the next segment. 'The phones are ringing off the hook!' he proclaimed gleefully.

'Who's winning?'

'It's weird. No one wants to pick a winner. Everyone's saying they love watching you and Drew interact. Well, except for the old guy who said you were both disgusting.'

She chuckled and headed back to the set, swaying her hips so Drew, who was behind her, got an eyeful.

The secret ingredient for the next round was shrimp. 'Predictable!' they heard Stephen Jarvis pooh-pooh. The couple's consultation was hushed, but Caroline thought she overheard an argument ensuing about the merits of garlic.

'We could do your shrimp kebabs,' Drew suggested. 'That's a great recipe. Or something Cajun or Southwestern. I can whip up a dry rub in no time.'

She shook her head, in part to dispel images implanted by *whip* and *rub*. 'Talk about predictable! That's exactly what the judges will expect from us. We have to think of something different.'

'Japanese. A cold noodle dish with shrimp and seaweed and ... something else. I'm not the Asian fusion expert – what do you think?' He bowed gallantly. Oh, oh, look at him trying to sway the audience to his side. Bastard!

'Cucumbers!'

Suddenly Drew looked less enthusiastic about his idea. 'Not cucumbers, Caroline. Please, not cucumbers.'

The studio audience tittered.

'But they're a classic Japanese ingredient. And wait until you see my way with a cuke, gorgeous!'

He tried to look away when she held up two cucumbers, both perfect specimens. OK, he was going to play it that way? Fine.

She turned to the audience, leaning on the work counter that separated the stage from the seating area, and held up both cucumbers. Batting her eyes, she asked, 'What do *you* think: short and thick or long and slender?'

The audience hooted and applauded, and she laughed along with them. That's right, get 'em on her side.

What the viewers saw was her being friendly and charming.

What Drew saw was her arching her back and presenting herself as if asking to be taken from behind.

She bit back a grin of triumph when Drew's voice cracked. 'I'll get the rice noodles soaking while you, uh, work on those.'

He moved behind her. To the viewers, it looked like he was just reaching around to grab the bag of thick rice noodles on the counter, maybe being a little playful, standing a little too close to get her back for the cucumber jokes.

They wouldn't know that he whispered in her ear, 'How about long *and* thick?' or that he pressed against her, pushing his cock into the crack of her ass.

From what she could tell, 'long and thick' was an apt description.

And it would be so, so very easy for him to slip it deep inside her. All he'd have to do was open his fly, raise her minuscule skirt, nudge her drenched panties aside. He could reach around and toy with her nipples through the dress. He'd start slow, with long even strokes that would nudge her higher, then he'd gradually increase the speed until he was diving into her, filling her ...

... and getting them both fired and probably banned from TV anywhere in the country except certain pay-per-view channels.

Caroline took a deep breath and a determined step to the right. Thank God nobody could see how her legs trembled as she did. She began carving cucumber flowers, first cautiously, not trusting her fingers. But, as she pulled herself together, she wielded the knife with a certain vengeful glee.

She really couldn't say how they got through making the cold noodle dish. Every time she tried to focus on the preparations, her mind wandered back to the feel of Drew's cock pressed up against her – and her body followed right along, rewarding her with more deep, aching shivers.

It probably wasn't a factor, but this time, although the judges had good things to say about the Japanese dish, the Jarvises' Spanish-style shrimp, hot peppers and garlic in olive oil got the nod.

'Remember, everyone,' the announcer said, 'this is an all-Saturday marathon. We need to give our talented chefs a short break, though, so for the next half-hour we'll be showing highlights from your favourite episodes of *Cooking With Caroline* and *Warning: Man Cooking*, as voted on by you, the viewing audience.'

'I *have* to get some fresh air,' Ally Jarvis proclaimed, and the geek couple wandered off hand in hand.

Caroline got herself a bottle of water from the tiny fridge backstage. 'Want one?' she asked Drew, who'd followed her.

'Thanks,' he said with a nod, and she tossed the bottle at him.

She proceeded to do a series of yoga stretches to work out the kinks in her back from the marathon session of standing.

Drew spilled water down his front. Which was probably a good thing for him, since the bulge in his jeans could use an icing down.

Dammit. The mental picture lodged in her mind of her wielding a pastry bag, drawing curlicues on his erect penis and then following the swirls with her tongue, tasting sweet powdered sugar and salty precome.

A taste sensation not found on any menu.

That's it. She had to hide in the bathroom, bring herself off. Clutching her water, she turned to flee, and nearly slammed into Lee.

'Both of you. Here,' the station manager said.

For a fleeting moment, in her aroused, fanciful state, she thought Lee meant she and Drew should do it right there. Luckily, she figured out he simply meant he wanted to talk to both of them.

'Phones are ringing off the hook,' Lee said. 'Audience is loving this. Real chemistry between you two. Who knew? Bonuses for you both. Now, back to work.'

Caroline bit back a groan as he shooed them back towards the soundstage. No quickie masturbation in the bathroom for her. At this rate, by the end of the show she'd have to wring out her panties.

'Yeah, who knew?' Drew whispered in her ear, his breath fluttering the loose tendrils of hair.

The lights went up on stage, and she had no chance to reply.

They settled into their places in the kitchen, standing far closer to one another than was really necessary.

Caroline tried to concentrate, focus on making an amazing dessert that would be a feast for all the senses. But the heat of Drew's body so close to her own and the way her insides felt as hot and sweet as molten chocolate whenever he brushed against her – and he was doing so a lot – blanked every recipe she knew from her mind.

The announcer came on. 'Because our chefs have been performing at such a high level, we're throwing out a special challenge. There are two secret ingredients for the dessert round: raspberries and rosewater. And sorry, you're not allowed to sprinkle the berries with the rosewater and call it a day!'

Caroline turned to Drew and smiled. 'I know we'd been talking about a –' she paused to give the words extra significance '– peach tart with whipped cream.' She winked at the audience, admitting they were in on the joke. 'But it looks like we need to be flexible.' She hoped the word would call to mind her yoga poses. 'Do you have any ideas about the best way to handle raspberries?'

'Delicately. Very delicately. More often than not, I like to nibble them plain.' He slurred a bit, so nibble sounded almost like nipple, but not so much so that it would get him in trouble with Lee. 'But I bet we could do something with them to give the peaches a lovely rosy colour.'

Then he gave her a searing smile. Her nipples felt as red and plump and tender as the berries heaped in a basket on their counter. She didn't dare to glance down, but she suspected they were popping out through the fabric of her dress, clearly visible to anyone in the studio and probably to the TV audience.

What she wouldn't give to have Drew's sensuous mouth closed around one of those ripe peaks now, suckling at her, drawing out her arousal until she was dizzied and begging for more.

Breathe. Remember to breathe – and to make sure Drew, too, was distracted. 'Maybe use some of them for a glaze,' she said breathily. 'Nothing makes a peach look prettier than a little moist sheen. And for a topping, how about a nice, warm crème anglaise?' She let the words sink in, watched Drew's eyes widen and darken.

She'd take his 'crème anglaise' in her 'peach' any day and she could tell he was thinking something similar.

The whirr of a food processor brought her back to reality. The Jarvises were already at work, grinding nuts from the sound of it. (A linzertorte variation with fresh fruit? She should have been paying more attention to them, dammit!)

'Flavour it with rosewater,' Drew added. His voice sounded a little shaky. 'Sounds good.'

'You start on the peaches and raspberries, Drew. I'll get to work stirring up the crème. It takes a little time for it to . . . thicken.'

As she passed him, heading to the refrigerator for cream and eggs, she cupped his ass briefly under the cover of the counter, just long enough to feel it was as firm and delicious as she'd suspected.

His sigh wasn't loud enough for the microphones to pick up, but she heard it.

He got her back, though, as he started to split the peaches. 'This peach is absolutely perfect,' he sighed. 'So juicy and succulent, with just the slightest hint of fuzz. I wish I could eat it right now!'

Even if she hadn't been sensitised already, that remark, in that tone of voice, would have zinged directly between her legs and gotten her speculating. As it was, she almost spilled heavy cream onto the floor, lost in a vision of Drew's tongue deftly playing over her slick lower lips and swirling in on the throbbing spot where she needed it most.

Then she glanced over their opponents. The Jarvises, lacking such distractions, were hard at work and their dessert looked well underway. Time to focus!

As they busied themselves with making the rich, rose-water-infused custard sauce, turning some of the raspberries into a delicate red glaze and basting it over the split peaches before sticking them under the broiler, the banter and surreptitious touches continued. A brush here. An innuendo there. Eye contact that lasted longer than was strictly necessary.

By the time the peaches came out from the broiler looking perfect enough for a glossy food magazine, Caroline's legs felt weak from frustrated desire.

Caroline carefully spooned the crème anglaise into the hollow of each peach.

Drew, not to be outdone, took one intact raspberry and placed it strategically on each peach, placing himself between the dessert and the camera so the results wouldn't immediately go out to the viewers.

They looked at the dessert and then at each other. 'Too much,' Caroline mouthed, trying not to burst into obvious laughter.

Before the camera could focus on the erotic creation, Drew sprinkled the remaining raspberries more casually over the plate and Caroline swirled the creamy sauce. Now it might classify as food-porn, but it was no longer porn made from food.

Both of them still stifling chuckles and giving each other amused but heated glances, they presented their dish to the judges.

'Ladies and gentlemen, we have ... a tie!' the announcer said. 'The judges are evenly divided between both teams. We didn't make provisions for a sudden-death round, so we're going to turn it over to you, the home viewers. Call the station and vote for your favourite team and their recipes. One call per viewer, please. We'll show you some more top highlights from *Cooking with Caroline* and *Warning: Man Cooking*, and we'll return in fifteen minutes with a verdict. Get those dialling fingers going!'

The station was so small that there was only one dressing room, a tiny box of a space with just enough room for a short couch, clothing rack, and vanity table and stool. Caroline made a beeline for it.

Not fast enough. She didn't get the door all the way closed before Drew pushed it open, and shut it behind him.

If the room had seemed small before, now it was downright tight. Drew's lanky frame took up a lot of space – and Caroline's libido filled in the cracks.

'Here's the thing,' Drew said. 'I know that you've been coming on to me to distract me, to mess me up.'

Her mother had always told her she was too competitive. 'Boys won't like you if you always have to win,' she said.

Well, the boys had liked Caroline just fine, although admittedly they all got along better when the boys weren't trying to get the same things Caroline wanted – like the top cooking show on WPVL.

Her mother could be right about many things, but she'd been as wrong about boys as she was about cooking. Her idea of tacos included Velveeta 'cheese', and she'd layered her lasagne with cottage cheese rather than ricotta. A healthy self-preservation instinct had driven Caroline to learn how to cook.

'Fact is, I respect that,' Drew continued. 'It was a slick move. It almost worked. Maybe it did work. But here's the thing.'

He stepped closer to her.

That same self-preservation instinct was failing her now. She backed up until her knees hit the arm of the sofa. She caught herself before she fell – but, oh, she wanted to fall, and pull him down on top of her.

'What I need to know is if you're feeling what I'm feeling,' Drew said, his voice husky. 'If the audience is right and the chemistry is real. Because as much as I like cooking against you, right now I'd rather be cooking with you. Figs and asparagus and cucumbers and peaches ... licking and sucking and –'

The hell with it. They weren't on stage any more. The cook-off was over.

Caroline grabbed the front of Drew's T-shirt and dragged him down for a kiss.

There was no time for subtleties, and no need for them, either. They'd been enjoying foreplay for hours already. Even as they kissed, his hands were behind her neck, unhooking the halter top. He dragged the front of her dress down and filled his large hands with her breasts, catching her peaked nipples between his fingers and rolling them, lightly pinching them, murmuring something about rasp-berries, until her thighs turned to jelly.

She might have slid bonelessly to the ground if he

hadn't insinuated his hand between her thighs and caught her in a most intimate way. His eyes widened, no doubt because he'd discovered how drenched her panties were. He hiked her dress up and she tugged the French-cut lace briefs down and he pulled them the rest of the way and she kicked out of them.

She popped the buttons on his jeans. No underwear for him. His cock was smooth and curved. She swiped her thumb across the bead of moisture at its tip, and brought it to her mouth.

He groaned.

She thought they'd make good use of the sofa, but instead he spun her around to face the dressing table. She was stunned by her reflection in the mirror: tumbling-down hair and dilated pupils and well-kissed, swollen lips.

'I've been dying to do this all day, ever since you leaned over the damn counter,' he growled in her ear.

She spread her legs and wiggled her hips, and he needed no further invitation. He sank into her easily, her inner walls plump and slick with her own juices.

Oh God, so good to be filled! Her eyes fluttered shut.

'No,' Drew said. 'Open your eyes. Watch what happens when I fuck you.'

She tried, she really did. But with every thrust he sank deeper and she pushed back harder, and an orgasm began to build, an ache deep inside her that expanded and grew and burned until it threatened to incinerate her. Bracing herself against the vanity with one hand, she reached between her legs with the other. His cock slid across her knuckles as she found her clit.

The fire flashed and consumed her. She gritted her teeth to keep herself from screaming as she came. The walls were thin enough that they would have heard her on stage. As she keened deep in her throat, she heard him gasp her name, a short thrust for each syllable as he found his own release.

In the mirror, they both looked rather stunned.

He toyed with her breasts. 'Casabas melons, indeed,' he murmured.

She chuckled, enjoying the feel of him twitching inside her as she moved.

'Caroline? Drew?'

It was Lee.

'Where the hell did you go? We're on air in thirty seconds!'

She'd never heard Lee speak in sentences that long or panicked. In a flurry of motion, she and Drew separated. He tucked his still-wet, still-half-hard cock back into his jeans. She grabbed a towel and swiped between her legs.

'Where are my panties?'

'Who knows?'

They raced for the stage. His shirt was untucked, and her hair wild. The audience roared their approval, clapping and whistling and stamping their feet.

Stephen Jarvis glared. Ally Jarvis did, too, although she also looked a little longingly at Drew. Or maybe Caroline.

The announcer tried to spread out the results, but the audience was having none of it. They started yelling all over again when they heard Caroline and Drew had won.

And, oh, how they'd won.

Once they were able to escape from the studio, they ran the only stop sign in town on the way to Caroline's house, where they spent the rest of the night playing with food. In bed.

On Monday, Lee called them both into his office and laid out a proposal for a new show: *In the Kitchen with Drew and Caroline.*

'*With Caroline and Drew*', Caroline countered.

'*Hot in the Kitchen*,' Drew suggested.

'Yes!' Lee said.

A month later, the show was syndicated.

Some episodes could not be aired in the Bible Belt.

Ice Creamed Heather Towne

Once a week during the summer, when I finally escape the office around six or seven at night, I stop in at an ice-cream parlour that's on my way home. The cool treats are sweet to eat, but what's sometimes even tastier, more mouth-watering, is the young men working behind the counter.

I'm pushing forty – backwards, rather than forwards – but I've always had a thing for the younger set, a woman who likes to play out of her own age group, so to speak. I exercise and eat right, cover up the foundation cracks as best I can, and use my flamboyantly orange hair and overly large breasts as my first line of offence with the younger crowd. It's a simple matter of bridging the generation gap, as I see it, and nothing lays the timber for that bridge to a young horndog better than a big set of knockers.

Rodney was the latest counterman I'd set my sights on. He'd started working at the shop in early July and, in striking up a conversation with the lad, I'd found out that he'd just graduated from high school the previous month, turned eighteen only a short time before that.

He was trying to earn tuition for community college in the fall, planning on taking business administration with a major in marketing. And he certainly had the personality and looks to make a good salesman: he was warm and enthusiastic, with straw-blond hair, a trim, sun-bronzed body and a handsome face punctuated by a dim-pled chin.

I quickly began assembling my own plans for the young man, but I wasn't about to wait until fall to implement them.

* * * *

'Hi, Valerie,' he chirped, when I dingled the bell over his door one Monday evening. He adjusted the paper hat that crowned his sunny blondness and asked, 'What'll it be?'

Given the late hour and cool weather, there was no one in the small shop but us two sugar junkies. I sauntered up to the display case and took a good long look at the frozen offerings, an even longer look at Rodney's sweet, caramel-coloured body. The ice-cream-slinger almost glowed in his all-white shirt and pants ensemble.

'Hmm...' I murmured, tapping a scarlet-tipped digit against my chin. 'What shall I have? What do you recommend, Rodney?'

'Everything's good here,' he responded, like a natural-born salesman. 'But my personal fave's the banana split.'

One of the most expensive items on the menu, I noted. 'Really? Well, every girl needs a good banana every now and then,' I quipped. 'Give me one of those.' It would ruin my diet for the day, but it would mean a long, sensual chew in front of impressionable young Rodney. As a businesswoman myself, I well knew that 'sell yourself' was the cornerstone of any successful direct-marketing campaign.

I was dressed in a pinstriped jacket and a sleeveless, plunging white satin top, a short, black leather skirt and sheer white stockings, my push-the-envelope business-pleasure attire. It'd been another long, frustrating day at the office, and a cool treat from a cool young man would hit the spot just right.

I watched Rodney as he peeled and split a banana, made a show of whipping together the tasty dessert. I took off my jacket and draped it over my arm, making a show of my freckled cleavage, my breasts squirming tightly against my blouse and my aroused, air-conditioned nipples indenting the thin fabric.

He scooped, spritzed and sprinkled, then handed me the completed banana split with a smile on his face and a cherry on top. 'Here you go,' he said, our fingers touching briefly as he handed me the calorific confection over the counter.

I admired his form and his presentation, and thanked him. Then I started spooning frosting and nuts and ice cream into my mouth, daintily and sexily, throwing in plenty of wet, satisfied lip-licking and smacking. He peppered me with more questions about the business world, about my job in the marketing department of a major telecommunications firm, seemingly oblivious to my come-on. I've always found dessert the most sensual of courses, but Rodney wasn't buying.

The ice-cream cone hands on the sundae-shaped wall clock soon read five minutes to ten, five minutes to closing. I'd been nursing my split like there was a looming banana shortage, waiting for the right time to implement my plan, and I decided now was it. 'I'm never going to be able to finish all this,' I said, pouting and, shrugging my shoulders so that my breasts jiggled. 'Can you help me polish it off, Rodney?'

He rubbed his brown hands on his white jeans. 'Uh . . .'

'C'mon. If you don't, we'll never get out of here,' I said, appealing to his need for work relief.

He eyed the half-eaten dessert, eyed the pair of heavy, nipple-flared tits that provided an enticing background to the hull-shaped container. I was showcasing myself and the dessert like a *Price is Right* girl, smiling sweetly and batting my lashes, blue eyes hopefully twinkling with encouragement. He finally swallowed the bait.

He scooped up a plastic spoon and hustled out from behind his protective counter. I held the treat up to him, my real treat drawing closer. He grinned, dipped his spoon into the gooey mess and lifted out a mouthful.

'Good, huh?' I cooed, watching his throat work. I slid a teensy bit of frosting and banana between my lips, tongued and sucked my spoon thoroughly, then reloaded it and held it out to Rodney.

He looked at the spoon, at my smiling face, his big brown eyes growing even bigger.

'Open wide. There's a good boy,' I teased, questioning his manhood in an effort to set the hook. I pushed the tip of the spoon against his plush lips.

He opened up, and I slipped the spoon and its sweetness and its promise inside. He swallowed hard and choked a little. I withdrew the spoon and licked up the bit he'd missed with my pink tongue.

I repeated the process, feeding him, fuelling him, trying to fire him up to the point of ignition. He swallowed everything I gave him, except my unspoken desire that he give me something back.

I popped the cherry into my mouth and sucked on it thoroughly, popped it out again and pushed the juicy fruit into his mouth, but he still didn't seem to get it. So, I turned up the heat even more, deliberately misaiming at his mouth and plopping a blob of frosting on his upper lip. 'Whoops,' I said, jumping to my tip-toes and brushing the goo away – with my tongue.

He just stood there and took it like a statue, and I started losing my patience. I was dolled up like a real dish, horny as a devil's food cake, no amount of sweet talk required to eat me up, but Rodney just didn't seem to have any appetite. I began to wonder if maybe he didn't like the taste of an older woman.

I sighed, took a frustrated chomp out of the banana split, and that's when the young man finally responded to my sales pitch. He dipped his finger in the ice cream and held it out to me. I leaped at it, eagerly licking it off, took his finger between my lips and sucked on it.

He dabbed some goo directly on my glossy lips, and then tentatively cleaned it off with his tongue. Ka-ching. I opened my mouth and shot out my own tongue, bumping it into his, and the now clearly excited young man pulled his own bait and switch, batting the banana split out of my hands and grabbing me in his arms. The hormones were raging, and I revelled in their hot-blooded embrace.

He kissed me just about on the lips, smearing lipstick and ice cream all over my mouth. I adjusted things so we were fully lip-locked and kissed him right back, gripping his broad shoulders and squeezing.

We stood in the middle of that frozen sweet shop and passionately snogged, our heated bodies melting together, both of us tasting sugar and spice and everything nice. I could smell the sharp tang of his boyish sweat and feel the hard outline of his burgeoning manhood pressing into my belly.

We swirled our tongues together, his hot breath flooding my face, my hands gliding down to his cute little bubble-butt and grabbing hold. He pumped his hips, anxiously dry-humping my stomach. I wanted, needed, his young cock inside of me, pistoning me to the land of sticky cumdrop wet dreams, so I pushed him back and grabbed on to his belt. I quickly and expertly unbuckled him, as he panted ice cream and banana.

I got him all unfastened, was holding my breath in anticipation of receiving the true treat of the evening, when the bell over the door suddenly jangled my nerves. An overstuffed man with an ecstatic look in his puffy eyes pushed through the door. He took no notice of the sticky situation Rodney and I were in; he was staring up at the hundred-and-one flavours listed on the signboard over our heads, and drooling.

I came into Rodney's ice cream parlour every night for the rest of that week, the wicked things I was going to do to the golden boy when I got my hands on him again dancing in my head. But I could never get him alone. My work suffered, my sheets sweated and I gained four pounds.

I suppose I could've just invited him to my parlour for some sugar, but something about capturing the young man on his own turf, in his all-white, all-bright outfit and clean-cut paper hat, just really appealed to my sweet tooth and sense of sexual adventure.

And finally, finally, thanks to an air mass flowing down from Canada, on a chilly, drizzly Sunday evening I got my ice-cream man all to myself again.

He set down his scoop and scoped me out as I sashayed up to the counter. I was dressed to thrill in an ultra-short, leopard-print skirt and matching, low-cut, form-fitting top, legs sheathed in sheer black stockings, boobs unrestrained by a bra. I was anything but a cool customer.

'H-hi, Valerie,' Rodney squeaked, devouring me with his eyes like the gooey tart I was. 'Uh, we just got some new flavours in today.... if you're interested. They're in the back.'

He gestured with his thumb, and I grinned like a kitten in a creamery. The guy was about as smooth as chunky monkey, but I wasn't exactly sweating subtlety myself. He lifted up a part of the counter, and I strutted on through.

He guided me into the back of the store, down a short hallway that led to a huge, stainless-steel walk-in freezer, my leopard-print stilettos click-clacking impatiently on the tile floor. And then he tugged the freezer door open and started heaving industrial-sized plastic pails of ice cream out into the hallway, right at my feet, like I was actually interested in any new flavours other than Rodney delight.

I got that frustrating, burning itch in my pussy again, the one that just has to be scratched by a cock. And I was about to say something to get the boy refocused on the task at hand, when he tripped on the lip of the freezer.

'Look out!' I shrieked.

He fumbled a tub of ice cream and stumbled straight into my arms, pinning me up against the wall. That was more like it. His body was hard and hot, especially compared to the Arctic wind blowing out of the open freezer. He held on to me for support, and I provided it gratefully.

'Sorry about that,' he foolishly apologised, his strong hands gripping my bare shoulders.

'No problem,' I murmured, looking up at him with my fluttering baby-blues. Things had worked out quite nicely, after all; I had the young hottie in my loving arms in a nice, secluded spot, right where I wanted him.

Rodney then warmed me up even further by dipping his head down and planting a dry one directly on my puckered lips. He kissed me again, harder and longer this time, with a lot more passion and just a little tongue, selling me on his skills – like I hadn't bought into the guy weeks ago.

'I've always liked you, Valerie,' he breathed, the one-scoop waffle cone in his pants pressing into my stomach.

'I've always had a warm spot for you, too, Rodney,' I responded, gazing into his eyes. The warm spot was between my legs, getting warmer and damper by the second.

He kicked the freezer door shut with his heel and mashed his mouth against mine. He really chewed on my lips, ground his rigid cock against my tummy. I slithered my tongue in between his parted lips and tasted his warm, crimson wetness, my hands sliding off his wiry arms and down over the top of his bum, cupping his impudent cheeks.

He grunted into my mouth, gripping and squeezing my breasts through the flimsy material of my top, sending shivers racing all through me. He pinched and rolled my jutting nipples, triggering a monsoon in my pussy.

'Can I fuck you, Valerie?' he asked, hands full of my tits, lips on my neck.

'One fuck, coming up,' I replied. I pushed him back to give ourselves some elbow room for stripping.

He started fumbling with his shirt, the brass 'Rodney' name tag jumping all over the place. I stopped his nervous hands and slowly unbuttoned the shirt for him. Then I slid my hands inside his shirt, brushing fingers and thumbs over his gloriously stiffened nipples. He closed his eyes and groaned, his body shaking.

I yanked his shirt out of his pants and pushed it off his shoulders, unwrapping his sun-kissed upper body. I ran my hands all over his chest, feeling his heat, his racing heartbeat, the baby-smooth texture of the man-boy's skin. Then I captured one of his nipples between my lips and sucked on it.

'Valerie,' he moaned, clutching my long, burnt-orange locks.

I flicked his nipples even further erect with my tongue, bathing them in warm saliva, licking and kissing and biting them. Then I traced fire over his burning skin with my fingernails, trailing them over his expanded chest and undulating stomach, down to his belt. I started unbuckling him like I had days earlier. Only this time, there was no one to stop me, to stop me from sealing the sexual deal with the ripe-for-the-picking young stud.

I quickly had his pants loose and down around his ankles, and he stepped out of them, slid off his Jockeys and tossed them aside. He was blazingly bronze all over, except between his legs, where he was blond and bountiful. His cock stood out like an exclamation point in the ice-cream-scented air, long and hard and quivering. I captured it in my hand, and his knees buckled. I squeezed his prick, rubbed the swollen length of it, cupped his furry balls with one hand and lightly stroked him with the other.

He tore at my own sales outfit, its seduction purpose achieved. I helped him get rid of my top and bottom, my hand never leaving his cock. I was soon as glaringly naked as he was, clad only in stilettos and stockings and a smile.

He grasped my hanging tits in his sweaty hands, and I jumped at his touch. My boobs went electric and my body flooded with heat. He played with my tits as I played with his cock, pinching my nipples as I lightly scraped his veiny surface with my nails. He twirled his tongue around one of my nipples, then the other. He latched his lips onto a blossomed bud and greedily sucked on it.

'God, yes,' I moaned. His warm, damp hands and mouth and tongue felt so very good on my tingling breasts, as he smothered them with attention. But when I spread my legs and steered the mushroomed head of his manly cock towards my womanly opening, he suddenly pulled back.

'Why don't we, uh, sweeten the deal a bit?' the naughty young man teased, his forty-something playmate panting for action.

He prised open the lid of a pail labelled JUICY ORANGE RIPPLE, and I found out why the guy had been so intent on lugging the stuff out of the freezer in the first place. He scooped out a handful of orange-marbled ice cream, held it up to my mouth and said, 'This flavour reminds me of you, Valerie.'

The classic bait and switch. Give a gal a feel of a hard cock, and then take it away, replace it with hard ice cream. Well, I was just kinky enough to bite. I stuck out my tongue and flicked it at the melting hunk. It tasted good, sweet and tart and tangy – just like me, in fact.

And it felt even better when Rodney lowered his hand, glooped it on my chest and started rubbing it in. The impact of the frosty cream on my heated tits made my head spin. He used both hands, massaging my breasts, smearing the streaming ice cream all over my heaving chest like a kid excitedly finger-painting, pushing me back against the wall and leaving me gasping.

'Hey,' I gulped, 'someone's going to have to clean up this mess.'

He dropped his sticky hands down to my waist and started licking the orange-white ice cream off my coated tits and nipples. I lifted my arms up over my head and surrendered my messy chest to him, the combination of the cool ice cream and his hot hands and tongue literally driving me up the wall.

And when the earnest young man finally had me some-what stickily clean, he promptly gouged out another double scoop from the pail and resmeared me, repeating the sensual process. I brought my arms down and cupped my slathered mounds, feeding them to him, watching and feeling his velvet-sandpaper tongue swirl all over my aching nipples, my trembling tits, lapping ice cream off my body and setting me ablaze.

He licked my breastplate cream-free again, and then I decided that two should play at this game. I wriggled out of his grasp and cracked open a pail labelled BANANA BUTTERSCOTCH. It seemed the appropriate choice for my blond, burnished lover.

'I wonder what this tastes like?' I mused, scooping out a handful. And before Rodney could hazard a guess, I dropped to my knees in the muck and plopped the dollop of semi-frozen cone-filling on his extended cock.

'Yeah,' he yelped, the cool treat hitting just the right spot.

I rubbed the banana-tinged, caramel-rippled ice cream all over his stiffened prick, my hand gliding up and down on him until he was rock hard and cream-coated. Then I gripped him at the furry, tangled base and started licking. I hungrily lapped at his cold–hot pole like it was a melting ice-cream cone, tasting both him and the exciting new flavour. I used his hood as the cherry on top, popping it into my mouth and tugging.

'Fuck, Valerie,' he groaned, staring down at me, his body quivering.

I winked up at him, my lips sealed around his cock head. Then I reached over to the ice-cream bucket and ladled out some more sloppy goodness. I plopped it onto his prick again, but this time I didn't lick, I sucked. I inched my creamy lips down his shaft, swallowing him and the ice cream at the same time, until his hood hit the back of my throat and I gagged.

'Too much of a good thing,' I gasped, spitting his frozen banana out of my mouth.

He nodded, and I devoured him all over again. I bobbed my head up and down, diving deep and then easing back, over and over, never breaking the sticky seal of suction.

Rodney managed to dig two handfuls of banana butterscotch out of the tub and press them against his balls, desperately trying to slow the boil down there. I wasn't slowing down, though, vigorously pumping the exposed portion of his shaft with my finger and thumb while I sucked on the rest of him, hot, humid breath steaming out my flared nostrils and onto his groin.

'I'm gonna come, Valerie,' he wailed, clawing at my hair, his slick body tensing with imminent release.

I hastily disgorged him before he salted the sweetness. I wanted the candy man fucking me, giving his sugar-mommy what she so desperately needed – a good and thorough reaming – with the two of us coming together in one big, gooey heap.

I climbed to my feet, and we cooled things down by playfully slapping more of the ice cream onto our over-heated bodies: he slathering my breasts and pussy with juicy orange ripple; me spreading banana butterscotch all over his torso and bum, the ice cream liquefying almost instantly now.

Then he shoved me up against the wall and covered my sex with his hand and stuck two sticky fingers inside of me. I was wetter than an ice-cream sandwich at a Hell's Kitchen picnic, and I gyrated against his probing digits. He pumped me faster and faster, finger-fucking me with a concentrated ferocity.

A bolt of sexual electricity arced through my body. 'I want your cock inside me,' I hissed, staring into his eyes. I didn't want to come on the boy's fingers, I wanted to come on the man's cock.

Rodney knew that the customer was always right, so he

yanked his dripping digits out of my pussy and shoved them into my mouth. I sucked on them, swallowing hot, tangy girl juice and cool, tangy ice cream. I grabbed the guy's prick and yanked him forwards, then pressed his head against my shiny entrance.

'Fuck me,' I breathed into his peach fuzz face.

He gulped and pushed forwards, cock pressing through my petals and into my pussy. He went balls-deep, filling me up like no dessert ever can. He started pumping his hips, sliding back and forth inside me, ploughing my gripping sex.

His powerful thrusts slammed me against the wall, the flimsy building seeming to shake with the strength of our passion. Our ice-cream- and sweat-coated bodies stuck and separated again and again, the youngster putting my more experienced lovers to shame with his stamina and intensity, his willingness to kink.

'Yes,' I gushed, my pussy erupting and flooding my body with bliss. I dug my fingernails into Rodney's buttocks, convulsing with orgasm.

He grunted and drove me harder, fast and brutal. Then his body jerked and he shot his own brand of cream deep into my being, coming over and over. Not even an ice-cream bath could've cooled the pair of us off just then.

We clung to each other when it was over, exhausted and exhilarated, our bodies glued together by sugar and spice. He churned his still-hard cock in and out of my soaking wet pussy, sweetly thanking me for the opportunity I'd presented to him. I covered his mouth with mine, swallowing his foolish, heartfelt feelings.

'You, uh, don't go in for just vanilla sex, do you, Valerie?' he asked unexpectedly, when we'd finally pulled ourselves apart like two sodden strips of Velcro.

'Huh? What do you mean, Rodney?' I said, my legs still shaky and my head still dizzy. I was a mess, in more ways than one.

'Well ... I was just wondering if, you know, you liked to

experiment with different flavours – besides ice cream,' he said, grinning and retrieving my clothes for me. 'See, I've got this girlfriend who's pretty wild, and I was wondering if maybe you and me and her . . .'

Off the Menu Toni Sands

'Fantastic. Come on, Millie – time for a glass of wine. Such a busy night, but did you see the size of the tip they left you?'

My boss Stella is in a good mood. The diners have gone home happy and, when things go with a buzz in the restaurant, she likes to end the evening with a drink and a chat. She's lively company and she gets a bit lairy when Monty's away.

Monty is Stella's partner. The relationship seems a bit nebulous to me but he travels a lot and on the occasions he's around, he seems pleased to be there. I guess you would call him her sleeping partner, though, with tongue in cheek. Stella's amorous adventures are strictly off-menu and I'm the only one she confides in. One of the reasons we get on so well is that I don't go telling tales.

Stella and Monty have converted the ground floor of a Victorian school into a restaurant with owners' suite. There are letting bedrooms upstairs. The austere old building still retains a scholastic flavour and in the restaurant they've placed the headmaster's desk near a blackboard, on which Stella chalks up the tasty dishes she's concocted. Tonight, our duties finished, we're chilling out on the small rear patio, drinking from goblets that Stella has filled to the brim with chilled Frascati. The heavy scent of jasmine hangs in the air and we're relaxing and watching a cocoa-coloured moth getting high amongst the tubs of night-scented stock.

'How are your guests getting on?' I ask.

'Good,' she says, offering paprika-dusted hummus with raw veggie chunks. 'Nice guys...' She scoops up the dip with a celery stalk and looks slyly at me before she nibbles. 'Pity you've been away. You've missed out on a good opportunity. Well ... almost ...'

'Now, now, Boss ... surely Monty's due back soon,' I tease.

'While the cat's away,' she says. There's a dreamy look in her eyes, a look that usually means one thing. Stella has a plan.

'OK,' I say. 'What are you cooking up and which one do you have your eye on?' It will be much more exciting if I take a fancy to the one she prefers.

'It would be hard to choose between them,' she tells me. 'One's fair ... tall – he's the quieter of the two, I think. I'm hoping still waters run deep. The other one's dark ... medium height. It's a pity they won't be back tonight so you can meet them, but they'll definitely be here tomorrow evening. Monday morning they're driving to Heathrow. They're off up north on another contract.'

These Canadians are helicopter pilots; crop sprayers over here for a few months' work. Just my luck to have booked a week in Spain with a friend and flown off before their arrival. I work as an office temp as well as help Stella, and my knots needed untying. We'd gone to a health complex so we could detox our systems and, as we'd hardly set eyes on a male, we'd undergone another sort of fasting. Now I'm sun toasted, with all my appetites sharpened.

'So they're eating in tomorrow evening then?' I ask, selecting a carrot stick.

Stella sips her wine and smiles. 'Definitely,' she says. 'I've already told them we'll have a farewell party for them. I'm counting on you, Millie ... especially since I've seen their reaction to your photograph.'

'You know I trust your taste in men,' I tell her, really intrigued now. Stella's themed evenings are normally available only to a privileged group of gentlemen so something about these two Canadians must have got to her. The thought of performing for two strangers I'd never see again sets a naughty pulse beating. 'And these two do know what kind of party you're planning?' I ask.

'Oh, yes. I've hinted at the culinary delights and other options ... they're up for it, never fear. Don't forget I've had a chance to get to know them in your absence ... prepare the ground. The menu fits our favourite theme. And they'll be ready for seven.'

I look sideways at her. 'Dressing for the part?'

'But of course,' she says.

'Just us and them?' I ask.

'But of course,' she says.

'Marks out of ten?' I ask, leaning forwards.

'I'd say seven with expectations of nine.'

I wouldn't put it past her to have already given these guys a taster but I play along. 'They're very trusting ... putting themselves in your hands?'

'I told you. They're impressed that they're being given the VIP treatment. And they'll be hungry,' she says and winks at me. That pulse is still beating and I cross my legs, gloating as I picture the two very special outfits Stella keeps tucked away.

'I'll try hard to be a good girl,' I tell her.

'But surely not too hard?' she says. We exchange glances, our laughter bubbling over the starry jasmine and dissolving in the soft night air.

Next day, twelve appreciative diners partake of Stella's Sunday lunch. The restaurant is small and Stella likes it that way. She enjoys her quality of life far too much to be worrying about expansion. Most people who eat at the Old School are regulars and she cherishes her loyal clientele. Monty's wine list is exquisite, with a high profit margin. The occasional, shall we say, intimate party is purely for relaxation and timed for when Monty is away on business. It's my good fortune to be able to share in the fruits of Stella's success.

I watch as she captivates the vicar and his wife, exerting

her sparkle and warmth on them as if they're the only people in the world she cares about and, as usual, I admire her style. If the local dignitaries had ever seen Stella as I have seen her ... now there's a thought. But the voluptuous siren I know has slipped off her apron and is a picture of refined elegance, wearing a sleeveless number that's the colour of fondant roses. I'm cool as a sweet pea in my uniform dress. Who says redheads can't wear pink?

Back in my tiny cottage on the village outskirts, I kick off my shoes. Stella and I have shared a salad and now I'll relax to get into the right mood. I choose some music and strip to my bra and thong, moving to the beat until beads of sweat appear on my skin. Upstairs, I've left my bedroom window open, curtains drawn, so that the room is cucumber cool. My thoughts drift to the two guys I've yet to meet. The thought of Stella's soirée excites me. Somebody always wants to try the à la carte.

I reach into my bedside drawer. Oil myself. Spread my legs and let the hussy take over. One hand teases and tweaks my nipples while the other wanders between my thighs, stroking, until my middle fingers slide inside the wetness and start to work their magic. I enjoy pushing under the tight edge of my thong, pretending I'm being invaded against my will. Meanwhile I picture two horny guys, one fair, one dark, each sitting at an end corner of the bed, watching my every move. It's only when I bring myself to the very brink that I allow one of them to peel off his jeans and come and lie down with me. Then he can work his way inside me with his eager cock while the other one ... must be patient until I am ready; unless of course he wants to come and sit on my pillow. This cerebral soufflé I've whipped up has me creaming and groaning with the sweet release so that afterwards I'm happy to catnap for a while.

When I return to the world it's still a brilliantly sunny day and the sky is an unreal blue, dotted with powder-puff clouds. I want a cool shower and I also need to shave my pubes before I put on the underwear I've selected. I lather myself and carefully create the girlish smoothness that's such a stark contrast to the wickedness of the sheer black nylon stockings I carefully ease on. Finally, I select a floral fragrance and spray a mist above my auburn head so that the scent of violets settles on my hair and skin. With a tiny shiver of anticipation I'm ready for whatever the night will bring.

The restaurant is nearby so I walk, breathing in the garden scents and admiring the lush greenery in the early evening sunshine. There's a rousing hymn being sung inside the church and I wonder what the congregation would think if they knew what I was about to do. I've never taken my knickers off in church but the thought is a provocative one. Then I notice a hire car parked outside the old school. The guests are back. And I go around to the kitchen entrance and sniff the tempting smells drifting through the open top half of the stable door.

'Hi,' I call as I look inside for Stella.

She is listening to a poetry CD. She beckons me to join her and pours me a glass of the French aperitif with which she likes us to start this kind of evening. We soak up the haunting, sensuous words ... words that are pure aphrodisiac, as if Stella's potion isn't lubrication enough. Stella smiles and tells me it's time to get ready. To go and slip into my uniform.

'Will I do?' I ask on my return.

'Perfect,' she says. 'Seams straight?'

I turn around and bend over so my navy-blue gym tunic rides up and I know I'm displaying the edge of my snowy cotton briefs and the band of bare thigh above each stocking top. My hair is in two beribboned bunches swinging either side of my face.

'Irresistible,' she says. 'Love the scarlet suspenders – did you buy them in Spain, you naughty nymphet? Shame on you! Now, keep an ear open and if the guys come down, pour them a drink. I shan't be long.'

She disappears to get changed and I finish my drink and stir the simmering nectar that she calls gravy. I hear footsteps on the staircase and I enter the dining room just as a pair of long legs in linen trousers comes into view and then I see the caramel-coloured shirt and a twirl of fair chest hair in the V of an open neck. The man's broad, handsome face breaks into a smile.

'Good evening, sir,' I say.

He's speechless for a moment then remembers his manners, saying, 'Well, hi there,' and I get the feeling he'd whistle if he weren't such a gentleman. Then his muscular colleague, who's wearing black denims and a white T-shirt, comes into view, jumping the last three stairs. He may be shorter but he's certainly built for action.

'Hi, you must be Millie. I'm Jack and this lanky guy here's Carl,' says the second one. Smiling, Stella slinks into the room.

'I've heard a lot about you,' Jack says, still holding on to my hand. And Stella, suitably prim, says, 'She's usually a good girl but sometimes we have to take, erm, corrective measures.'

'You don't say,' says Jack in his crisp Canadian accent.

I'm delighted I trusted Stella's judgement; they're better looking than I expected and exude a brawny, earthy manliness. I wait, eyes lowered, whilst the two guys take in my pale-blue shirt, navy-blue and gold tie and my mid-thigh-length navy gymslip, tightly tied with a turquoise sash. I'm wearing shiny black shoes with very high heels. Stella is identically clad but she has a prefect's badge pinned to her gymslip. She's taller than me barefooted when I'm in heels. The stilettos make her legs look even longer.

Drinks are poured and I move to the blackboard menu to point out the food and ask them what they want to eat. The dark guy, Jack, is devouring me with his eyes and the feeling's entirely mutual as I lick my lips, wondering if he and I will actually make it as far as sitting down to eat. His colleague, Carl, is downing his lager so fast that he's halfway through his drink before Jack even sips at his glass. A vase of flame lilies, their throats speckled with black, stands in the inglenook. I bend to touch one bright stamen with my forefinger, conscious of the men's gaze. The front door is locked and Stella has, I know, switched on the answering machine.

When the two guys sit down, I stand behind Jack and nudge his shoulder with my breast as I pick up the linen napkin he's let fall to the pine floorboards. As I drape the napkin over his knees, I brush his groin and I know we can both feel the energy sparking between us.

Carl says, 'I'd like to try the speciality of the house,' so I stand beside him and pretend to write his order down, deliberately letting my beribboned bunches flick his face before I retreat to the kitchen.

'On a scale of ten?' asks Stella, airlifting grilled French bread with tapenade onto a dish: her version of Marmite toast.

'I think,' I say, picking up the dish, 'on first sight I could go seven out of ten. Seven and rising.'

A cool jazz combo CD plays while we leisurely eat our first course. Then the two guys are exclaiming over the Schoolroom Sausage Twist with garlic and parsley mash. The mushroom gravy is laced with brandy and herbs, the red wine is flowing and I'm feeling both mellow and seductive. I know my boss is too. She changes the music to something more sultry.

Jack tells us that his grandfather came from Wales. 'I should really try to visit there one day,' he says.

'I have some Welsh ancestry,' I tell him.

'Maybe we're related from way back,' he says.

'I hope not,' I say.

He laughs then reaches out and gently strokes my wrist. 'Well, ma'am, they do say vice is nice but incest is best.'

That pulse is beating again. I start working my second sausage, speared on my fork so I can rub the tip against my mouth and lick it before my lips open just wide enough for me to push the savoury meat inside. My aim is to remain demure, as if totally incapable of any depraved thoughts. Both guys look at me as if they can't wait to see what I'll do next and I'm wondering if the dining table will rise a few inches when I think of what those two must be hiding down there beneath the pink cloth.

Then Stella clears our plates and I move to the menu board where, hand on hip, I rap the blackboard pointer against each dessert, while reading the choices out.

'I'd like the bread and butter pudding, please. Must keep my strength up,' says Carl, though I can't believe he'd have any problems with stamina.

'Ahem ... apple tart for me, please, Millie,' says Jack, with a mischievous grin.

'I expect you'd like custard with the tart, Jack, ... and maybe a little whipped cream with the bread and butter pudding for you, Carl ...'

I know they're watching my slinky derrière as I swing towards the kitchen. Stella mouths 'So fuckable' at me as she spoons out their puddings and asks me, 'Some of my special ice cream, sweetie?' I nod on both counts and carry the bowls back to the waiting men, knowing when Stella brings our ice creams to table they will contain a dash of what she calls her magic ingredient.

Stella's cooking skills are unparalleled in the locality. But she is a hard taskmaster, expecting perfection of presentation and service. While we're all eating dessert, I see her frown as she notices a drop of custard staining the cloth between my place and Jack's. But she bides her time, knowing that my imagination will be running wild as I wonder when she will call me to task.

The guys are enjoying their puddings. And Stella and I are lapping up the soft ice cream, as such manna deserves. Chunks of morello cherry are threaded through the rich chocolate sauce; a combination so scrumptious that all too soon the last sinful spoonful slithers down my throat. Stella finishes just before me and, when I lick my lips after my final mouthful, she leans forwards.

Oh! I didn't mention Stella's breasts? They are lush and round and heavy and she pampers them with exotic body lotions and designer lingerie. On her last visit to the kitchen she must have undone her top blouse buttons and now she lazily unravels her tie so it hangs loose around her creamy neck. I tingle, then shiver with anticipation, because I know what's going to happen next. I can only imagine the effect she's having on the two guys, especially when she lets the tip of her pink tongue protrude between her soft full lips.

'Could I have your attention, gentlemen?' she says.

Instantly the atmosphere is heightened and Jack puts down his spoon, saying, 'See what a good boy I am?'

Interestingly, it is Carl who dares to disobey. He takes his time, swallowing his last morsel of pudding and giving me a lascivious wink before he looks his hostess straight in the eye. Stella's body language tells me that she finds this bit of devilment tantalising.

'I'm so sorry to tell you this, but I feel it necessary to punish Millie for being a naughty girl.' Stella speaks softly so that the men instinctively lean closer to her and I know they're drooling over those luxuriant breasts, straining against the starched blue fabric of her blouse.

'Oh, please, Mistress,' I whimper. Jack and Carl turn towards me, then glance at each other and Carl mutters something to his friend. When I hear Jack reply, 'Hell, yes,' I know they're both entering into the spirit of the evening and my breathing becomes more rapid.

Of course, it's no good my pleading. Stella rises and goes across to the headmaster's desk where she picks up a long slim cane and gives it a little swoosh. It ripples through the air before she walks slowly back to us. I stand up, turning around so my back is towards the table. Stella has dimmed the lighting to an intimate rosy glow.

'Bend over,' she instructs me in that same low voice. I obey and I feel her raise my skirt. As if she's flipped a switch, a frisson of excitement fizzes around the four of us. The wine has relaxed any lingering inhibitions and I'm remembering that I haven't enjoyed the attentions of a red-blooded male for at least a month. I know Stella will give me only a playful caning but my pants are already damp. The cotton is stretched tight over the cheeks of my bottom and I'm well aware that three people are viewing my suspenders and stocking tops.

'So soft, so smooth,' croons Stella, reaching out a hand to brush the top of my left thigh. Her touch is like silk. My clitoris, I know, is swollen, and I feel a surge of lust and I whimper, aching to be touched again. And my wish is granted because now a firm hand is feeling the flesh between my stocking top and my knickers. Now we're cooking.

'Carl, feel how soft she is,' purrs Stella. So I know whose fingers are stroking me and I wonder whether Carl will explore further as I remain bent over, in that vulnerable position. Then I feel Jack's touch as well ... harder than Carl's caress. He brushes the nylon behind my knees then his fingers slide up the seams to my stocking tops. When he pinches the inside of my right thigh, I'm melting like hot butter.

Then there's no more stroking: only the whippy cane whooshing through the air as my boss switches me. I feel a stinging sensation on my bottom but it's a pleasurable burn with a thrilling effect. The second switch increases this feeling and I gasp and start to plead for another. Stella always pauses before administering her third and final stroke and the anticipation is delicious. I hear the swish again and close my eyes, shivering as the heat of the after-burn spreads over my skin and I become even wetter between my thighs.

'Please ... someone, oh, please. Jack ... Carl ...'

'Behave, bad girl. Nobody's going to save you. Go and stand in the corner,' snaps Stella in mock anger.

'Shan't,' I call. Then I run into the kitchen and I hear Stella telling Carl to go and deal with me. I know the way her mind works. She will have her eye on Carl but she wants to savour the moment ... have me warm him up for her. We're past masters at managing our menu.

My excitement mounts as he comes into the kitchen but I giggle and dart through the stable door as he approaches and next thing I know we're on the cushions of the lounger and his hard-on is straining against his trousers so I help him forget he's a gentleman as I unwrap my prize. I curl up beside him and he groans as I start licking and flicking my tongue where I think he'll like it best. He takes hold of my cheeky bunches of hair and pulls me down so my soft wet mouth fastens on to his cock. But he's more than a match for me and he takes control, pulling at my pristine cotton and peeling the fabric down my thighs so he can knead the cheeks of my bottom. I know he's turned on by my demure yet naughty image as I tell him how disobedient he is and I'm rewarded as he moves away and kneels in front of me. He starts unbuttoning my blouse and cups one breast so he can reach the nipple. Then he tells me I taste of violets and I whisper that he will eventually reach the honey. He pushes me backwards, parts my legs and sucks at my naked mound, with his tongue right inside my ruffles. He laps faster and faster and the lounger rocks as my hands are holding his head against me.

I'm aware that Jack and Stella are standing in the doorway watching us. Stella's blouse is fully open and Jack has his arm around her shoulders, is fingering her sweetmeats and tweaking them through the lacy wrapping of her bra. This image is the last trigger and I'm spinning: dissolving in a blissful shower of sparks.

Then Stella breaks away from Jack and disappears inside for a moment. She returns to throw a fleecy blanket down on the tiled patio and I sink onto it and stretch like a cat in the cool evening air. Before I know it, Jack is beside me with a glass of wine. He dips his fingers into the ruby liquid and starts to rub my lips and inside my mouth and then I get to my feet and stand in front of him, Millie the mischievous schoolgirl. He pulls off my tunic and dishevelled blouse and I hear his intake of breath as he unfastens the severe white bra so that my pert breasts, their dark buds standing up from Carl's attentions, await his wandering fingers and lips. But first he loosens my hair ribbons so auburn strands tumble round my face.

Stella and Carl are entwined on the lounger. I know they're watching Jack tongue his way down my body and, judging from the sounds, they're as aroused as we are. And I guess Stella is using those long, cool chef's fingers of hers on Carl, to finish what I started. I'm incapable of stopping now that the naïve schoolgirl has become a demanding bitch. My hands reach for Jack's trouser zip and his cock springs free into my greedy fingers. It's so smooth, so velvety, yet rock hard and I can't wait for it to be inside me but suddenly I scramble upright and run off inside, inviting chase. Jack follows me and when he comes into the restaurant I'm draped over a bar stool, thighs apart, clinging to the wooden struts and calling out, 'Please, don't spank me. I'll be a good girl now.'

I feel the flat of his hand smack me twice and I sense his urgency but still he moves away. I turn my head and watch him approach the dining table and dip his fingers into the bowl of whipped cream. When he starts to rub one creamy finger around my tight dark rim, I'm climbing the walls: still stretched out, powerless to move, with my butt in the air. He moves his hands down and underneath my hips, raising me, so I'm longing to feel the length of him inside me. His fingers are circling and teasing until he pushes the index finger inside my opening, driving me so crazy that he must feel my muscles tighten round his finger.

'Jeez, Millie, I have to have you properly,' he gasps and next thing he's lifting me in his arms and I'm lying on the polished bar top like a virgin awaiting sacrifice. I'm whimpering with wanting now but his hard cock is soon sliding into me and I'm so close, so close ... and I go with the sensation and when I cry out he's rocking faster and faster until he finishes too.

Stella and Carl have been upstairs for a while. I have a wicked thought as Jack and I regroup.

'How about a nightcap, Jack?' I ask.

'Yes, ma'am,' he says. 'God, Millie ... I could eat you all over again.'

'Then you'd like seconds?' I suggest as I pour him a brandy.

'Depends what's on offer,' he says.

'Wait here while I check the menu,' I tell him and I climb the stairs, a naked ghost in the dimly lit corridor. Before I get to Carl's room, the door opens and Stella appears. I say nothing, just nod, and she pushes a little bottle into my hand and moves aside so I can enter. Carl must be in the bathroom so I go over to the bed and wait for him, amusing myself by imagining Jack's reaction as Stella descends the stairs, those luscious breasts demanding his full attention. And I'm such a greedy girl that I wish I hadn't left Jack quite so soon and I'm just reaching for that little bottle when the connecting door opens and Carl almost catches me in the act.

'Stella said she had a surprise for afters,' he says and his voice is husky.

I'm trembling as I move over so Carl can join me and reap the benefit of Stella's thoughtful gesture. I let a few drops of fragrant massage oil roll onto the palm of one hand and move astride him so I can give him the attention he deserves. And all the time I'm whispering mischief to him, asking him what it felt like to be squeezed between those heavy, perfumed breasts.

'Tell me, Carl. Did Stella make you watch while she

played with herself?' I demand. 'Did she lie back, licking her lips? Did she make you suck on her cherries to help her come?' And all the time he's becoming more and more aroused and my hands are rolling and teasing and caressing until I lift myself and climb on top of him so I can sit on his beautiful, firm shaft.

I adore being on top: almost as much as I adore the man being on top of me. And Carl is a force to be reckoned with. For such a shy, sweet guy, he has an enviable talent for murmuring sweet nothings and soon he's giving as good as he got as he tells me what he wants me to do to myself while he's inside me. He's got me oiling my fingers and touching my breasts, until my nipples are swollen and glistening. He's demanding me to tell him in intimate detail what Jack did to me and what I did to Jack.

The shocking words spill from my lips, fuelled by the erotic images I cherish, until the two of us are lost in that sensual limbo land where nothing matters but the moment. My pelvic writhing makes him shudder with pleasure as I squeeze myself around his lubricated cock, then relax, then squeeze again, then almost withdraw myself. But a pilot keeps his head in an emergency and he remains inside of me, rolling us over so he's on top now and he pushes a pillow under my hips so his rhythm intensifies as he rides me, working towards putting the icing on my cake.

'Push harder . . . pinch my nipples . . . hurt me,' I demand. And this time he's obedient. And I get my just desserts . . .

Fantastic.

Stone Touch Natasha Rostova

His hand was dry and slightly cracked, rubbing against her palm as he clutched her fingers and drew away. When he was no longer touching her, she became aware of the assault on her other senses. Spices, body odours, smoke, petrol. Thick, weighty air. Rattling cars, motorbikes, a dog barking, incoherent shouting. And heat. Intense heat. Miranda could feel the sun scorching the skin of her face and neck. She welcomed it, wanting to be warm, wanting the heat to penetrate her skin to her very bones.

'Welcome to Bhubaneshwar, Miss Watson. Your hotel is not far.' The words were braided with a precise and deep accent. 'John has told me much about you.'

'Thank you. Please call me Miranda.' She hesitated. 'Hastin.'

'Miranda, then.' She felt his smile, pictured his teeth white as rice. 'I have a taxi waiting.'

John put his hand on Miranda's lower back and guided her into the taxi. The interior smelled like cheap upholstery and cigarettes, baked by the ever-present heat. She put her hand on the seat. The vinyl was burst open to reveal gritty folds of foam rubber.

'John tells me you have not been to India before,' Hastin said from the front passenger seat.

'No. We just arrived in Calcutta yesterday.'

The car jerked to a start. Horns blared incessantly, seeming to add even more density to the air. Miranda imagined black-and-yellow taxis pimpled with dents and rust, sugarcane carts with rotating wheels that squeezed the juice out of the stalks, wagons pulled by sullen oxen, cows meandering with total complacency through the streets. And people, dozens of people, children in ragged clothing with eyes the colour of ink, fashionable women with silk saris and jewellery glittering like stars, rickshaw wallahs playing cards on the sidewalks.

'It is too hot here for you?' Hastin asked.

'No.' Nowhere is it too hot for me, Miranda thought.

'Thanks again for your offer to be Miranda's tour guide,' John said. 'She's been wanting to visit some Indian temples.'

'I have arranged for you to see Konark tomorrow,' Hastin told Miranda. 'The temple of the sun. You will find it most interesting.'

'Hastin,' Miranda murmured almost to herself. 'That's a nice name.'

He chuckled. 'Not the meaning, I am afraid. In Hindi, it means elephant.'

Miranda smiled faintly. 'Elephants are very noble creatures.'

'Ah, yes. Like myself. A very noble creature.' She felt him look over his shoulder at her. 'I assure you, I resemble an elephant only in character. Not appearance.'

'I believe you.'

Miranda knew he was still watching her, even when the car started moving again.

The hotel lobby was bathed in coolness and quietude. Miranda sat in a chair near the reception desk, her arms crossed against the chill. She listened to the low conversations around her, to the clicking noise of shoes against the tiled floor. The desk clerk had a pleasingly melodious voice, like the sound of gentle ocean waves.

'Miranda?' A hand touched her shoulder, the callused edge brushing against the tender naked juncture of her neck. 'It is Hastin here for you.'

'Hello, Hastin.' She turned towards his voice. 'I hope this isn't too much trouble.'

'I can think of nothing I would rather do than show you our sun temple,' he said grandly. 'Is John not here?'

'He left about fifteen minutes ago. He didn't want to be late for his meeting.' Miranda smoothed possible wrinkles from the loose cotton dress she was wearing and stood. One hand curved around the handle of her cane, the other around the back of the chair. She felt Hastin's eyes on her, then his fingers skimmed across her arm.

'You have goose flesh,' he said. 'Are you cold?'

'I'm always cold.'

He hesitated. 'You have not been blind for long.'

It wasn't a question. 'Just a few months.'

Hastin was studying her. She sensed the intentness of his expression, the furrow between his brows.

'And yet you have expressive eyes, Miranda. Very beautiful.'

'Thank you.'

'Why have you come to India?' Hastin asked.

'I heard that it was hot here.'

'Why do you long so for the heat?'

'You would, too, if you lived in ... if you lived like I do.'

'How is that?'

Miranda knew she could never explain how her world had become so frozen, so lacking in colour. How her blood chilled with fear of the unknown, and how she wished that her whole being could somehow thaw.

'In a place where everything is like winter,' Miranda said. 'Stark and cold.'

'Winter can be beautiful,' Hastin countered. 'Many shades of grey and blue. I think you do not yet know that there is heat where you live.'

Miranda's mouth tightened with irritation.' How would you know?'

'I don't. I am making a guess, but perhaps I am correct. Come. I will take you where you will find warmth.'

Miranda's heart thudded abruptly when Hastin put her hand on his arm. He was taller than she was, but his body seemed to lack the comforting bulk that John possessed.

She could feel Hastin's thinness in the edge of his elbow and the bone of his forearm as she tightened her grip on it.

'Would you tell me something before we go?' she asked.

'Certainly.'

Miranda lowered her voice a bit. 'What does the desk clerk look like?'

'The clerk?' There was a pause, during which Miranda imagined he was looking at the other woman. 'She is pretty. Perhaps in her mid-twenties. Very big eyes lined with kohl, and black hair that almost reaches her waist. Indians would say that her skin was wheat-coloured.'

'Wheat-coloured,' Miranda repeated.

She knew that 'wheat-coloured' was not a particularly flattering term by Indian standards, but it held a certain poetry for her. The association brought to mind endless fields of flaxen grain swaying, waterlike, with the wind. It wasn't only an association with nature; it was an association with the most fundamental nourishment. To Miranda's mind, 'wheat-coloured' conjured up images of freshly baked loaves, masses of dough between her fingers, the yeasty smell of bakeries, and the ripe satisfaction of sinking her teeth into a warm, crusty slice of bread.

'What about you?' she asked Hastin as they went out to the car.

'Me?'

'What do you look like?'

'Oh, I am very good-looking,' Hastin said. 'Fine features, an aristocratic forehead. Like a Mogul prince. All I need are silken pillows and an embroidered robe. And one or two courtesans, perhaps.'

Miranda was unable to prevent a smile. 'Courtesans, hmm?'

'Ah, the Moguls were great lovers of pleasure, did you know that?'

'Like yourself?'

'Indeed like myself. The Moguls knew how to create,

how to love, how to eat. They ate korma, kebab, biriyani, pullao – all perfectly spiced to both warm and cool the body. They served food on gold and silver platters and drank from jewelled vessels. Their porcelain dishes were perfumed with rose petals, adorned with saffron and crisp, toasted pistachios. Sometimes they were even decorated with sheets of pure silver and gold, thin as a tissue and entirely edible. Can you imagine? Placing pure gold upon your tongue. I imagine it tastes like the sun.' He sounded wistful. 'Delicious food is one of the great joys of life, don't you think?'

'One of them,' Miranda agreed.

His fingertips barely touched her elbow as he guided her out of the car. They stepped into a cool space whose silence was broken only by the hum of an air conditioner. A shiver skimmed down Miranda's spine.

'This is my cousin's restaurant,' Hastin explained. 'John told me you have not yet eaten Indian food. I will remedy this chasm in your culinary experience. Come and visit the kitchen first.'

As Hastin led her through the restaurant, Miranda breathed in an increasingly pungent and intricate array of scents. She imagined that the walls of the restaurant were whitewashed, perhaps lined with cracks and decorated with colourful batik wall hangings. There would be glossy potted plants in the corners, tables draped with white linen and adorned with glass vases bearing a single flower.

She heard Hastin speaking briefly with a man she assumed was his cousin.

'You are welcome in my kitchen, memsahib,' a deep, mellow voice said with great politeness.

'Thank you.' She pictured him as a stocky man with an open, wide face and bristly moustache. 'Don't let me disturb your work.'

'You would like to sit?'

'No, I'll stand.'

Miranda felt for the doorway and leaned her shoulder against the jamb. Heat flowed from gas burners, enveloping her in a cloud of warmth. She listened to the rhythmic tattoo of a chopping knife hitting a wooden cutting board. She heard the sizzle of oil bubbling in a pan followed by the smell of frying onions. A spicy cloud began to rise in the kitchen. Miranda drew it into her lungs, feeling as if it were entering her very bloodstream. Although she hadn't yet tasted Indian food, she loved the names of Indian spices as much as their flourishing scent. The words were poetic; cumin, cardamom, turmeric, coriander. Like flowers or gemstones.

Hastin began speaking with his cousin in Hindi. The sound of their voices was a pleasing complement to the music of the kitchen. Miranda listened hard to try to identify all the various instruments. A heavy butcher's knife slamming down on the cutting board with a thud. The moist, rhythmic sound of someone kneading a ball of dough. Crisp green beans snapping in two. The paper-tearing sound of an onion being peeled. Running water, a kettle filling. Potatoes dropping into a boiling pot. Aromatic seeds crushing and splitting open under the weight of a granite pestle.

'You are hungry, Miranda?' Hastin asked.

Miranda's stomach rumbled in response. She smiled. 'Very.'

'I will show you where to sit.'

He situated her at a table and took her hand. His touch felt more certain, as if he were more confident now that she was on his territory. He wrapped her fingers around a cold damp glass.

'Mango lassi,' Hastin said.

Miranda brought the glass to her parched lips. She shuddered as she welcomed the velvety, sweet liquid into her throat and beyond.

Footsteps approached the table, followed by the clinking

noise of metal dishes. Steam rose, flavoured with a blend of spices, curried meats, various oils, seasoned vegetables, mesquite. The fragrance was tantalising.

'Here is clean water.' Hastin took her hands between his long fingers and guided them to a bowl. 'For washing. Food eaten with the hand is better.'

Miranda washed her hands and dried them on a towel. Hastin took her hand again and helped her touch the plate in front of her.

'My cousin has prepared a variety of dishes for you to taste,' Hastin explained. 'We would not normally eat all of this together.'

He began to place food onto their plates, the metal spoon hitting each bowl with a clink. 'You should start with the pakora,' he recommended. 'Vegetable fritters coated with chick-pea flour.'

Miranda accepted one of the crispy fritters. Her teeth bit through the delicately fried exterior to the moist filling of onions, cumin and a touch of mint. The flavour was mildly spicy and subtle, as if preparing her taste buds for future delights. At Hastin's urging, she dipped a shrimp fritter into a smooth mint-and-coriander chutney whose aroma was as delightful as the fresh, tangy flavour.

'I have put samples of each dish on your plate,' Hastin explained. 'Please, try. This is a bread called paratha. Wheat layered with ghee and cooked on a griddle. And this is makki ki roti, a bread made of maize flour. Very typical Punjabi breads. You can use the bread as a spoon to eat the curry. It is very pliable.'

Miranda broke off a portion of the paratha with her fingers and brought it to her mouth. The flaky bread was saturated with the earthy flavour of toasted whole wheat glistening with butter. A kernel of enjoyment broke open inside her, emitting a tiny, luscious glow.

'It is good?' Hastin asked.

'It's delicious.' Miranda darted her tongue out of her mouth to capture a crumb she felt clinging to her bottom lip. She was suddenly ravenous, hungry to be filled with both food and pleasure. 'What's next?'

'This is korma, braised chicken in a sauce of coconut milk, cloves and ginger. Cooked gently over a low heat so that the meat absorbs the flavours. And matar paneer, peas in a sauce made with paprika and fresh coriander. The dish contains pieces of fresh home-made cheese that have soaked up the flavour of the sauce. We have more bread, of course, a naan bread. This is an unleavened bread cooked in the tandoor oven.'

Miranda bit off a piece of warm naan, delighting in the chewy, slightly charred taste, and then sampled the paper-thin, crunchy pappadams made of lentils. The matar paneer burst with the flavour of sweet green peas, with the cheese proving to be a moist and fresh accompaniment. In an attempt to eat the Indian way, Miranda scooped up a portion of korma with her fingers and somewhat awkwardly brought it to her mouth. The chicken was delectably tender, bathed in a rich, silky sauce whose various spices melted together in a taste that was almost illicit in its ability to give pleasure.

Miranda closed her eyes, sucking a drop of sauce quickly from her thumb. She didn't feel as if she could eat enough. She sampled juicy kebabs stuffed with dried fruits and nuts; sautéed potatoes that had absorbed the tangs of ginger and cumin; and succulent lamb drenched in a raisin and pistachio sauce, then seasoned with saffron. She ate purple eggplant that had been slow-roasted over an open flame and blended with fresh peas, onions and tomatoes. She used the soft bread to ladle a portion of smooth, puréed lentils sprinkled with slivers of garlic and thickened with butter. She bit into a floret of cauliflower curry sharpened with chilli, which spread a sharp, hot tang across her tongue.

'Too hot?' Hastin asked. 'Here. This is raita. It will ease the sensation.'

Miranda wrapped her fingers around a small metal bowl

and drank a small portion of the refreshing yogurt flavoured with lemon and cilantro. The coolness was a welcome contrast to the peppery cauliflower, but the chilli had a delicious, lingering effect. Miranda wiped away a trickle of sweat that ran down her temple, absorbing the spectrum of flavours from cool to warm to outright fiery. Although the room was cool, she felt her body warming from the inside out, an agreeable warming like the slow kindling of a fire.

'Are you all right?' Hastin asked.

'Yes, of course. It's just such an array of ... of sensation.'

'Pleasurable?'

'It's like eating colours.' Miranda paused. 'Are you having anything, Hastin?'

'I am more enjoying watching,' he said somewhat apologetically. 'You are ... you have a very sensual way of eating. As if with your whole being.'

Miranda flushed. The glow expanded inside her, spilling light into her blood, to her very core. She became aware of the cushion of the chair underneath her legs, the soft, glossy texture of the bread between her fingers, the way her cotton dress draped over her shoulders and breasts. The feeling of Hastin's gaze on her.

She patted her lips with a napkin. She imagined that Hastin's eyes and hair were as dark as peppercorns, that his skin was wheat-coloured – a rich brown, like tea diluted with a few drops of cream. And his hair, the black glossy colour of a vanilla bean. Miranda wished that she could see the expression on his face and wondered if it complemented the hint of awe she heard in his voice.

'You must tell your cousin how grateful I am,' she said in an effort to distil her growing fascination with him.

'I will,' Hastin promised. 'Here is a special dish he has made, a prawn curry. The prawns are fresh from the bay. They are seasoned with coconut, tamarind pods and chilli, then dusted with garam masala.'

'What is that?' Miranda asked. 'Garam masala.'

'Ah, the masala ... the blend of Indian spices,' Hastin explained. 'Cardamom, cinnamon, black pepper and cloves are the four original Mogul spices. Now we add coriander and cumin. You sprinkle a bit on the food prior to serving for additional flavour. Like tying a pretty bow on a package. And this you must try, a special Mogul biriyani, rice layered with lamb and vegetables then cooked in a mixture of ginger, onions, crushed almonds, spiced yogurt and saffron. Saffron, the spice of kings.'

'And Mogul princes,' Miranda said with amusement.

She tried the curry first, sinking her teeth into a thick juicy prawn. The coconut proved to be a sweet and tasty counterpart to the piquant chilli, like two opposites who formed a perfect whole. The biriyani was perfectly seasoned, a complex array of textures that were a pleasure to discern. The long-grained rice was tinged with the flavour of saffron, the lamb moist and laced with a creamy marinade of cinnamon, cloves and cumin. The crunchy almonds were a delectable contrast to the soft rice and tender meat, with the entire dish containing an undercurrent of rich butter.

Miranda scooped up a mouthful with a piece of spongy, poppyseed-decorated naan. She closed her eyes again with the bliss of intricate tastes, unable to prevent a murmur of sheer pleasure from escaping her lips.

'I wish you could ...' Hastin's voice trailed off.

Miranda licked a few morsels of rice from her fingertips. 'Wish I could what?'

'I wish you could see the food,' Hastin said. 'The saffron imparts a beautiful yellow to the biriyani, and the raita is a creamy white strewn with bright green. When dishes were set before the Mogul kings, they were often made to look like jewels. Each grain of rice would be painted with a red vegetable dye so that it resembled a bowl of rubies. The dishes are a pleasure to the eye as well as the mouth.'

'How lovely.'

'You would care for more?'

'So delicious, Hastin, but I can't possibly eat more.'

'I am pleased you enjoyed it so,' Hastin said. 'I will ask Sanjeev to pack dessert for us to take.'

As they prepared to leave, Miranda washed her hands and accepted a small handful of fennel, aniseed and sugar pods that were perfumed with rose. As Sanjeev explained, these were to aid digestion and freshen her mouth. Miranda thanked him copiously for the meal before she and Hastin left for Konark.

Miranda sat in the passenger seat, both replete from satisfaction and with a heightened consciousness of her body. She was aware of how the spices had conspired to cool her physically from the heat and yet simultaneously create an inner warmth that infused her blood. She was all at once languid and alert, softened and intensified. She rubbed her hands over her thighs, felt the silk of cotton sliding between her legs. A trickle of perspiration slipped into the valley between her breasts.

'We have arrived,' Hastin said as the car slid to a halt.

They got out of the car. A breeze undulated through the trees, playing leaf music with delicate precision. Miranda gathered her loose hair and lifted it into a sheaf. The air caressed the back of her damp neck with a movement as luscious as a kiss.

'You are warm?' Hastin asked.

'Warmer,' Miranda admitted.

'The temple of the sun god will thaw your winter, Miranda.'

Miranda closed her eyes, feeling the sunlight on her face. 'Is this a Mogul temple?'

'No. Konark was built in the thirteenth century,' Hastin explained. 'It is a monument to the sun god, Surya. It is meant to be his chariot carved from stone, although sadly much of it is in disrepair. But you can see ... you can tell that it was once glorious. As Mogul cooking is a celebration of the pleasure of the senses, Konark is a celebration of artistry, religion and life.'

Miranda tried to imagine the looming Konark temple before her. In the light of the sun, the stones would glow the colour of saffron, the edges of the sculptures softened, yet still hard and immobile. What a contrast they must form with the movement of surrounding trees, the lush greenery nurtured by frequent rainfall and rich soil.

'This temple is not big,' Hastin said. 'It is not a complex like Khajuraho.'

Miranda turned towards the sound of his voice. 'Would you allow me to do something?'

'Yes.'

'I'd like to touch your face. If you don't mind.'

He was silent for a moment, which caused Miranda to fear she had offended him. Then she felt him take her wrist and guide her right hand to his face. The air seemed to thicken between them. Miranda drew in a breath. Hastin was very still.

She spread her spice-scented fingers against the plane of his face, the high ridge of his cheekbone. She felt the straightness of his nose, the thick arch of his eyebrows and the feathery softness of his eyelashes. His lips were shaped like a bow, the skin slightly dry like his palms, the lower lip full and tender. His breath was warm against her fingers, and she imagined that he tasted like cloves and cinnamon.

'You're right,' Miranda said, her voice foreign to her own ears. 'You look like a Mogul prince.'

She drew away, still feeling his breath against her fingertips. 'Would you take me to the temple?'

'Of course.'

He brought her hand around his elbow. He manoeuvred with infinite care around the rocks and broken stones that littered the area around the temple.

'We are now before the horses of the chariot,' Hastin said. 'The front of the temple. There are seven of them, all pulling the magnificent god across the sky, and a set of steps leading to the entrance of the chariot. The chariot is huge with a roof like a pyramid, and there are lion and elephant sculptures.'

'How big are the animals?' Miranda asked.

'Some are life-sized and fully carved, but attached to the structure, like the wheels of the chariot. The wheels are most extraordinary, but only one remains intact. Over the centuries, invaders have come and attacked the temple. It is most unfortunate.'

They moved slowly around the temple. Miranda encountered rocks with almost every step, but Hastin was so cautious in his movements that her fear over what lay ahead began to dissipate slowly.

He stopped. 'This is the intact wheel. All of the carving is intact, decorated with symbolic and auspicious designs to protect the god.'

Miranda lifted her eyebrows. 'They didn't quite protect him from the invaders.'

'Miranda, sometimes even gods cannot be protected.'

She put her hand out towards the wheel and grasped a fistful of air. Hastin guided her closer, then placed her hand on the warm stone. Miranda's fingertips followed the intricately carved arc of the huge wheel, each spoke leading to the centre hub. A filigreed design embellished the outer edge, so detailed that she couldn't help but think of the artisan who had created it with such apparent capability.

'There are twenty-four wheels,' Hastin said. 'For the twenty-four hours of the day.'

Miranda stroked her palm over the curve of the wheel, enjoying the sensation of the rough stone underneath her hand. 'I wonder which hour this one represents.'

'Perhaps it is midnight, both the beginning and the end.'

Miranda smiled. 'And maybe that's why it hasn't been broken.'

'Yes.' His voice was smiling, too. 'I think you are correct. The beginning and the end remain a perfect circle. You think the stone should be cold, but you can feel that it is not. It shimmers with heat from the inside out.'

Like me. 'Can you show me some of the other figures?'

He coughed slightly. 'Yes, but I'm afraid some are ... well, they are of the erotic variety. I do not want you to be offended.'

'I won't be offended. I promise.'

Hastin guided her hand to a relief, this one of a guardian or a charioteer. Miranda touched the outline of the relief, running her hand over the figure's features, the draping lines of his clothing, the ninety-degree angle of his arm.

'Are there any women?' she asked.

'Um, yes.' He sounded slightly embarrassed, but led her towards another sculpture. 'This is a *yakshi* figure, a fertility goddess. In Indian art, many of the woman are very ... voluptuous because they are associated with nature and fertility.'

Miranda felt for the wall, then leaned her cane against it so both hands would be free. The woman was carved in such deep relief that she was almost sculpted in the round. Miranda started at her feet, the toes chiselled with such care from the stone that even her toenails were evident. She touched the woman's legs, examining the slope of her calves and the fullness of her thighs. The sculpture was all womanly curves, her hips tilted slightly to the side as if she was resting her weight on one foot. That angle gave her body a strangely rhythmic quality, one that Miranda followed with her hands.

Over her hips, across the expanse of the stone pelvis, her fingers dipping into the slight indentation between her legs. The woman's belly button was a perfect circle, her waist inclined with artistic precision up to her breasts. And what glorious breasts the artist had bestowed upon her, so full and round, like mangos ripe for picking. Her nipples stood out in a perpetual expression of arousal. Miranda slid her fingers under the swells of the *yakshi*'s breasts, then cupped them in her hands and felt the nipples poking against her palms. Miranda reached up further and put her fingertips against the mouth, stroking full lips that were turned into a slight smile.

She experienced a momentary rush of sadness that this woman had been relegated to a life of stone rather than one of living, breathing flesh. What a sight she would be in movement, her hips swaying with every step, her breasts bouncing with a natural tempo, her jewellery jingling to announce her presence. And warm, she would be so warm, her skin pulsing with blood and heat, her lips moist, her eyes flashing with lively curiosity. And what incredible pleasure to make love with such a woman, to melt against her abundant curves and move with the rhythm of the seasons and the tides.

Miranda pulled away reluctantly, unwilling to sacrifice her fantasy of the *yakshi*, but aware of Hastin's presence. She fumbled to find her cane. Hastin took her arm and put the cane in her hand. His elbow bumped against her side.

'Are there more?' Miranda asked.

She felt his gaze on her, could smell the faint scent of incense on his clothing.

'Yes, there are many more.' He didn't move for a moment. 'You must remember much.'

'Yes. Sometimes John doesn't even have to describe things for me. I can recall them immediately.' She turned away as much as she could without letting go of his arm. 'Would you take me to another one, please?'

Hastin fell silent as they made their way towards another sculpture. 'This one is a bit low. Please watch your step.'

Miranda steadied herself on the stone as she knelt in front of the sculpture. This artist, or perhaps it was the same one who carved the *yakshi*, had found a man and a woman embedded in his block of stone. Miranda was momentarily disconcerted to reach out and touch a male body, as she had been expecting another woman. These two bodies were so intricately entwined that it was a bit difficult to determine which limbs belonged to whom. She rubbed the man's face, the sharp lines of his nose and chin, even his carefully carved ear. Then she ran her hand over his shoulder, following his arm as it reached out and curved around the woman's neck. Her head was thrown back slightly, her throat arched in a graceful movement as if offering it to the glide of Miranda's fingers.

Miranda smoothed her palm over her breasts and over her belly before reaching the juncture of their union. She flushed hotly since she knew that Hastin was watching her, but she couldn't help touching the sculptures there, sliding her fingers over the man's erect penis, which was poised at the entrance of the woman's sex. Her heart thudded with a strange excitement as she deliberately fondled the stone erection, the woman's spread legs. She pressed her thighs together, feeling the throb of swelling arousal.

Hastin hadn't moved away. Miranda could tell that he was standing right behind her. She hadn't noticed before that the temple grounds were filled with a portentous silence in the early afternoon, as if all the world waited with breathless anticipation as the sun god commanded the day to continue.

Miranda stopped, resting her hand on the woman's thigh, her breathing erratic.

'She is very beautiful,' Hastin said. His voice sounded a bit thick. 'She is in submission to their union, to him. It is about the universe, these sensual sculptures. The joining of the most basic divine principles, male and female.'

'They're not joined yet, though.' Heat bloomed over her skin.

'Yes. Yes, they are.'

Miranda heard him take a few steps towards her, then the shifting of his body as he knelt beside her. He picked up her hand, sliding his fingers over the back of hers as he guided her back to the sculpture. Her fingers touched the hard ridge of the man's thigh before Hastin drew them up towards the penis again. His breath brushed against her hair as he slid her hand over the erection to the woman's vulva.

'There,' he said. 'You feel how he disappears inside her?'

Miranda nodded, stunned by how much she liked the feeling of him next to her, the sensation of his hand on hers. The high sun burnished their backs, creating a delicious glow of warmth.

'I . . . Miranda.' His voice wrapped around her name as if he were eating a chocolate.

Miranda drew in a breath. Hastin untangled his hand from hers.

'I have . . . would you like to try the dessert?' he asked.

'Dessert?' Miranda's mind spun.

'Yes. I have brought it.' There was the sound of paper rustling, as if Hastin were attempting to occupy himself with another task. 'You didn't have any earlier.'

Miranda sank to the ground, her palms flat against the stone beneath her. 'Um, sure.'

'This is gulab jamun,' Hastin said. 'Little balls of milk curd fried and then marinated in a sugary syrup of rosewater and cardamom. If you would . . .'

His fingers brushed against her mouth. Miranda parted her lips.

'Like the moons of heaven.' Hastin placed one of the gulab jamun against her lips.

Miranda bit through the soft, damp globe as her mouth filled with a thick sweetness perfumed with rosewater. A trickle of syrup ran down her chin. She wiped it away with her finger, then darted her tongue out to lick her finger.

'More?' Hastin asked.

Miranda nodded. He slipped the rest of the dessert into her mouth. His fingertips, sweet with syrup, slid against the moist interior of her lower lip. Miranda wanted to kiss them.

Hastin fed her a chilled, creamy pudding that carried

the flavours of sweet carrots and pistachios, and a firm custard made of almond milk and cream, then garnished with plump pomegranate seeds. The flavours were velvet on her tongue, the pomegranate seeds bursting with crimson light between her teeth.

When Hastin began to draw away, Miranda reached out to grasp his wrist.

'May I touch your hands?' she asked.

'My hands?'

'Yes. They seem so long and elegant. I'd just like to touch them.'

'Please.' There was a faint clatter as he put down the container and spoon.

His dry, rough skin was becoming familiar to her. The backs of his hands were covered with a light matting of coarse hair. Miranda felt his tapered fingers, drawing them through hers with careful concentration. She fixed the tactility of his fingers in her mind, the rigid feeling of his bones, the thickness of his nails and the way they came just slightly over his fingertips. He had a scar in the shape of a half-moon on his thumb and calluses on the pads of his hands. She traced the lines criss-crossing his palms, felt the pulse that beat so rapidly at his wrists.

'You have a touch like rain,' he said.

Miranda smiled, pleased by the simplicity of the compliment as she touched the tendon of his wrist, and then she couldn't resist moving just a little farther up. His arm hairs brushed against her fingers, then against the palm of her hand as she flattened it against his inner arm. His skin was so warm that Miranda imagined she could feel the blood rushing through him. She let her fingers pause at the crook of his elbow. That soft, tender crease was unbearably erotic. She parted her lips to draw in air.

His arm turned, his hand coming to rest on her knee. Sweat broke out on her forehead, but she didn't stop him as his hand slipped to her inner thigh. The thin cotton of her dress provided a minimal barrier between her skin and his hand. Miranda grasped onto a sculpture to steady herself as Hastin's fingers crept closer to her sex. She could hear his breathing as if his lips were against her ear, smell his skin so acutely that it was as if he was lying on top of her. She wondered what his slim body would feel like against her, his sinewy chest pressing against her breasts, his legs winding with hers, his gentle hands stroking over her skin. There would be no sense of oppression, of heaviness. Only of freedom and pleasure.

Miranda gasped when Hastin touched her. His forefinger slipped into the folds of her sex with a precision that nearly undid her. The flimsy cotton barred them both from direct touching, but the sensation of the material against her labia made her tremble. Her body swelled with the pressure of that one finger. She felt Hastin shift, and she wondered if he was also touching himself. She imagined him stroking a long slender cock with the same skill he used to touch her. His hand was clutching the shaft, sliding up and down with a rhythmic motion, the skin warm and tight. The sun grew hotter, sinking into the stone temple and into her blood. Melting her.

She leant towards him, felt his responding movement, his body colliding with hers. Their mouths met in a frenzy of heat and sugared sweetness. She had been right; he tasted like cinnamon, like rosewater, like edible gold. Like the sun.

Miranda rested her head against the statue and closed her eyes, letting him stroke her until pressure tightened in her lower body. His tongue thrust into her mouth, his capable touch growing stronger, more intense, as if he sensed the increase of her arousal. Miranda cried out, her hand tightening on the sculpture as her body came apart. She heard Hastin make a guttural moan, his body tremble. She sagged against the wall and tried to absorb the overabundance of sensation and bright, vivid colours.

They didn't move, didn't speak. His breathing still sounded in her ears. Miranda heard a bird chirping noisily nearby and felt with growing awareness the hard rock underneath her knees, the heat burnishing her face, the living, pulsing, breathing rhythm of the temple and the sculptures that had protected it for so many hundreds of years.

'I ... I should be sorry,' Hastin said, the words ragged. 'But I am not.'

'No.' Miranda's heartbeat began to slowly calm. 'Neither am I.'

He helped her to her feet. Miranda tucked her arm through his as the sun god continued his ritual of the centuries.

'You would like to continue looking around?' Hastin asked.

'No,' Miranda said, warm, thawed, melted. 'I've seen enough.'

Vanilla with Extra Sauce
Jessica Donnelly

Becky knew she should never have agreed to go on the hen weekend when the blonde girl in charge started handing round the plastic police truncheons.

'And these are for what, exactly?' asked Becky, before dropping her truncheon discreetly on the floor of the mini-bus and vowing never to touch it again.

'Spanking naughty boys!' shrieked the blonde, 'Isn't that right, girls? What boy doesn't need a good spanking?'

The group of fifteen women crammed into the minibus yelled their approval at this sentiment, with the exception of Becky, who pulled on the eye mask she always carried with her and plugged the headphones of her iPod firmly into her ears. Noting the quizzical look of the girl sitting next to her, she stated, 'I get travel sick,' and stayed firmly enclosed in her own world for the three hours it took for the bus to travel from London to the West Country.

The only reason Becky had joined the party of hens heading for a weekend's fun at the seaside was that Ruth, the blushing bride-to-be, was a cousin of hers who had recently moved to the same part of London. In a spirit of friendship that was, frankly, unlike her – and one she was already regretting – she had accepted the invitation to celebrate Ruth's forthcoming nuptials by spending Saturday night in some ghastly B & B in a rundown sea-side resort on the coast with a horde of overexcitable women she had never met before and had no desire to meet again.

By 7 p.m., this crowd of women were spilling from the

minibus onto the seafront of the resort, already a little worse for wear, having drunk the best part of a crate of champagne. Most of them were proudly waving large, brightly-coloured vibrators, which they had been ceremonially presented with on the journey.

'This is it, girls!' shouted the blonde girl, who was called Maria. 'Our new home – the Sea View Guest House. It may be cheap and cheerful but it's good enough for the likes of us! Whoops! I've dropped me dildo!'

'Let's get unpacked, get dressed up and hit the town!' added Ruth in a drunken shriek, her comedy bridal veil slipping over one eye as she dragged her suitcase up the steps of the Sea View Guest House.

Becky surveyed the scene before her and concluded that if there was anything that had once amounted to a 'town' in this last outpost of civilisation, it had already been hit one time too many and had given up the fight. The old-fashioned Edwardian seafront curved gently along a sandy beach where pedalos and plastic canoes had been pulled up out of reach of the sea for the night. Strings of coloured light bulbs hung between the lamp-posts, though, as only a few of them appeared to be working, they added little to the ambiance. And whatever ambiance a full set of working light bulbs may have provided, it would have been instantly crushed by the parade of elderly couples shuffling along the seafront, out for their evening stroll. Shuffling, Becky thought, to their deaths.

'Oooh, smell that sea air,' said Maria as she dragged what looked like an inflatable sheep from the back of the minibus.

'I think I'm in hell,' replied Becky politely.

'Where's your vibrator gone? Didn't I give you one?' asked Maria.

'Tell me, Maria,' said Becky, fishing in her bag for a cigarette, 'what is the point of our having vibrators? Are we going to use them on each other? Or on the bride? They used to do that, you know, in some ancient cultures –

penetrate the virgin bride with a phallus before her wedding night, to ready her for her husband. Mind you, I can't say I'd mind penetrating that young redhead you were sitting next to on the bus.'

Maria blinked and laughed awkwardly. 'Ruth said you were funny,' she said doubtfully. 'Come on now, have my vibrator. Get into the spirit of things. You'll feel so much better when you have a drink in your hand and you're out there on the dance floor – especially when we're all in our rubber policewomen costumes!'

'I'm think I'm allergic to rubber,' said Becky, staring along the length of the seafront in what she hoped was the direction of London, where normal people were going out for normal nights out, which involved neither inflatable sheep nor policewomen costumes. She could hear Maria still twittering on in her ear as she found her gaze catching on the figure of a man moving chairs and tables about outside a seafront shop. Tall? Check. Broad? Check. And if her eye for the male physique wasn't deserting her, those were some good legs. Oh yes, they were.

But then Maria was looming in front of her, blocking her view with the inflatable sheep and pushing her into the floral-wallpapered prison that was the Sea View Guest House.

It only took one hour of drinking with the hens before Becky made a break for freedom. She'd lost count of the number of drunk men she'd had to insult brutally in order to make them leave her alone. Apparently, the rubber policewoman costume was extremely popular with the locals – many of whom seemed to think women from out of town were easy game. Walking back to the guesthouse, her costume safely concealed beneath her long coat, she marvelled at how quiet the town was at night – just the occasional slam and shout of a drunk leaving a pub. Turning a corner, she came upon the sea: a mass of silky black beneath the night sky, small waves sliding gently up the shingle before pulling away with a hissing noise, tumbling the pebbles beneath them. She stood for a moment and breathed it in, before remembering the man at the stall – she was never one to forget a good pair of legs – and when she turned in his direction, she found he was just ten feet away and looking right back at her. Becky felt a little thump in her chest. Now this was what you came to the seaside for.

'Did you want an ice cream?' he said, as she sauntered towards him.

'What?' said Becky, instantly confused.

'I'm just shutting up for the night, but I saw you waiting around and I thought you wanted one.'

'An ice cream?'

'Yes, an ice cream. An ice cream from my ice-cream shop, here. This one that sells ice creams,' he said and Becky caught the hint of a tease in his voice that pleased her.

'Oh right,' she said, stepping towards him, 'Yes, yes, sorry – I was in a world of my own. I do want one.'

'An ice cream?'

'Yes,' she said, pausing and taking him in with her eyes. 'Yes, I want an ice cream, please.'

He was tall, she'd been right about that, with dark hair shaved short. He was wearing flip-flops, faded shorts and a T-shirt and had a deep tan and creases round his eyes that suggested he spent most of his time outdoors. As he stood in the light that came from the shop behind him, his face was half in shadow, but she sensed there was something mischievous about him that she liked. Here was a way to forget the horrors of the evening, she thought. A good old-fashioned anonymous fuck. Her speciality.

'What flavour?' he asked, stepping back into the shop to go behind the counter and gesturing at a blackboard with a list of different varieties of ice cream written on.

Becky said the first one she saw: 'Raspberry ripple.'

'Excellent choice, madam,' he said and reached for the scoop.

'Madam?' said Becky, leaning on the counter. 'Do I look old enough to be a madam?'

'Well, not in terms of age, no,' he said, 'but I couldn't help but notice you are wearing a rather provocative rubber skirt.'

Becky opened her coat to show him the full glory of the minuscule rubber outfit, gave him a twirl and topped it off with a flirtatious wink. 'Hen night,' she said, 'or hell night – depending on how you look at it.'

'And how do you look at it?' he asked, handing her a cone filled with ice cream.

'Hell,' she said, catching his eye as she licked up a drip from the cornet. 'Utter hell.'

'Not a fan of the seaside then?' he said, leaning his long arms on the counter.

'I'm more of a city girl, though the view from here is very nice,' she said slowly, emphasising her words while looking directly at him, 'and the ice cream's not at all bad. Want to try?'

He caught her gaze and held it, a smile twitching the corner of his mouth.

Becky lasciviously licked her way round the ball of ice cream she held in front of her, before adding: 'Or have you had your fill of ice cream?'

'I don't think one can ever have enough ice cream,' he said evenly, looking at her with a mix of curiosity and cautious enthusiasm. 'My name's Dan, by the way.'

Becky, who found she tired of conversational formalities very quickly, turned behind her to push the door of the shop shut and said: 'I'm not interested in your name.'

'I –' began Dan, but he was quickly silenced by Becky striding around the counter while taking a scoop of ice cream from her cone with one deft finger, which she then slid quickly into his mouth.

'What I like about ice cream,' she said, gently moving her finger inside his warm mouth in teasing circles, 'is the way it melts on your tongue – the way the initial cold dissolves with the heat of the mouth – the way it turns to liquid.' She watched his surprised eyes carefully, assessing whether he would be willing to play the way she wanted to. And it seemed he was. He reached up with one hand to grip her wrist and slowly pulled her wet finger from his mouth. With his other hand, he reached beneath the counter and scooped up two fingers worth of vanilla ice cream which he then slid into the mouth she opened eagerly, her dark gaze flashing approval.

'What I like,' he said, 'is giving people ice cream.' And with that he reached forwards and kissed her, his tongue replacing his fingers, sharing her mouth with the sticky chill of the ice cream, a vanilla-flavoured kiss. And that was it: the connection was made. He knew what she wanted and had responded in kind.

Becky quickly swallowed the ice cream in order to taste him better. He kissed her slowly and deeply, in a confident way that made her feel dizzy. She was beginning to like this man. She'd chosen well. With a practised move, she slipped her coat from her shoulders then slid her hands beneath his T-shirt. His stomach was firm and warm; fine hairs tickled her fingers. She moved her hands down as their kissing became more urgent and, to the delicious ripping sound of his fly unzipping, she felt herself pulse inside with eagerness and knew she would already be wet for him. She always liked a man willing to be quickly undone.

They moved faster now. Dan pulled his T-shirt off and pushed Becky gently but firmly backwards until she half-lay on a nearby freezer compartment. Her squeaking rubber skirt was pushed roughly up around her thighs and Dan, his unzipped jeans now hanging about his knees, slid his hands up between her legs, where he soon discovered that Becky was the kind of girl who didn't like wearing underwear on a hot night. He obviously approved of this attitude, as he quickly pushed her knees up on either side of her so she was suddenly open before him, and ducked his head down and into her with a sudden passionate rush. Becky felt his tongue sweep up the whole length of her, making her gasp, before he quickly moved back to ring it rapidly around her clit, the sudden flickers of pleasure making her body buck beneath him.

Dan stood up briefly, still holding her knees apart so she was splayed before him shamelessly. They looked at each other, momentarily thrilled by their own daring. Then she reached her hand down to where he had been, never afraid to add to her own pleasure, and used two fingers to slide up and down either side of her clit, making it swell with feeling.

'I liked what you did there,' she said.

'I'm not going away,' he said, quickly reaching back with one hand to stick his fingers into another tub of ice cream beneath the counter, which he then smeared over her busy hand and onto her tremulous clit and then down inside her. The cold was shocking and Becky jolted and gasped. Dan returned his hands to her knees to hold her apart then lent in to lick the ice cream from her. The warm relief of his tongue and mouth against the cold of the ice cream sent shudders through her as he lapped at her slowly and tenderly, finding every last drop, dipping his tongue up inside her to push her open and spread her where she was already aching to be filled. The more he swirled that hot soft tongue of his over her clit, the more she felt herself open to him and she pushed her pelvis up, asking for attention till he took one hand from her knee and, keeping his tongue teasing her, slipped a finger into her slick pussy. Becky moaned and moved against him, wrapping her free leg about his head to pull him closer, muffling him between her thighs. She pulled open the top of her policewoman's uniform, freeing her breasts so she could toy with her own nipples, the twinges of pleasure seeming to set off little corresponding sparks in her similarly swollen clit. She tipped her head back and abandoned herself to the blood rush of sensation that made her body vibrate, her approaching orgasm building somewhere deep in her pelvis. All she wanted now was to be filled and fucked to capacity and it was then, with a flash of ingenuity, that she remembered her regulation hen-night vibrator. While Dan continued his selfless work between her legs, she reached for the handbag she had dumped beside her on the freezer, pulled out the garish pink sex toy and tapped him with it on the shoulder.

He looked up, vaguely bemused. 'You want that?'

'I want that . . . and I want you. I want both,' she replied. 'In for a penny, right?'

Dan half-laughed with surprise then licked his lips devilishly. 'I guess I have to keep my customers satisfied,' he said, pulling her up from the freezer, 'but you should go first and show me how it's done.'

Becky quickly tried to figure out the logistics of what she had suggested, and realised, not for the first time in her life, she would need to be bent over something. She moved to the ice-cream counter and slowly bent at the waist as if to sample another flavour. While her left hand took a finger of mint choc chip to pop in her mouth, her right hand flicked the switch on the vibrator so it began to whirr and she pressed the tip of it against herself. Stepping her legs further apart, she moved it back and forth, each stroke a little closer to going inside her, the vibrations against her clit making her arch her back with pleasure, till finally, with a small moan of relief, she pushed it slowly inside, feeling each inch as it expanded her. She closed her eyes, sucking her ice cream-covered fingers, while her other hand worked the vibrator in and out. She felt Dan move behind her, then his long body bent to cover her so he could reach for more ice cream to fill her mouth. She sucked greedily on his fingers and he moved his hand in and out between her lips, as if fucking her mouth. With his other hand, he pushed her skirt up over her buttocks to reveal her naked arse before taking his wet fingers from her mouth and using them to spread her apart to find her hole.

Becky, lost in the electronic thrills of the vibrator, knew only that she wanted him to join her inside herself, and pushed back against him, encouraging him to gently force one, then two fingers into her, relishing the pleasure of being stretched open. She stepped her legs apart, her hen-night high heels ensuring that her naked arse was conveniently hovering just before his straining boxer shorts, which he quickly pulled down out of the way. She felt him hold his cock to run it up and down between her cheeks, once pulling away to reach down and lick her, then moving back to use his own wetness to lubricate himself as he pushed gently then firmly to get inside her.

'Slowly,' murmured Becky, as he steadied himself on her hips. 'Do me slowly.' She slowed her own movements with the vibrator in order to match him, just keeping the tip carefully slipping in and out of her pussy, teasing herself, while the plastic length of it brushed her clit, humming against it, tingling. They stayed there, hung tremulously together, the vibrator buzzing and Becky panting softly, then Dan exhaled as he gradually increased his pressure and forced himself carefully into her from behind. Becky mirrored him, moving the vibrator deeper inside the front of her, till both items were fully consumed and each way she rocked, she was moving onto something. Each time Dan moved partially out of her, she swung back to catch the full length of his cock as he returned, and when she moved away from him, leaving that delicious internal gape where he had been, she pressed the vibrator inside her, like a see-saw of penetration. As they slowly gathered pace, Dan used one hand to balance on the counter and the other joined her at her front, rubbing gently on her tender clit as she felt herself tipping into climax, thrusting backwards and forwards, all self-consciousness gone, till her sex spasmed and clenched repeatedly at him, constricting around him in jerks as she came. He came seconds later, groaning and collapsing gently onto her back. Becky half-opened her sleepy, satiated eyes to look out over the ice-cream counter, through the shop window, to the sea, which still moved there in the dark, reflecting a low half-moon. The hen night had turned out better than expected, she thought.

The following morning, the hungover hens in the Sea View Guest House pulled themselves from their beds and readied themselves for Sunday's chosen activity: pony-trekking. From beneath her duvet, Becky murmured something about having a migraine and told them she would join them later. It had been late when she had returned from the ice-cream shop. She'd bid Dan farewell in her usual style, saying it was nice to have met him, and strode quickly away. Deal done. But this morning, lying in bed, she remembered how he had responded to her demands with that unexpected quiet confidence and she found she had an itch to see him again. First, however, she had a mild hangover to deal with that required a full cooked breakfast and a day's sunbathing. She was at the seaside after all.

After eating a plateful of bacon, eggs, sausages and toast, she took herself onto the sandy beach that lay opposite the guest house, and spread herself on a towel, enjoying the mild aches and strains she had sustained the previous night. Occasionally, her mobile phone bleeped to let her know she had a text from a hen wondering where she was. She ignored them and let herself fall into a gentle doze, letting her mind switch off in the heat of the sunshine, the soothing sounds of the sea whispering in the distance.

She was woken by a voice saying: 'You look like a girl who likes ice cream.'

Without moving or opening her eyes, she replied: 'Stan was it?'

'Dan,' he said, 'but you're not interested in my name.'

'No,' she replied, 'I find it complicates things.'

She heard him sit beside her and opened her eyes. If anything, he seemed more handsome in the daylight. His lean, long body in its scruffy beach wear looked perfectly at home on the sand. He had a certain self-possession that intrigued her.

'You'll notice I didn't even ask you your name,' he said and Becky felt momentarily outsmarted. She wasn't used to her conquests beating her at her own game.

'That's probably best,' she said, 'I'm going back to London tomorrow and you will never see me again.'

'What do you do up there?' he asked.

'I make lots of money for people I hate,' she replied, 'I drink too much, I smoke, and I live in an extortionately expensive flat that is smaller than the towel I am lying on.'

He laughed. 'I used to do that.'

'What?'

'I used to work in London. In advertising. For five years. Then one day I woke up and realised there was absolutely nothing about my life I enjoyed at all. So I quit. Travelled a bit. Bummed around. Ended up here.'

'Ended up running an ice-cream shop?'

'Frankly, I'd run anything anyone asked me to run if it meant I could wake up, look at the sea and know I didn't have to put on a suit and get on a train with hundreds of other people in suits to work in an air-conditioned office nine to five, five days a week, for the rest of my life,' he said evenly. 'I know which I prefer.'

Becky looked at him, then turned to look at the sea. To her surprise, she found she could see what he was talking about. The view to the horizon seemed endless. When was the last time she looked at the sea? When was the last time she had slept on a beach or sunbathed for that matter? She seemed to spend most of her time running from the office to the bar to home and back again. Normally in uncomfortably high heels.

Dan sighed in a relaxed way, then reached out a hand

and picked up Becky's bottle of sun lotion. 'Need creaming?' he asked politely.

Five minutes later they were in the back of the ice-cream shop, which had been hurriedly closed, a sign saying OUT FOR LUNCH left swinging on the door.

'I want to give you a lesson in ice cream,' said Dan, pushing her gently to a chair. 'Sit here.' He had already pulled her cotton sarong from around her waist and quickly tied it around her head, as a makeshift blindfold.

Becky sat obediently in the darkness, wearing nothing but her skimpy bikini. She listened as Dan moved about, trying to guess what he was up to.

'First, chocolate,' he said, his quiet voice closer now. She felt his face close to hers, then his lips brushing gently against her mouth, teasing her open with his tongue, which he used to slip a scoop of chocolate ice cream into her mouth, before withdrawing tantalisingly. 'Taste it,' he said. 'Chocolate is rich, dark. We use the finest organic products when we make it. It tastes indulgent. It tastes like late nights and bitter cocoa. It's decadent, luxurious, sinful.'

Becky sucked the sweet chilled creaminess in her mouth and swallowed hungrily. She couldn't remember the last time she had had chocolate ice cream, living, as she did, on a diet of calorie-controlled ready meals.

'Next, strawberry,' said Dan, and his mouth was there again, slipping her a taste. 'You tell me what strawberry is like.'

Becky rolled the ice cream in her mouth, then felt a sudden chill on her breast.

'I seem to have dropped some,' said Dan, his mouth moving downwards to lick it up greedily. 'I'll just see to that while you tell me what strawberry tastes like.'

Becky shivered as she felt him remove her bikini top and gently tongue her stiffening nipples before sucking them, pulling at them till they stood upright.

'Strawberry is fruity, sweet,' she said huskily. 'It tastes

of strawberries and cream. It tastes of Wimbledon. It tastes of . . . summer. And Pimms. And garden parties.'

Dan's hands were on her bikini bottoms now and she lifted her hips slightly so he could ease them down her thighs and take them off, leaving her completely bare.

'Next, my favourite,' he said. 'Vanilla.'

'Vanilla is your favourite?' said Becky, her voice breaking slightly as she felt his hand moving tenderly up her thigh.

'Vanilla gets a bad press,' said Dan, his voice muffled as he licked around her breasts and caressed her thighs. 'People think it's boring and plain, but it's not. We make it with clotted cream. Done properly, it's luscious. Smooth, delicate . . .'

Dan's hand had now reached the top of Becky's thighs and gently inched between them. With a careful single finger, he parted her to find her glistening wetness. Slowly, he ran his finger up her inner lips and down again before gently slipping it inside. Becky moaned and gripped the edges of the chair, pushing her pelvis up to allow him greater access.

'Let me taste it,' she whispered. 'Put it on you and let me taste it.'

Dan stood up and the next thing to nudge against Becky's open mouth was his ice cream-covered cock. She took it in eagerly, sucking at it, savouring the gentle vanilla taste of the ice cream and, underneath that, the dirty sweet taste of him. She moved her head backwards and forwards, running her tongue along the underside of his cock. Her hands moved to his arse so she could pull him forwards, greedy to take all of him, the ice cream dribbling down her chin.

'Vanilla is subtle,' said Dan, his voice husky now. 'You can get a real taste for it.' He lent down to her so she could feel his breath, smell the salt of his sweat. 'Vanilla tastes like you,' he whispered, nudging his cock further into her mouth.

Becky wanted him then. She wanted this man who made ice cream, who smelled like the sea, who was long and lean and quietly filthy. She wanted him inside her. She pulled back and ripped off the blindfold. Dan stood before her, his tanned body entirely naked, a hazy look of lust in his eyes.

'Now you sit,' Becky said, standing up. He did, and she wasted no time swinging her leg over him to straddle him, her pussy immediately grazing the tip of his long upright cock. He moaned and reached up to grab her hips, pulling her suddenly down onto him, the exquisite pleasure rushing through them both like a drug injection. Becky found herself moving on him almost unconsciously, her hands gripping at his shoulders, his neck, overtaken by a feeling of want so strong it was almost like anger.

'Fuck me,' he whispered, licking her neck, her breasts, nipping at her nipples, running his teeth over her body, the pair of them almost frantic now.

Becky rose and fell with Dan's encouraging hands at her hips, keeping the rhythm, their bodies joining fully then pulling apart, the ache of withdrawal rewarded by the sweet pulse of bliss as his cock returned to deep inside her. They kissed now, their mouths open wide, tongues desperate, Becky's hands holding his face. They moved faster and deeper, grinding and slamming against each other, till Becky felt her climax come in a sudden, overwhelming rush and she cried out. Dan placed his hands on her shoulders and pulled her down hard in one last thrust and came inside, shuddering against her, his cock squeezed again and again by her contracting pussy.

'Well,' Becky panted, from her post-come slumped position, her face buried in his neck, 'that was quite a lesson.'

'Every good teacher learns from his pupil,' said Dan, and he turned to kiss her softly on the cheek.

'And every good pupil deserves special treatment,' Becky replied and paused, before reaching in to kiss the ice-cream man gently on the lips. He looked at her cautiously, then smiled and said: 'What about a beer?'

Sipping her fourth bottle of beer while sitting at the water's edge, Becky could clearly see the members of the hen party loading their belongings into the minibus.

'What did your text message say?' asked Dan, inscrutable behind his sunglasses.

'I told them that by some freakish coincidence I had bumped into a long-lost maiden aunt of mine, who lived nearby. And that I was going to spend some time with her before returning to London,' she said, watching as Ruth helped Maria manoeuvre the inflatable sheep into the minibus before returning her gaze to the sun, which was slowly setting over the sea, casting a peachy orange glow over the beach.

'Do you think they believed you?' asked Dan, leaning back into the sand.

'Unlikely,' she said, 'but I'm not sure I care really.'

Dan looked at her. 'Before you go off to this imaginary maiden aunt of yours, there's something you should try,' he said.

'More ice cream?'

'I was thinking sex in the sea. Right now, in fact. I think you should try that now. I encourage all our visitors to try that while they're here.'

'I suppose I could fit that in,' she said, standing up and reaching out a hand to pull him to his feet, 'as long as we have ice cream afterwards.'

'Oh yes, there's an awful lot of vanilla ice cream that needs to be eaten,' replied Dan. 'We could be eating it for days, weeks even.'

'I was thinking about that actually,' said Becky, walking towards the evening sea, feeling the cooling sand beneath her feet. 'You may think plain vanilla is best, but personally, I'm of the opinion you could use some sauce to make it even better. Just to top it all off. I think you need extra sauce.' She turned to face him, reached out a hand and gently but firmly gripped his cock through his shorts and pulled him purposefully towards her. 'I'm Becky, by the way,' she added.

Salsa Estelle Blake

Salsa. Sounds sexy, doesn't it? I mean, no one ever named a dance after the English equivalent – the Sauce?

I had been perfecting my recipe for years. Since I had visited a café in downtown San Pedro Sula, in fact, where the salsa was so good that I got the chef to write down his recipe. I still have it now – a piece of yellowing paper ripped from a notebook, Sellotaped into my collected recipes book. '*Receta para salsa picante*' it says in a curly foreign hand.

Sitting in a small, out-of-the-way café late at night, I was eating enchiladas with refried beans, grilled onions and crumbled goat's cheese. In the middle of the table was a rough terracotta bowl of gloopy green-speckled redness. It filled the immediate space with a rich smell of ripe tomatoes and spices. I was cautious at first and put a tiny amount on the edge of my plate. I love food and new tastes but I am not the type who considers it a point of honour to eat thermo-nuclear chillies and curries uncomplainingly. More than once I have had to spit out a mouthful of hot coals in food form to save blistering my tongue. So, I dipped my bread into the sauce and bit into it. The flavours were so intense that I put the bread down on my plate, the better to concentrate on the taste in my mouth. Palms flat down on the table, I moved my tongue around my lips and savoured the sweet tang of the tomato, the clean, fresh coriander and the cheeky sharpness of just the right amount of chilli.

I had come late to the restaurant and the food had been, in true Central American mañana-style, a long time in the preparation and service, but I had happily read and filled in my notebook to pass the time. When my meal arrived, I looked up into the face of the crinkly old Indian waiter as he put my plate in front of me, and I heard the *'Buenas noches!'* from the only other table of late diners as they rose to leave. I raised my eyebrows in query but the waiter patted my wrist reassuringly. He didn't seem in any hurry for me to go. He bowed and smiled as he backed away, then started to take a leisurely turn around the other tables with a damp cloth, blowing out unnecessary candles as he went.

As soon as I tasted the salsa, I knew that I had to have the recipe. Part of my joy in travelling was the food I tasted and, wherever possible, I begged the recipe from the chef. I'd come up with some beauties: a really special green curry from a tiny beach hut restaurant on a Thai island – thick, coconutty and tangy with lime leaves; a laksa from Malaysia, with its chunks of seafood and sub-aquatic nest of noodles. My mother, a passionate cook, awaited my emails with excitement and, if I sent her one without a recipe, she'd be (only just) mock angry.

> *Kate, I realise you're having the time of your life, scooting around the world with nothing but a pair of flip-flops and a spare pair of pants, but do you think you could, next time, indulge your mother with some useful local information (like a recipe!!!?).*

She'd love this, I thought … summer coming, salads, barbecues and the perfect salsa. I spooned a huge dollop of it into my mouth and relished the hot–cold, smooth–bumpy sharp–sweetness of it as it ran over my tongue and into my belly.

A few minutes later, I was following the old waiter down a corridor to the kitchen. Somehow, my bad Spanish (*'La receta, por favor?'*) and gestures with my notebook had been enough to make the old fellow understand what I wanted. He leered at my chest as I rose and nodded as he moved to the back of the restaurant. I left a note large enough to cover the price of my meal and went after him.

At the end of the corridor was a doorway hung with a colourful plastic curtain of ribbons. The waiter popped his head through and rattled off something to whoever was beyond, in a dialect I didn't understand. Then, he reached right in and came out with a greasy white baseball cap, which he pulled onto his balding brown head.

'*Buenas noches*, señorita,' he said to me and gestured into the kitchen with his hand before turning and going back down the corridor into the restaurant. I heard the outside door close and then there was quiet.

He was formal at first, bowing to me as I peeped through the ribbon curtain. I nodded back at him and glanced around the small, tidy kitchen, thinking how this tall man could probably reach the walls from one side to the other if he stretched out his arms. My imagination fed me pictures of the Angel of the North and the statue of the Christ Redeemer in Brazil. Word association then led me to remember the Brazilian waxing I had had done earlier that day and I blushed as if I'd actually shown it in public.

'Señorita?'

'*Si!*' I focused my attention back on to the chef and mastered my self-inflicted embarrassment.

He was wearing a spotless white T-shirt and a stained apron tied at the waist. His arms were thick, brown and smooth and there was a tattoo of a long red chilli pepper, with a cheeky curl at its tip, on his right bicep.

'Mmmmmm,' I remember thinking to myself. I took a deep breath and tried again to explain what I wanted. '*Buenas noches*, señor. *La salsa es muy buena ... Como ...?*' I mimed chopping and stirring and he smiled at me.

He put down the cleaver he had been using to dice tomatoes at one end of the table, wiped his hands on his apron and motioned me forwards with a long finger. I looked at him questioningly and considered the danger of being alone at night in a strange place with a powerful man. He nodded, beckoned me again and smiled encouragingly. He was probably thirty or so. He had smooth olive skin, slightly oriental black eyes and cheekbones that could slice chorizo. His smile was warm and humorous – not the sleazy grin of the groper, which I'd come to recognise on my travels alone – and I decided to trust him, not least because a jolt of excitement fizzed through me when he smiled.

He mimed writing, so I took a notepad and pen out of my bag and passed them to him.

'*Receta para salsa picante,*' he wrote and then underlined it with an artistic squiggle. I was impressed that he was giving me the time to do this properly – not just a hastily scribbled 'Salsa' – so I looked up at him and gave him a big wide smile. I held out my hand.

'*Me llanan* Kate.'

He swapped the pen into his left hand and took mine with his right. It was warm and I could feel the calluses, which had formed from, I guessed, gripping his chopper. He gave a gentle pressure and a small shake.

'Garcia. *Encantado.*' His eyes crinkled at the corners and I got the feeling that he was teasing me with his old-fashioned 'Enchanted' so I gave him a mock frown and pointed at the page.

'OK, Kate,' he said, scratched his head for a second with the end of the pen and then wrote, '*Cilantro (fino).*'

I made the international sign of the uncomprehending idiot – bottom lip out, chin tucked in, shoulders raised and hands held out. Garcia laughed and took hold of my hand again. This was starting to feel like a game and I let him lead me into an open pantry at the far end of the kitchen.

The three walls of the pantry were covered with floor-to-ceiling shelves on which stood hessian sacks, terracotta jars, enamel bowls and huge catering-sized square tins. On one of the lower shelves was a bowl full of herb posies. Garcia leaned down and picked one of them out of the bowl. He put the pen and notepad in the back pocket of his baggy trousers and held the bunch of leaves up to his nose. He tore one of the delicate, emerald-green fronds, inclined his head and inhaled deeply with his eyes closed. I already knew that what he was holding was fresh coriander, but this was starting to mesmerise me and I too put my face into the bundle and pulled in the smell.

I wasn't prepared for the intensity of the scent – perhaps it was the heat of the kitchen, the variety of the herb or the experience of being given something so sensual by this dark stranger, but I let out an involuntary 'Ohhh!' and put my head back, eyes closed.

'*Si. Cilantro. Fino*,' said Garcia and mimed chopping finely.

Garcia next took an empty bowl from a shelf and put the coriander bundle into it. Then he took the notepad and pen and wrote, '*Chilli picante.*'

He reached up and took down a jar from one of the top shelves. As he did, I saw a tuft of black silky hair escaping from under his arm, and smelled his warm biscuity scent. Being in this small space with this man was beginning to agitate me. I was starting to sweat and could feel it trickling between my breasts. I could also feel the crease under my bum cheeks getting sticky with moisture. Despite the heat and the sweat, my scalp was tingling and the hairs on my arms rose. The sensation spread down my neck and up my arms to reach my breasts and my nipples suddenly sprang out. I looked down and the sight of them excited me more.

I could feel the syrup from my fanny starting to ooze and wondered whether my pants could withstand it. I remembered the way I had looked after my waxing – I had hurried straight back to my hotel room and tilted the mirror from the ancient dressing table so that I could see myself, newly-shorn on the bed.

I had expected the experience in the salon to be humiliating but had found it, instead, highly erotic. I stripped from the waist down, just leaving on a tiny vest to cover my tits. The girl was a jet-haired sugarplum called Consuela. She wore a clinging white uniform, which gaped over her breasts so that I could see the lace of her bra. She asked me to climb onto the table and get down on all fours. Consuela gently pushed my head further down and pulled my hips up higher and then moved her hand between my thighs to force my legs further apart. I felt like a porn star, ready to take it from behind, and I thrust my bottom higher into the air and arched my back as Consuela slapped the warm honeyed wax onto the lips of my fanny and around to my bottom. I rested on my upper arms and looked up at my tits hanging down towards my face. I dug my fingernails into the table top and resisted the urge to wiggle my bottom and push back onto the spatula, but enjoyed the experience of being basted by this Latin honey. Consuela's fingernails were long, filed to a taper and painted pomegranate red. As she moved her hands backwards and forwards over my fanny and bottom, I willed her to stick one of her slim brown fingers with its bloody tip into my bum, but she denied me. By the time she had peeled the wax and my hair with it, I was sweating, breathless and hungry to stick my fingers into my sex to bring on the climax that had been building.

When Consuela had finished, she handed me a mirror and I looked down at myself. I remembered myself as a girl as I looked at the pink hairless lips. Surrounded by the molasses colour of my suntan, my fanny looked like a sliced peach in chocolate sauce. The remaining tiny tuft of black hair like an exotic garnish. I felt all the way around to my bottom and marvelled at the smoothness.

'*Si?*' asked Consuela as I held the mirror pointing up between my legs, the better to see my shorn bits.

'*Si!*' I laughed at the ridiculousness of the situation and handed her back the mirror so that I could dress.

Back in my hotel room, I ripped off my skirt, vest and pants – leaving on my high-heeled sandals and a string of turquoise beads hanging between my breasts. The mirror confirmed what I had seen in the salon – I was clean, satin-smooth. I was greedy for something to put into that fresh new place. I posed for a few seconds on the bed – legs spread with my heels in the air, legs wide apart, flat on the mattress, and then I found the perfect pose for viewing my fluffless muff – the waxing position. I got onto my hands and knees and looked at myself in the mirror over my shoulder. My bottom looked good, golden brown and fat enough to show off the narrowness of my waist. My breasts hung down and I gave one of my nipples a pull. I arched my back, pushed my bottom out and opened my legs wide to see the raspberry pink of my labia. I reached behind, put a finger into the wetness and felt my muscles contract. Urgently, I stretched over to the bedside table, grabbed my travelling companion – six inches of vibrating purple plastic – and rammed it, whirring, into my sex. It took only seconds before I was moaning and biting the pillow with sheer bliss.

'*Si, chilli picante,*' I said slightly breathlessly and tried to concentrate on Garcia's ingredients-gathering.

'OK?' he asked, evidently noticing that I was hot and flustered. I had leaned back against the arched entrance to the pantry; my hands were holding the wall behind me for support. There was concern in his eyes and he reached for my elbow, sending a spasm of heat and excitement through my body. 'You sit?' he asked.

I shook my head

'I'm OK, *gracias*, Garcias.'

We laughed nervously at my mixed-up Spanish and, when we stopped, we looked into each other's faces until I turned away.

I bit my lower lip and looked back up at him through my lashes, trying to control my breathing and my heartbeat. He was still looking at me and holding the jar of chillis and the pen and paper. I could hear his breathing – heavy and expectant. I reached up and took the things out of his hands, bent and put them in the bowl with the coriander. He was smiling now, nodding and waiting for me to make the first move.

I held my hands up to him and took his face between my palms. He closed his eyes and turned to kiss my wrist. Then he pulled me to him and held me close, burying his nose in my hair. He was so tall that I barely reached the middle of his chest and I could feel his cock against my belly. He bent his knees and reached down for my legs. He gripped the backs of my thighs and effortlessly lifted me so that I could wrap my legs around him. He held me with one arm and pulled my head towards him with the other and we banged noses in our haste to taste each other's mouths. His flavour was sweet coffee and I drank him in. His tongue was strong and mobile, exploring the shape of mine.

I gripped him with my thighs and wrapped my arms around him. I felt the muscles of his upper back through the fabric of his T-shirt. His kissing became more intense and I could feel his urgency as his free hand moved down my back and up under my vest. His warm strong hand sent a thrill through me and I reached down and grabbed his buttocks, pulling myself into him. He was hard and soft at the same time, like a loaf of freshly baked crusty bread, and the thought of him naked and brown caused me to moan.

Garcia took my cue and carried me out of the pantry to the kitchen table. He laid me gently on my back and then looked me up and down as I turned my head and wriggled for him. My legs were bent up, feet on the table. I was wearing a long gauzy white skirt, which had gathered around my knees. Garcia took hold of the hem in both hands and lifted it up towards my waist.

'Oh!' he gasped and closed his eyes, tipping his head backwards.

I was wearing the tiniest pants imaginable – white and barely wide enough to cover the wisp of hair left. Garcia took hold of the cloth in one hand and pulled the gusset of my pants up between the lips of my moist sex. I arched my back and pressed my bottom into the table to increase the friction of the fabric. I reached for Garcia's head and held him, looking him in the eyes as I squirmed under the pressure of my knickers.

'I eat you,' he said and stooped to my crotch.

He took the damp cloth between his teeth and pulled it taut against his fingers until the lace ripped. He yanked the ruined panties off, threw them on the floor, and then turned back to me. By now my sex was twitching and I was wild to feel his tongue, his fingers, his cock inside me. I pulled up my vest to bring my thrusting breasts in. I was braless and still erect and Garcia was distracted. He drew the vest over my head and then pressed me against the table as he took my breasts into his hands and sucked hard at one of my nipples. I wrapped my legs around him and pressed my desperate sex against him.

After sucking both of my breasts until I squealed, Garcia moved to my ribs and licked delicately along them while still squeezing my nipples between his fingers. He reached the bunched up cloth of my skirt and his fingers left my nipples to undo the zip and pull the skirt away. I was now naked on the table except for my espadrilles, laced midway up my calves.

Garcia took hold of my thighs and deliberately parted them wide, gripping me as I pushed my hips up towards his face. He looked at me, smiling, and inclined his head slowly, slowly . . .

'Yes, yes, eat me,' I begged him, feeling myself open up for him, and he plunged his tongue deep inside me. 'Garcia, oh!'

I was so wet and eager I could hear him slurping and enjoying my juices. He found my clitoris and gave it a playful stab with his tongue.

'Ahhh.'

My hands were in his hair now and he took hold of my wrists and pinned them down by my hips. He flicked his tongue against my clitoris again and I struggled against his grip, excited by the pain and the constriction. He sucked me and flicked me rhythmically, knowing that I couldn't bear for him to stop as I bucked against his face and pretended to try to free my wrists. My tits were bouncing and I could see my feet in their tightly laced shoes bracing against the table's edge as Garcia's head moved against me and I felt his floppy black hair against my pubis. He sucked and flicked and nibbled at my sex until I reached that place where my body becomes a purely physical thing – no intellect, no emotions, just pure sensation, noise and taste. I held his head between my thighs as I shuddered and jerked against him and cried his name.

When I came back to the real world, I was stretched out across the table, legs wide apart, head thrown back and my hands were clutching at my breasts. Garcia held me by the waist, supporting my arched back. My hair was hanging down over the side of the table and I could feel sweat at my temples.

'Wow!'

I was still swooning as I lifted my head to look at Garcia. He was looking down at me, licking his lips and smiling. He crossed his arms, gripped the bottom of his T-shirt and pulled it over his head. His torso was even more exquisite than I had imagined – chocolate brown, undulating and gleaming like waxed mahogany. His nipples nestled in short silky black curls. I sat up and wrapped my arms and legs around him. Still throbbing and wet, I pressed myself against him. He held me and I felt his hardness through the cloth of his apron.

I turned him around to undo the strings. When the apron had fallen away I took the waistband of his pants and pulled them down to see the perfect roundness of his caramel-coloured buttocks. Garcia reached back and held the table edge as I knelt and pressed my breasts against his back. My nipples were like champagne corks and I rubbed them against his shoulder blades. I draped my hair over his shoulder and kissed the nape of his neck as my fingers flickered down his flanks.

Garcia leaned back against me and took his cock in both hands. I slithered off the table behind him and kissed my way down his back. When I reached his bottom, I took his buttocks in both hands and pulled the cheeks apart. Garcia spun around and I followed until he was leaning over the table, supporting himself with one hand and pumping his cock with the other. I was desperate to see it, taste it and feel it but I stayed behind Garcia and pushed my face into his bottom. I found the tight creased hole and pushed my tongue in as far as it would go. Garcia tensed and I reached around to take hold of his balls. I licked along from his anus to the seam under his balls. By now, I was on my knees with my head up between his legs and he was grunting with increasing pleasure. I took his balls in my mouth and used my tongue to massage them, feeling the hard kernels inside the skin and rolling them around. Then I eased my way up in front of Garcia to kneel between him and the table. He let go of his cock and it bounced in my face, huge and dripping, the colour of an aubergine. I could hardly wait to get him in my mouth and I grunted greedily as I gulped him in. He was magnificent and tasted briny and clean. I stroked his balls with the fingertips of one hand and eased a finger from the other into his hole, still slippery from my tongue. Garcia groaned. He took my head in his hands and pulled me onto him. He thrust gently into my mouth and I felt his hole tighten around my finger.

I could feel the pressure mounting in his cock when he pulled out of my mouth and lifted me under the arms to throw me back onto the table.

'Yes?' he asked me as he took his cock in his hands and held it quivering by my sex.

'God, yes!' I yelled and he rammed it into me.

The size of him almost knocked the breath from my body. I closed around him and felt him throb. Slowly at first, he moved in and out of my wetness. At every push the tightness pulled at my clit and I felt his balls swing against my bottom.

'Harder!' I ordered him and he grunted.

With closed eyes, his face contorted and he gave me his full length. He pumped into me faster and faster and stars whirled before my eyes as I felt the orgasm build in us both. He gripped my bottom and pulled me deeper onto him with each stroke and his animal noises grew louder. I held onto the edge of the table behind my head, and pushed up against him. The sight of his cock thrusting into my naked sex excited me more.

'Nngh, nngh, *si, si, si,* aaaarrrrggghhhhhh!' He jerked and shuddered and I felt him release into me as I reached my own heights. 'Yeeeeeeeeeeeeeeeeeeeeeeesssssssssss.'

We thrashed together on that table as the orgasm built and subsided and built again and then faded. I squeezed him as I came, wringing him of every drop of creamy salty delicious spunk.

Garcia lay on top of me and I gripped his back with my legs. As the spasms withdrew and we relaxed, he laid his head against my breast and I felt the brush of his eyelashes against my nipple. I started at the sensation, giving Garcia's cock one more squeeze. He laughed and moved out of me and I felt the slipperiness of him against my leg.

Standing up, Garcia looked down at me still sprawled on the table. My breathing slowly returned to normal, but my skin was glowing, and damp with sweat – his and mine – and I could feel that my hair was glued in crazy squiggles to my forehead and cheeks.

I put my feet down and made to lift myself onto my elbows. Garcia reached forwards and pulled me towards him by the shoulders. He stood between my legs and folded his arms around my back, pressing my face into the warmth of his chest. I could feel his breath in my hair and he kissed the top of my head.

'Kate,' he whispered.

I looked across his body at the arm over my shoulder

and saw again his tattoo. I traced the outline with my finger and the shape of it followed the curve of his muscle. As I drew the chilli, thoughts of the salsa, which had brought me into this kitchen, caused my mouth to water. I leaned over and licked the pepper and was almost surprised when I tasted, not sweetness and freshness, but salty warmth. I looked up, smiling.

'*La receta*, García.'

'*Si, querida . . . Mañana.*' And he stooped to kiss me.

Hello Mum,

I was going to travel up to the Bay Islands tomorrow to do some diving, but I've been persuaded to stay in San Pedro Sula for a while longer.

I had a Brazilian waxing yesterday so that I could pose in my bikini, but I suppose I can get another one before I finally go. It's actually not as gross as it sounds, being stripped and waxed with your bum in the air!

The reason I'm staying is that I've made a new friend, who you'd love. He's a chef and I met him when I ate some salsa in his restaurant and sought him out for the recipe. It's to die for, Mum – sweet, juicy, piquant and fresh – and he's teaching me how to make it. We made a start last night but it was late and something came up.

His name is Garcia and he's going to give me the rest of the recipe this evening, which I'm excited about – so far, all I have is coriander and chillis! When I have the complete recipe, I'll send it to you as I can see you serving it up at one of your picnics. It's gorgeous with goat's cheese and enchiladas.

I'm off for a siesta now because it's really really hot and I've got a busy evening ahead of me.

I'm having a fantastic time, so don't worry about me. I'm well and happy and looking forward to my next salsa lesson!

Love and kisses, Kate xxx

WICKED WORDS ANTHOLOGIES –

THE BEST IN WOMEN'S EROTIC WRITING FROM THE UK AND USA

Really do live up to their title of 'wicked' – Forum

Deliciously sexy and explicitly erotic, *Wicked Words* collections are guaranteed to excite. This immensely popular series is perfect for those who enjoy lust-filled, wildly indulgent sexy stories. The series is a showcase of writing by women at the cutting edge of the genre, pushing the boundaries of unashamed, explicit writing.

The first ten *Wicked Words* collections are now available in eye-catching illustrative covers and, as of this year, we will be publishing themed collections beginning with *Sex in the Office*. If you never got the chance to buy all the books when they were first published, you can now complete your collection and be the envy of your friends! Look out for the colourful covers – guaranteed to stand out from everything else on the erotica shelves – or alternatively order from us direct on our website at www.blacklace-books.co.uk or through cash sales – details overleaf.

Full of action and attitude, humour and hedonism, they are a wonderful contribution to any erotic book collection. Each book contains 15–20 stories. Here's a sampler of what's on offer:

Wicked Words

ISBN 0 352 33363 4
£6.99

- In an elegant, exclusive ladies club, *fin de siècle* fantasies come to life.
- In a dark, primeval forest, a mysterious young woman shapeshifts into a creature of the night.
- In a sleazy midwest motel room, a fetishistic female patrol cop gets dressed for work.

More Wicked Words

ISBN 0 352 33487 8
£6.99

- Tasha's in lust with a celebrity chef – it's his temper that drives her wild.
- Reverend Billy Washburn needs salvation from Sister Julie – a teenage temptress who's set him on fire.
- Pearl doesn't want to get married; she just wants sex and blueberry smoothies on her LA poolside patio.

Wicked Words 3

ISBN 0 352 33522 X
£6.99

- The seductive dentist – Nick's encounter with sexy Dr May turns into a pretty unorthodox check-up.
- The gender-playing journalist – Kat lusts after male strangers whilst cruising as a gay man.
- The submissive PA – Mandy's new job fulfils her fantasies and reveals her boss's fetish for all things leather.

Wicked Words 4

ISBN 0 352 33603 X
£6.99

- Alexia has always fantasised about being Marilyn Monroe. One day a surprise package arrives with a sexy courier.
- Bridget is tired of being a chef. Maybe a little experimentation with a colleague is all she needs to get back her love of food.
- A mysterious woman prowls the back streets of New York, seeking pleasure from the sleaziest corners of the city.

Wicked Words 5

ISBN 0 352 33642 0
£6.99

- Connor the tax auditor gets a shocking surprise when he investigates a client's expenses claim for strap-on sex toys.
- Kate the sexy museum curator allows a buff young graduate to make a thorough excavation of her hidden treasures.
- Melanie the interior designer and porn fan swaps blokes with her best mate and gets up to nasty fun with the builders.

Wicked Words 6

ISBN 0 352 33690 0
£6.99

- Maxine gets turned on selling exquisite lingerie to gentlemen customers.
- Jules is stripped naked and covered in cream when she becomes the birthday cake for her brother's best mate's 30th.
- Elle wears handcuffs for an indecent liaison with a stranger in a motel room.

Wicked Words 7

ISBN 0 352 33743 5
£6.99

- An artist's model wants to be more than just painted, and things get pretty steamy in the studio.
- A bride-to-be pays a clandestine visit to the bathroom with her future father-in-law, and gets much more than she bargained for.
- An uptight MP has his mind (and something else!) blown by a charming young woman of devious intentions.

Wicked Words 8

ISBN 0 352 33787 7
£6.99

- Adam the young supermarket assistant cannot believe his luck when a saucy female customer needs his help.
- Lauren's first night at a fetish club brings out the sexy show-off in her when she is required to wear an outrageously daring rubber outfit.
- Cat's fantasies about hunky construction workers come true when they start work opposite her Santa Monica beach house.

Wicked Words 9

ISBN 0 352 33860 1

- Sarah gets a surprise when she and her husband go dogging in the local car park.
- The Wytchfinder interrogates a pagan wild woman and finds himself aroused to bursting point.
- Miss Charmond's charm school relies on old-fashioned discipline to keep wayward girls in line.

Wicked Words 10 – The Best of Wicked Words

- An editor's choice of the best, most original stories of the past five years.

Sex in the Office

ISBN O 352 33944 6

- A lady boss with a foot fetish
- A security guard who's a CCTV voyeur
- An office cleaner wIth a crush on the MD

Explores the forbidden – and sometimes blatant – lusts that abound in the workplace where characters get up to something they shouldn't, with someone they shouldn't – someone who works in the office.

Sex on Holiday

ISBN O 352 33961 6

- Spanking in Prague
- Domination in Switzerland
- Sexy salsa in Cuba

Holidays always bring a certain frisson. There's a naughty holiday fling to suit every taste in this X-rated collection. With a rich sensuality and an eye on the exotic, this makes the perfect beach read!

Sex at the Sports Club

ISBN O 352 33991 8

- A young cricketer is seduced by his mate's mum
- A couple swap partners on the golf course
- An athletic female polo player sorts out the opposition

Everyone loves a good sport – especially if he has fantastic thighs and a great bod! Whether in the showers after a rugby match, or proving his all at the tennis court, there's something about a man working his body to the limit that really gets a girl going. In this latest themed collection we explore the sexual tensions that go on at various sports clubs.

Sex in Uniform

ISBN 0 352 34002 9

- A tourist meets a mysterious usherette in a Parisian cinema
- A nun seduces an unusual confirmation from a priest
- A chauffeur sees it all via the rear view mirror

Once again, our writers new and old have risen to the challenge and produced so many steamy and memorable stories for fans of men and women in uniform. Polished buttons and peaked caps will never look the same again.